Mystery Cunnin X
Cunningham, Richard
Maude Brown's baby : a novel /

34028083151325
KW $14.95 ocn820148966
07/17/13

3 4028 08315 1325
HARRIS COUNTY PUBLIC LIBRARY

P9-AQC-091

MAUDE BROWN'S BABY

~~~~~

a novel

Richard Cunningham

Enjoy!
Richard Cunningham

WITHDRAWN

MAUDE BROWN'S BABY
Copyright 2012 by Richard Cunningham
All rights reserved
ISBN-10:1478201517
ISBN-13:978-1478201519

Cunningham Studio
Houston, Texas
USA

HISTORICAL NOTE

The hurricane that struck the island of Galveston, Texas on
September 8, 1900, claimed up to 10,000 lives.
It remains the worst natural disaster in U.S. history.

Maude Brown's Baby is a work of fiction that follows the life
of an aspiring photojournalist in the fall of 1918.
While much of the historical setting is real, the people in this story
live only in the writer's imagination.

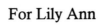

For Lily Ann

The Letter

Tuesday, September 11, 1900
John Sealy Hospital, Galveston, Tex.

My dearest Ida Mae,

No doubt you have read accounts of the horror that transpired here Saturday last, but words can not convey the dreadful calamity that has befallen our beautiful island city. How grateful I am that my little family is safe in Fredericksburg! Please make no attempt to return here, my love, for all is in ruin. For now, may it ease your mind to know that I am safe and still working as best I can here at the hospital, which was greatly damaged by the storm.

Forgive me if my thoughts ramble. I have slept less than six hours in three days. Five doctors and a dozen nurses arrived from Houston this morning, so our staff has finally some relief. We are all beyond exhaustion, but I wanted you to know that I am alive and will come to you as soon as conditions allow.

I hear that our home is badly damaged, although I have been unable to see it for myself. Was it just Saturday morning when I was last there? It seems so distant now! I arose at dawn, dressed and shaved. I had no desire to linger, the house being so void of life without you and the children, so I hurried to our little corner restaurant for breakfast. Already the clouds were darkening. I carried an umbrella, and by the time I had finished eating, a light rain had begun.

My morning was routine. I saw three patients, all with minor complaints, and dispensed some pills. One man had passed during the night, Mr. Hixson. You may remember his wife, Leona.

As I was completing my report, I noticed from my window that water had accumulated several inches deep in the street. I recall thinking it odd that a carriage rushing by created a wake large enough to push water onto an adjacent lawn.

Around noon, a new patient reported that breakers had wrecked buildings on the gulf side of the island. Having finished my report, I decided to venture out for lunch before the weather grew worse. It would be my last meal for two days! At the restaurant I learned that the street cars had stopped running, and that a section of track along the beach had washed away.

When water began seeping into the restaurant, the proprietor said he was closing for the day, so I returned as quickly as possible to Sealy. Walking was difficult as the wind had picked up, and water was soon above the tops of my rubber boots!

The electric lights went out before the worst of the storm. We struggled by candle light and lanterns to move patients away from the windows, and it is good that we did. All but six were smashed by debris carried by the terrible wind.

Around 8 p.m., water from the bay and from the gulf met, and the entire island was at once submerged. Morning revealed that miles of land and buildings were simply gone. What remains are great walls of wood and steel, boats, trees, wagons, furniture and every possible item of daily life, along with those who owned them.

It sickens me now to look outside. Another corpse wagon just passed, with two men walking silently beside. Their frightful cargo is the third I have seen today. The newspaper says 6,000 are dead in Galveston alone, and many more up and down the coast.

It has been impossible for me to grasp all that has happened here. I suppose our minds work that way to protect us, but one small thing has occurred that, at least for me, reveals the face of this disaster.

On Saturday, upon returning to the hospital from the restaurant, I was standing at the entrance pouring water from my boots when a woman clutching a baby rushed by me through the door. I followed and found her pleading with a nurse.

The poor woman's clothes were soaked through. Her hat and combs were gone, her long hair matted about her face. She was sobbing, trying to explain that she had been caught out when the street cars stopped running. She had another child nearby and needed to reach her, but was afraid she could no longer manage the rising water with a baby in hand. Would the nurse please keep him until she returned?

Without waiting for an answer, she thrust the baby in the nurse's arms and wheeled for the door. She stopped abruptly, took a photograph from her handbag and pressed the card between the folds of the child's blanket. As she raced out she cried, "I'll be back!"

That was three days ago, so I fear the young woman perished in the storm. The child is healthy and cheerful enough, and he has become the delight of the staff. The photograph is of the boy—the nurses have named him Donald—seated in a chair. It is a recent picture, surely taken within the last week or two.

We know that Donald was born on January 1 of this year, for there is a note to that effect on the back of the card, but neither the child's real name nor the photographer's is on the card. The photograph itself is little help. A penciled note across the bottom simply reads, "Maude Brown's baby," but no one recognizes that name. If the woman who left him does not return soon, one of our nurses will take the boy we call Donald Brown to an orphanage in Houston.

Well, my dearest, I must close now to get this letter in the post. Please write to me here at the hospital. I long to know that some place in this world is still whole, and that you and the boys are well.

Your loving and devoted husband,
Charles

4

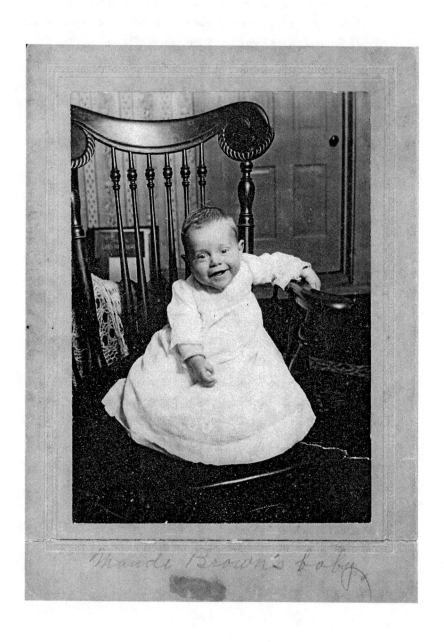

Maude Brown's baby

Chapter 1

Sunday, September 8, 1918

"GET ON WITH IT," said a voice in Donald Brown's head.

"Give me a minute!" he complained to the empty room. He leaned against the iron bedstead, tilting his head back to feel the cool metal against his bare neck. He breathed out, cheeks puffed, and reached for the envelope.

Slowly, Donald worked two fingers under the loose bow that held the flap closed and let the ends of the ribbon fall away. Lifting the flap released the faint smell of age. With a thumb and forefinger, he pulled the letter and photograph slowly from the manila sleeve.

The doctor's letter to his wife was on top. The testimony of a witness. No need to hear it again; Donald knew every word by heart. He held the fragile pages in his lap a moment longer, then set them aside. It was the photograph he needed, but dreaded, to see.

"Inhale ... hold ... exhale ... hold," Mrs. Carhart would say. "Learn to calm yourself, dear boy. Control your breathing and relax. It is a skill that will help you through life."

He closed his eyes and traced the edge of the card. His thumbs moved up the embossed border, left the roughness of the pasteboard mount and began gliding slowly over the print, which was smooth and cold as a marble headstone.

That's enough, he thought.

Outside, Houston's Fourth Ward was coming to life. A dray passed, still empty by the sound of it. The heavy wagon's iron-clad wheels rattled over the brick street, offset by the slow clomp of hooves. "Mornin' Sam," a neighbor called. "Mornin' James," the driver replied, but didn't stop to talk.

Donald leaned on one elbow toward the shed's only window, but even that slight movement disturbed a bit of lint from Naomi's quilt. Distracted by the white specks tumbling through a beam of sunlight, he studied the particles for a few seconds, saw how quickly they slowed, then puffed to set them moving again.

Donald raised the photograph almost to the tip of his nose, and the blurry portrait grew crisp as the day it was made.

"You have a wonderful eye for detail," Mrs. Carhart told him once, "but it is also your defense against things you do not wish to face."

"Maybe so," Donald said aloud. "Maybe so."

He angled the print to catch more light. The sitter was a nine-month old boy—himself, Donald knew—propped in a chair. The child's left hand rested on the arm of the chair, right hand in his lap, thumb and first finger just touching. Without thought, Donald's hand did the same.

Through the spindles of the chair, he saw wallpaper and the corner of a shawl. Books leaned in soft focus against the back wall. The boy in the picture gazed not at the camera, but toward a point slightly right of the lens. Below the image, a penciled note read, "Maude Brown's baby." On the back, a more deliberate scribe had printed in ink, "b. January 1, 1900."

The simple contact print was well lit and properly exposed, any amateur could see that, but Donald saw details only a professional might notice: the quality of the light, the tonal range, the skillful depth of field. He looked up, peering over the top of the print and into the blurry corners of his room.

"Who are you smiling at?" he asked the child on the photograph. He ran his fingers over the penciled note at the bottom, "And please, who wrote these words?"

"Do you really want to know?"

"Stop it!" he said to the empty room.

"Inhale ... hold ... exhale ... hold," the room replied.

He focused again on what he knew for sure. The card was not from a portrait studio. There were no trees or Greek columns painted on the background, and no grim-faced sitters, stiff and miserable thanks to the steel braces pressing at the backs of their heads.

"What about the pose?" said the voice in Donald's head. "Babies don't smile this way at strangers. That's you. What did you see?"

"Too young to remember," Donald whispered under his breath.

What he could not see in the print, he saw in his mind: first the heavy wooden tripod, then the camera itself, bellows reaching for the child. He imagined the photographer, head and shoulders under the black cloth, composing the shot. He wanted to warn them both, "Leave now! Leave Galveston while you still can!"

Donald leaned forward, resting an elbow on one bent knee. He squeezed closed his eyes and dropped his forehead in his hand.

Laughing? Donald's head popped up, instantly back in the present. He listened hard, but heard only chickens clucking in the yard. He slipped the photo and letter back into their sleeve, lowered the flap and retied the ribbon. He stretched the stiffness from his joints, then patted the table for his glasses. The base of the kerosene lamp felt cool. His fingers tapped across two books that Mrs. Carhart suggested he read. Reaching farther, Donald's forearm swept left to right. His fingertips found a brass lens cap, then an empty film spool, which dropped from the table and rolled under the bed.

No glasses.

He turned toward the rough table that was both his writing desk and nightstand, but it was little help. He squinted at the objects just beyond his reach. A screwdriver, pliers and a small wrench were all lumps of equal volume. Three more pats, and Donald's hands fell on the wire rims and thick lenses that were his windows to the larger world.

In one motion he sat up, pulled the glasses to his face, guided the steel loops behind his ears and twitched his nose to settle the heavy lenses in place. He paused to admire this simple, fluid action, one he'd practiced a dozen times a day since he was nine.

"My portholes," he called them, a joke shared only with himself.

Donald climbed from bed to retrieve the metal spool, then tucked it behind the curtain of his darkroom. Its walls and ceiling were black, the flatness broken only by a handful of black and white prints pinned to the walls. A small red lantern sat in the middle of one shelf, a reminder to replace the candle.

Floorboards creaked under Donald's bare feet. The shed was just large enough for his single bed, a workbench, a chair and of course, his darkroom. Above the workbench, a row of apple crates screwed to the wall overflowed with cameras and spare parts. One caught his eye. He took it from the shelf and laid his glasses aside.

"That should work!" he said aloud. Taking a Barlow knife from the bench, Donald freshened the point on his pencil, allowing the shavings to fall into the pail that served as a trash bin. He licked the tip of the lead, opened his journal, laid it flat and began to draw.

"When ideas come to you, write them down at once," Mrs. Carhart said when she gave him the odd little book with blank pages.

He drew quickly, jotting notes in the corners and linking them to his sketch with straight lines. Satisfied, he wrote the date: *Sunday, September 8, 1918, anniversary of the Great Storm.*

Donald closed the book, slipped it into his camera bag and lifted a pitcher to fill the baking pan he used for a sink. He splashed water on his face and had just reached for the fresh towel Naomi left for him each night when the screen door behind him swung wide. Clarence Stokes leaned in, one calloused hand gripping the edge of the screen, the other pressed flat on the outside of the shed.

"Good, you're up! Saves me the bother of wakin' you myself. Missus says breakfast will be on in ten minutes."

"Thanks, Pa, just a second." Donald patted the table for his glasses and slipped them smoothly over his ears, but the wooden slap-slap of the screen told him Clarence was already walking back toward the house. "Tell her I'll be right in."

"Come hungry, she's fixin' her Sunday feast," Clarence called over his shoulder. "And hide that poster afore your ma sees it."

Donald watched him go, suddenly sad for the gray in Pa's hair and the limp that remained after his accident last year.

Poster? Donald forgot he'd left it on the chair by the door. He flattened it on the bed. A stern Uncle Sam with piercing eyes pointed a finger at Donald's chest. "I want YOU for the U.S. Army," the headline read. A recruiter had pressed it on him the day before, along with a registration form to complete.

I have until September 12th, Donald thought, four days more. What then? He rolled the draft registration form inside the poster, tied it with a scrap of twine and tucked the tube out of sight under his bed.

Donald hung his nightshirt on a nail and pulled clean BVDs from his drawer. He buttoned the fly of his denim pants, slid his arms into his shirt, stuffed the tail deep into his pants and rolled the sleeves neatly to his elbows. He preferred a simple workman's shirt to the button-on collars that made his neck itch. He wiped his cheek; a shave could wait.

Donald scanned the shed once more. "You can sleep in his room," Naomi and Clarence told him after their son left for the Army, but Donald preferred the roughness of the shed. Naomi kept it clean and a stealth tabby named Jones kept it free of mice. Compared to the dormitory bunks in the children's home, this was luxury.

Donald pulled on fresh woolen socks, tugged at his boots and stamped each foot twice to plant the heels. His feet had grown over the summer, as had his shoulders and arms. He was already taller than Clarence. Naomi's cooking had filled him out.

He dragged a brush across his thick brown hair and patted a cowlick, but stopped when he caught his reflection in the window glass. Startled, Donald froze as if confronting a stranger on the street: Lean face. Strong jaw. Good teeth.

"Owl Eyes!" he said aloud.

The kids in school had called him that, and worse. He had to admit, they were right. The rims of the thick round lenses caught the light. They distorted his face, so that when anyone looked him in the eye, they saw the pinched sides of his head. The effect was comical: an owl with brown eyes ringed in white. He turned away in shame and disgust.

"Inhale ... hold ..."

He smelled bacon. Donald grabbed his flat leather cap from a nail by the door and stepped onto the boardwalk he'd built to keep from tracking mud into the house on rainy days.

He thumped the outhouse door with his boot to check for snakes. A minute later he crossed the rest of the yard to be joined at the back porch by the Stokes' yellow hound. Dropping to one knee, he tugged Bosco's ears before opening the kitchen door.

"Morning, Ma! What's cooking?"

"You know perfectly well, young man," Naomi said, wiping flour from her hands onto the sides of her apron. "Bacon, eggs, gravy and grits, and biscuits with butter and honey." She stood on tiptoe to kiss him on the forehead. "Now wash your hands and pour yourself some coffee."

Donald thought back to his time before the Stokes and couldn't see life without them. At ten he'd begun helping Clarence repair things around the old Washington Avenue orphanage, fetching tools and the like. Just months before the children's home moved to its new address, Donald grew restless and the Stokes were glad to take him in.

"We're going to miss you, Donny," Naomi said, picking up a conversation they'd been having for a week. "You sure you need to join the Army?"

Donald stood in front of the icebox and sighed as he leaned back against its heavy wooden case.

"It's my time, Ma. The new law says eighteen-year-olds have to register, but that doesn't mean I'm in. Anything could happen. They might not want me because of my eyes. They didn't take Elton on account of his asthma. Besides, he says the war will be over in a few months."

"Pshaw. For three years now, smarter people than Elton Sparks have been saying the war will be over in a few months. I don't mean to be uncharitable, but that man doesn't know to come in out of the rain."

"He may not be smart, but he sure likes you."

"He likes my apple pie, that's what. He can smell one clean from here to Sunday."

Donald laughed. He loved to egg her on. "Not just your apple pie."

Naomi turned from the stove, knowing his game.

"He loves your cornbread, too."

She wrinkled her nose and flipped a dish towel as Donald pretended to duck. "It's a wonder Elton made it all the way through high school," she said, her attention back to the bacon cooking slowly in her largest iron skillet. "Is he still running errands for the reporters?"

"He's been at the *Chronicle* since he took that job as a copy boy, but Jake Miller is teaching him photography. Elton's trying hard. He bought a good camera, and a few months ago, Mr. Foley started giving him assignments."

"Where does Elton live now? He doesn't have any kin nearby."

"He's been at Jake's rent house since April. Jake wants me to move in, too. If the Army doesn't take me, Jake says I can live there and work at the newspaper."

"As an errand boy?"

"No, I'd be a photographer right off, and in a year or two I could be writing some of the stories. Jake's going to ask his editor about that."

"Donny, I'll swear you trust that man more than I do, and a lot more than you ought to yourself. A rent house and room to yourself all the way downtown? Jake's filling your head with ideas. Besides, none of that matters if you're in the Army."

"I know."

Naomi picked the bacon from the pan, turned down the burner and wiped the stove with a rag. She poured half the grease into an empty coffee tin, leaving the rest to fry the eggs. Donald kept quiet, but felt the muscles at the back of his neck growing tense. Naomi wasn't done with her advice.

"It's one thing for him to help Elton," she said. "He certainly needs it, but you should know better. Jake just wants somebody to pay the rent on that place he bought."

Donald tipped his head forward and kneaded his neck muscles with both hands. He'd heard all her arguments before.

"Neck bothering you again?"

"No."

"You've been doing that a lot lately."

"I'm all right."

"You need some Ben-Gay?"

"No, Ma. What were you saying about Jake?"

"That rent house. What's he going to charge you, anyway? And come to think of it, where'd he get the money to pay down? Jake's just a newspaper photographer. He can't earn that much. How old is he, twenty-four? Twenty-five? He never studied business. You said yourself he's not a great photographer. All he's good at is finding lady friends. Who in their right mind would loan that glad-hand money to buy a house?"

Her last question caught him off guard. He raised his head, leaving one hand on the back of his neck. Jake never said where he got his money, and Donald never thought to ask.

"Jake wants ten dollars a month, but I can make fifty at the paper as a photographer. The office is two blocks away, so I won't even have to take the trolley to work."

Naomi cracked an egg harder than she meant to on the edge of the frying pan. Half of it fell on the stove. "You can stay here for free, you know, and Clarence can use your help."

"I know, Ma."

"Think about it, Donny."

"But the Army..."

"Jake's right. You won't be drafted. Just be thankful they won't take you, not with your bad eyes."

Inhale ... hold ... exhale ... His eyes weren't bad, just different. Donald kneaded his neck, rolled his head, straightened his back and answered Naomi.

"Maybe so. Either way, I need to move on. If I don't pass the draft physical, then I'll take the job."

"Fifty dollars sounds like a lot jus' for takin' pictures," Clarence said, tugging his suspenders and dropping with a grunt into his chair by the window. He left his gimpy leg straight under the table.

"Morning, Pa."

Clarence took his time spreading the Sunday *Chronicle* on the kitchen table, sweeping both hands wide to flatten the pages. He tilted his head back, squinting down the bridge of his nose.

"Says here this cool front's goin' to stay a few days. 'Bout time." Clarence consulted the headlines, tracing two fingers down the page. War stories mostly, and two about the draft. He looked toward Naomi, but held quiet on the news. He asked instead about Donald's new job.

"An' what happens when you fellows run short of stuff to foe-tow-graph?" Clarence loved drawing out the word. Donald laughed as he poured coffee into a battered pair of blue enameled mugs. He set one in front of Clarence and kept the other for himself. Naomi already had her fancy bone china cup on the counter by the sink.

"That's not my concern, Pa. I just worry about getting it all in. Mr.

Foster keeps his photographers pretty busy. Besides, the newspaper is short-handed with so many boys fighting overseas...." Donald bit his tongue. "Sorry."

"Me too," Clarence said, glancing at Naomi's back as she worked at the stove. He slid the sugar bowl next to his coffee cup and added two large spoonfuls.

"Only one, Papa," Naomi called without turning around. Clarence looked up from his coffee cup to Donald, shaking his head.

"That woman has eyes at the back of her head."

"I just know you, old man," Naomi said, still facing the stove, one hand on her hip as she flipped the eggs.

Clarence added a third spoonful of sugar and second splash of cream, then made a point of stirring noisily until the sugar dissolved. "You're the boss," he called to his wife.

Donald added one sugar and a bit of cream, then listened thoughtfully as his spoon clanked against the metal cup. "How long have you had these, Pa?"

"Them cups? They was the first things I remember buyin' when we come here from Galveston after the Great Storm." Clarence raised his voice so Naomi could hear. "Remember, Mama? That feed store over on Washington had 'em two for a nickel. We bought three plates to match and three knives, forks and spoons. They was all the dishes we had for more than a year."

Naomi turned back toward Donald. "Today is the day, isn't it, when you pull out that old photograph and the doctor's letter?"

"I did it this morning, Ma."

"Donny, them times is done," Clarence offered. "You've got to let it go and move on. You do this ever' year an' all it does is make you sad for a week."

"I'm trying, Pa."

Donald stirred until a vortex formed, then reversed to set his coffee swirling in the opposite direction. He licked the spoon dry and set it on the table with a click.

"So now you're takin' advice from Jake Miller?" Clarence said, steering the conversation back to Naomi's original tone. He licked his own spoon front and back. "Thought you'd want to be shed of him by now."

"Jake's all right, Pa. I know he's annoying, but he's taught me a lot."

"Didn't he get all the credit for that picture you took when the ship channel opened?"

"That was four years ago, Pa. Jake was with the dignitaries, so I got the shot when that drunken senator fell in the water."

"And Jake told the editor the picture was his," Naomi said from across the room.

"It was his, Ma, sort of. He gave me the film that morning and had it developed soon as we got back. I wasn't even sure I got the shot until I saw it in the paper."

"But didn't Jake tell Mr. Foley he took it himself?"

"He had to, Ma. With a half-dozen news photographers around, how would it look if some kid took the best shot of the day? What would his editor say?"

"I say you was cheated," Clarence said, "jus' like you was cheated with your first camera. That pawn shop owner took your six dollars slick enough, but forgot to mention the camera was busted. You spent all summer earnin' the money."

Donald thought of it often. Jake wanted to force the pawnbroker to refund the sale. Donald wouldn't let him, but it felt good to know Jake would stand up for him.

Clarence laughed. "But then you showed us all what for," he said, rapping his knuckles on the table. "You took the darn thing apart and used them close eyes of yours to find out what was broke. I sure as hell couldn't see it, but you did. By the time you finished, that old Kodak worked better 'n new. Wished I could've seen Jake's face when you showed him."

Yes, that was fun, Donald thought. When Jake saw the pictures Donald made he was speechless, and anything that made Jake Miller speechless was impressive.

At the stove, Naomi shook her head. "You boys want some eggs?"

Jake's new electric Klaxon sounded just as Donald was helping clear the breakfast dishes. Bosco and three other dogs chimed in when Jake hit the horn twice more. Donald's jaws grew tight. In the last year, his boyhood hero had changed. Donald still defended Jake to Naomi and Clarence, but he wasn't sure why.

Clarence walked to the screen door and looked out. "Well, I'll go see what his lordship wants while you help your ma with the dishes." Truth was, Clarence liked Jake, but he couldn't let it show around his wife. He stepped onto the back porch to quiet the dog, then limped down the path toward Jake's car.

Two minutes later, Donald set the last of the dishes in the sink.

"Here you go, Ma."

"Thanks. You run on now."

Donald paused as Naomi scraped leftovers onto the old cookie sheet she used to feed the chickens. She'd toss them table scraps while the dishes soaked. Later, Clarence would wash while Naomi dried. She'd put everything back in the cupboard, upside-down glasses on the left, plates right, silverware in the drawer with the spoons and forks in neat stacks, while Clarence cleaned the stove. Always the same.

That's it! Donald almost said out loud.

He knew what they were going to do today, tomorrow and next week, but Jake was likely as not to conjure something Donald never considered, like the time he talked that circus owner into letting Donald and Elton sit on the elephant, or when he snuck the three of them into the Rice Hotel to see Thomas Edison. Whatever Jake's reason for stopping by, Donald wanted to be part of it. He tugged on the bill of his cap.

"Bye, Ma."

"You're going with Jake?"

"Yeah. He's probably headed for the newspaper office."

"Well, you just behave yourselves," Naomi said as she dumped the last of the scraps onto the cookie sheet.

She always said that.

Chapter 2

"What's up?" Donald called to Jake and Clarence from the back gate. The air was fresh and unusually dry for Houston, with dozens of small clouds drifting across the morning sky like tufts of fresh-picked cotton.

Clarence had a foot on the running board and an elbow atop the hinge of the Model T's folding windshield. He raised one hand to shade his eyes as he turned toward Donald.

"We was jus' discussin' the baseball game. Jake won himself five dollars from some boys at the paper, and now he's goin' to collect." Clarence winked at Donald and poked a thumb toward Jake. "Bet against this man and you'll lose your shirt!"

Jake tilted his head toward Clarence, who slapped his own knee and laughed. Donald couldn't hear the joke over the noisy engine, which Jake had left running so he wouldn't have to crank start it again.

Jake stood three inches taller than Clarence and weighed forty pounds more. The weight had served him well in his high school football days.

Glancing toward the house, Jake slowly crossed his arms. He saw Naomi first when she appeared on the back porch. The wooden screen door slapped shut behind her, and Donald and Clarence turned at the sound. She took the steps slower than she used to, right hand braced against the side of the house, the other holding a cookie sheet to her hip.

The chickens came, flapping and squawking loud enough to drown the noise of Jake's car. Dust and loose feathers rolled behind them in the air.

"What foolishness are you discussing now?" Naomi called across the yard. At her feet, fat white birds pecked furiously at each other and the morsels she tossed their way.

Donald smiled. He knew his ma considered chickens dumb as fence posts, but she respected their ability to turn garbage into eggs.

"Hello Naomi," Jake called, "you get prettier each day."

"Save that for your lady friends," she called back.

"I thought you were my lady friend," Jake replied. Naomi laughed, unconsciously patting her hair.

Donald studied his friend. Jake's smile stretched thin and hard across his face, and stubble remained on his cheeks and chin.

Jake caught Donald's eye and nodded, but didn't speak. The look meant, "let's go."

Jake patted Clarence on the shoulder as he walked around to the driver's side. Clarence grinned in return and stepped back toward the gate.

"Get in!" Jake called over the growing rattle of the four-cylinder engine. Donald had barely lifted his boot from the running board when Jake took off, dropping him hard into the horsehair-padded seat. The Model T's little door slammed shut by itself.

In an instant, Jake's good mood was gone.

"What's wrong?" Donald said, just as the car's wood-spoke wheels bounced over a deep rut, banging his knee against the dashboard. Jakes' hands gripped the wheel as if that alone would move the little Ford any faster.

"Come on, Jake, slow down!"

"Elton," he shouted over the engine, then lowering his voice, "He's missing." Donald braced one hand against the firewall and used the other to keep his cap from blowing off.

"Elton? What happened?"

"Foley sent him to Galveston to get pictures of that new section of the seawall."

Jake bounced the Model T down Dennis Street toward Main. Luckily the narrow dirt lane wasn't crowded, or he would have had a pedestrian on the radiator. As it was, only chickens and stray dogs were at risk. Donald gripped the base of the windshield, waiting for Jake to continue.

"Elton took the Interurban down Thursday morning." Jake glanced over to check Donald's reaction. "When he didn't come back Friday, I figured he stayed over with someone he met down there. I wasn't worried, but Foley was, so he called Galveston. Nobody's seen Elton."

Donald didn't respond.

Jake raised a hand and dropped it hard on the steering wheel.

"He's out having fun, but damn it, he should let me know! I wasted half the night looking for him."

Donald tugged the bill of his cap to shade his glasses from sunlight flashing through the trees. Jake's eyes remained on the road, somehow unaffected by the same flickering light.

"He was a year behind me in school," Jake said, relaxing by degrees and easing slightly on the throttle. "Teachers called us Mutt and Jeff."

Donald remembered.

"I haven't talked to Foley yet," Jake offered, measuring his words. "I went over to Goose Creek Friday, shooting the Simms gusher and Humble's new wells in Tabbs Bay."

"Heard they lost another man."

"Dangerous work," Jake agreed. They rode another three blocks, each in his own thoughts, before Jake spoke again.

"I was supposed to have the weekend off, but after I turned in my film and got Foley's message yesterday, I drove straight to Galveston. I've got friends down there and figured they might know where Elton was."

Odd, Donald thought. He felt his jaws tighten. Jake's voice changed as he went on.

"Foley left me a message Saturday morning," Jake repeated, as if Donald might forget. "Someone found Elton's camera bag behind one of the cheap hotels along the beach."

Donald turned away, furious now that Jake was holding back. For the first time, he was afraid. Elton wouldn't give up his camera without a struggle. Donald took a long deep breath, then kept his voice flat and clear.

"Just the bag?"

Jake's eyes narrowed. "His camera was wrecked." He glanced sideways at Donald and kept looking as he spoke. "Something happened at the hotel and the night manager called the police. They're investigating now."

Jake turned his attention back to the road but seemed to sag behind the wheel.

"You said you haven't talked to Foley?" Donald asked.

"Not yet. I had to get to Galveston."

"But why go yourself if the police are investigating?"

Jake looked sharply at Donald.

"The folks I know don't talk to the police."

Donald started to respond, but Jake's tone warned against it. From the corner of his eye, he saw the flash of a bicycle crossing the road. He shouted and braced for the impact. Jake, with an athlete's reflex, jerked the wheel just in time to miss the bike's rear tire. Through the dust behind them, the rider yelled something Donald couldn't hear. Just as well.

"Close!" Donald said, but Jake had already forgotten it. He continued in clips about his trip to Galveston.

"Made it in less than three hours, even with a flat ... Busted my lip when the damn jack slipped ... Just got back this morning." He turned again to Donald. "Hey, you got any money on you? I'm hungry."

Not waiting for an answer, Jake aimed left toward the Hendrix Café. Donald gritted his teeth and fished his pockets for change. Damn you, Jake Miller.

To save gasoline, Jake liked to coast whenever he could. He depressed the clutch pedal, switched off the engine's magneto and the little flivver shook itself silent, coasting on the wrong side of the road the final half block into the restaurant's oyster shell parking lot. As the narrow tires crunched to a stop, a latent backfire—loud as a gunshot—rolled down the alleys and set hounds barking a block away on both sides.

A half-dozen customers watched Donald and Jake climb from the car. Thelma Hendrix herself brought coffee to the booth while her father hunched over an omelet at the grill.

"Hi Foots!" she said, placing one cup in front of Jake and sliding another toward Donald. He was impressed at the view of Thelma's backside.

"I was worried when you didn't show at Blake's last night."

"Something happened."

"Well, I hope the something wasn't too pretty."

"Not pretty as you." Jake looked up, forcing a smile. Thelma noticed the fresh purple bruise on his lip.

"Did she give you that?" Thelma said, reaching for his chin.

Jake twisted his face toward the window. "Not now, Thelma, just bring me something to eat."

Offended, Thelma went heavy on her heels back to the counter. Jake continued looking outside, not staring so much as keeping watch. The morning light raked across his face, outlining the dimple in his chin and giving his eyes a greenish tint. He often looked like a hawk watching a prey, Donald knew, but when Jake wanted to, he could make you feel like you were the only other person in the world.

Suddenly Jake turned, searching Donald's face. He lifted his cup but didn't drink. "Elton could at least let me know where he is. I should never have taken him ..." He turned back to the window without finishing his thought. His own reflection made it look like he was staring at himself.

An elderly gentleman in his Sunday suit came by, paused at the discrete "WHITES ONLY" sign on the restaurant's door, then passed from view.

Thelma returned with fried eggs and toast and set the plate clunking on the table. Jake didn't notice. Her father watched from the kitchen as she turned to Donald.

"You sure you don't want something, too?" It was the first time she'd asked.

"No, thanks."

"Still early for the church folks to be in," Jake said after a loud slurp of coffee. Donald only nodded. Shoulders to the wall, he draped an arm over the back of the booth and scanned the room, composing mental photographs and analyzing everything Jake said.

At the counter, a policeman had snagged Thelma in conversation. She leaned on her elbows toward the officer, the toe of one shoe hooked behind her other heel. The pose showed off her figure and made her skirt rise an extra two inches until the hem reached mid-calf. It would have been a shocking display two years before, but no more. Short dresses were patriotic now, more fabric for the war.

Thelma laughed each time the policeman did, but glanced more than once toward Jake. Mr. Hendrix, scrubbing the waffle iron harder than he needed to, glared at them both through his eyebrows.

Jake dumped more ketchup on his eggs and stabbed a forkful. Now fully focused on food, he used his left hand to dip toast in his coffee, then added the dripping morsel to the eggs already in his mouth. Donald sipped his coffee and looked away. Jake's sketchy account was beginning to take shape.

"You said the camera bag was behind the hotel?" Donald asked, but Jake, finally distracted by Thelma's progress with the policeman, missed the question.

"Was the bag just lying in the middle of an alley?" Donald repeated, somewhat louder.

Jake looked up from his plate and hesitated a instant too long before answering. He slurped the last of his coffee, then let the empty cup clatter in the saucer. "The bag? No. It was behind some garbage cans at the back of the hotel."

"Why do you think Elton didn't come back Thursday night?"

Their eyes locked for a moment.

"Beats me," Jake said finally, reaching for his hat. "Let's go."

"Maybe there's a message at the office," Donald said.

"Yeah. And remind me, I've got Elton's camera. Fix it if you can, but I think all it's good for now is spare parts."

Jake turned and walked away. Donald paid for Jake's meal and coffee, left a nickel for Thelma, then hurried for the door. Jake was already in the car. "Give 'er a crank," he ordered from behind the wheel.

"Key off?"

"Yep."

Donald bent forward at the waist to reach the crank at the base of the car's radiator. He gripped the wooden handle with his left hand, fingers underneath in case the engine kicked back. He turned the handle two half-cranks to the right to prime the carburetor, each time bringing the handle back to its original position.

"Key," he called to Jake, who turned the key on the wooden dashboard to "magneto" and adjusted the spark advance and throttle levers on the steering column.

"Ready."

Donald grabbed the right fender for leverage and pulled his body hard to the right, tugging the crank with his left hand. The engine, still warm, fired on the first try.

They reached the *Houston Chronicle* building at the corner of Travis and Texas a few minutes later. Jake parked at an angle to the curb, grabbed Elton's dusty camera bag from the trunk, handed it to Donald, then quick-stepped down the sidewalk to the building's main door. Donald trotted to keep up.

Some in the newsroom shouted greetings over the din of a dozen Underwood and Royal typewriters. Donald waved back, taking it all in, mentally composing the scene. Trails of cigarette smoke rose from nearly every desk into a haze that hung just over the heads of the reporters. Morning light from the east windows turned the smoky haze gold and put distant things in soft focus. Donald tried to imagine himself working there.

A copy boy burst from the Linotype room, his ink-smudged hands full of proof sheets. "Excuse me!" he said, then raced on.

"Hey, Jake," a reporter called from two desks away, "Foley says still nothing on Elton."

"Damn," Jake said softly, flipping his new straw boater onto the hat stand and hanging his jacket on a nearby hook. "When I find Elton, I'm going to strangle him—if Foley doesn't do it first." He took a moment to brush dust off one sleeve, then dropped full weight into his wooden chair, letting his momentum roll it back. He surveyed the piles of paper and photos on his desk as if he'd never seen them before.

A gust from the open windows lifted a proof sheet from Jake's desk to the floor at Donald's feet. There, wedged between an ad for men's shoes and another for Liberty Bonds, a one-column filler noted the anniversary of Galveston's Great Storm.

"Ten thousand people lost in one night." Donald murmured. "Hardly worth mentioning now."

"What?"

"It's nothing, Jake. Nothing at all."

The drone of typewriters, Linotype machines and conversations settled into the background. It always reminded Donald of iron wheels clicking under a freight train half a block away.

Jake read a note someone left on his desk, stared briefly, then tossed it in the trash. He wiped his face slowly with both hands.

"Damn! What a night!"

Jake sat up when he noticed another short note, this one in red.

"What is it?" Donald asked. He pulled up a side chair and straddled it backwards, knees wide and arms crossed over the chair's wooden back.

"Foley wants me back in Galveston. He still needs the seawall photos Elton went to get."

"Do you think Elton's in real danger?"

Jake looked up from the editor's note. He lowered his voice and rolled his chair over to Donald, even though the closest man in the noisy room was two desks away.

"Look, Don, Elton likes to drink. Don't tell Foley, but I've seen him go on three-day binges before. I figure he's done it again. If he's got a woman down there, then ..."

A boy ran up, thumped stiff-armed against the desk, struggling to catch his breath.

"Jake ... Mr. Foley wants you over at Union Station by 10:00 ... Troop train's coming in. Lots of soldiers sick. Some died on the way. Looks like flu, only worse. Show the nurses ... helping them. Enoch's writing the story now. Mr. Foley wants pictures for the morning edition."

"Damn, that's half an hour," Jake said. He thrust his arm out and crooked his elbow to expose his new watch. It was the kind you wore right on your wrist, and Jake liked showing it off.

"Sorry, Don, no time to run you home."

"Sure," Donald said. "Get your shot. I wanted to see your rent house anyway." Jake didn't hear, he was already checking his camera bag to be sure he had enough film.

Donald flipped on his cap, stood and swung his leg over the chair. "Later," he said to the top of Jake's head.

"Wait!" Jake looked up, one hand reaching toward Donald. "Don, I could use some help on this thing with Elton."

"Sure, Jake, come by this afternoon."

When Donald found the address of the rent house, a two-story Jake said he "acquired for a song" from a gambler down on his luck. The front door was locked, but Donald didn't care. His thoughts were still with Elton, and the nagging feeling that Jake wasn't telling the whole truth.

Action always helped him think. He set Elton's camera bag on the ground and recovered his own Kodak Autographic from his jacket.

A small hand patted the side of his leg.

"Whatca' doing?"

Donald looked down to see a dusty boy standing beside a girl who was maybe a year younger.

"I'm going to photograph this house. Would you like to be in the picture?"

"Yes!" the boy shouted. Giggling, he pulled the girl forward, until they both stood stiff and barefoot on the grass between Donald and the white picket fence that surrounded the house. He studied the children for a moment and looked around.

"Over here," he said, directing them to an ancient stump in the shade of a young red oak. "Is this your sister? Fine. Let her sit here and you stand in back."

The girl scrambled on and looked cautiously toward Donald.

"Perfect!" Donald said, "Now stand behind. Yes, behind her, like that. A bit to the side. Put your hands on the stump and lean forward."

He focused first on the pair, then readjusted to a point just beyond them for maximum depth of field. He checked the film counter, looked down into the viewfinder and pressed the release button. At the sound of the click, his subjects moved.

"Wait!" Donald said, raising his index finger. He advanced the film until the number 2 filled the red counter window on the back of his camera. He bent lower to show more of the house, then took a second picture. He advanced the film knob two complete turns, bringing up the number 3.

"Now both of you look to the right, toward that magnolia tree across the street." The camera clicked a third time.

"All done, thanks," Donald said.

A woman's voice got their attention. Waving back at him, the boy and his sister ran across the dirt street, up the stairs and onto the wide front porch where two women sat, each repairing portions of the same quilt. They smiled at Donald, who raised his hand their way before securing his camera inside his jacket. He opened his journal, wrote the date, location and time, then added a note to print copies for the family.

Donald could have ridden the trolley from there, but it was the first cool day in months. He decided to save the nickel and walk. Twenty minutes later, he was home. Naomi was hanging laundry on the line and the sight made him laugh.

A bed sheet kept her from seeing Donald. Below the sheet he saw her black lace-up shoes, sagging stockings and an inch of white fabric hanging below the hem of her blue dress. Behind the sheet, Naomi's plump silhouette—both arms reaching above her head—shifted sideways twelve inches at a time. Above the sheet, her fingers moved like legs in a tiny chorus line, pushing clothespins down over the corners of the cloth. Donald jerked the sheet aside and Naomi jumped.

"Hi, Ma!"

"Don't do that!" she cried, hands on her chest. "You'll be my death!"

Donald steadied her by the shoulders, kissed her cheek and Naomi relaxed. He stooped to gather the clothespins she had dropped.

"Nina Carhart telephoned a few minutes ago," Naomi said, patting the combs in her hair and arranging her simple white collar. "She'd like you to come by today."

"When?"

"Around noon, so you have just enough time to wash up. Don't you go over to that fancy house looking like some farm hand. I'll bring you a clean shirt and collar—and wear your good shoes."

"Sure, Ma. Do you know what she wanted?"

"That magazine you like came in." Naomi knew something was wrong when Donald didn't respond. "What's in the bag, Donny?"

"Elton's Speed Graphic. Jake brought it to me."

"You've got yourself a good little business now, fixing cameras for the newsmen and building tripods in your spare time. I suppose Jake did help you get it going; I'll give the devil credit for that."

"I wish it was just a broken camera."

"What's the matter?"

"Elton didn't come back from Galveston when he was supposed to. Jake thinks he's been drinking again, but I'm not sure."

Chapter 3

Donald walked up Bailey Street as far as West Dallas, even though it was a block out of the way. Italians owned the grocery store at the corner of Bailey and Sutton, and Donald stopped there often. The store was closed Sunday mornings while the family was at church, so today, only their arrogant tabby watched Donald from an upstairs window.

Funny how things change, he thought, returning the cat's gaze. Mrs. Carhart had taught him that each part of town had its own unique story. "Remember," she would say, "I really do live in the Heights of Houston! People used to travel all the way up here just to escape the mosquitos!"

Donald's part of the game was to make his eyes big. "And how high up do you live, Mrs. Carhart?"

They'd both laugh at her response: "Why, more feet than you can imagine!"

It was all true. He really was ascending—all of thirty-three feet—to get from the dusty, low-lying streets of his neighborhood to her home in "The Heights." She had taught him to appreciate the odd mix of houses and people around him. He resisted at first. His head often ached with all the knowledge she tried to cram in.

He passed the white mansions with crumbling columns and leaded glass doors (Greek Revival!). A few blocks down were rows of tiny houses just two rooms deep (slave cabins!). Nearby, he saw apartments and stables, then farther along, a handful of workmen's houses like the one owned by the Stokes.

"Open your eyes to the history around you," Mrs. Carhart demanded. In the beginning it seemed pointless. Now, he couldn't stop. Former slaves settled Freedman's Town, in the area known as Houston's Fourth

Ward. Immigrants came later, drawn by the cheap land. Here, races and nationalities lived side-by-side. Cheap land even drew survivors of the 1900 storm.

Oh Lord, that storm.

When Donald reached Montrose, dozens of people were emerging from a nearby church. Children, finally released from ninety minutes of good behavior, darted between the slow-moving adults.

"Damnation!" a man bellowed, jerking the reins of his mule while tugging the hand brake of his two-wheeled cart. A pair of church ladies, hats big as their parasols, scurried away. A second mule cart stopped suddenly behind the first, and a Buick swerved to miss them both.

Donald rushed to steady the wild-eyed mule, who was straining to see around his blinders. He finally calmed the animal while its owner retrieved his lost load of fence posts from the street.

Donald thought again of the Great Storm and tilted his head toward the sky. Eighteen years ago it would have been much darker. He looked back to the carefree families milling by the church. Had everyone forgotten this dreadful anniversary?

A few blocks on, Donald heard bells and sprinted the last hundred yards to the trolley stop, where the Westheimer route met the line running north to the Heights. He slipped a nickel token into the fare box and reached for one of the handrails that ran the length of the car. He sat by an open window and leaned back. Sparks crackled from the trolley's pantograph as it sucked power from the overhead wire. He closed his eyes to focus on the wind in his face. It meant he was moving on.

Donald left the Heights trolley at 11th Street and pulled a gold watch from his vest pocket. As always, he ran his thumb over the engraving before opening the lid. Cletus Stokes bought the watch from the Sears catalog, then had his name engraved before leaving for France last fall.

"Keep this until I get back, little brother," Cletus told Donald the day he boarded the troop train for New York. "I hear it's muddy over there."

Donald pressed the release and the lid snapped open. A quarter to noon. He decided to go one block east to Harvard Street where the taller trees offered more shade. Walk tall. Shoulders back. The all-knowing Mrs.

Carhart had taught him that, but she didn't say to tighten his chest and arms to build muscle, or stretch to keep his body loose. Those things he'd learned on his own.

Nina Carhart's home was not the largest mansion along Heights Boulevard, but it had the most land. By taking Harvard north instead of Heights, Donald came to the rear of the estate first. A low hedge lined each side of a path to the back gate. From there he saw the older of two Italian gardeners who lived on the property.

The men no longer spoke to each other, even though they were from the same village. Mrs. Carhart said the dispute had begun two years before over a bottle of olive oil.

"Che bella, Albino!" Donald called in less-than-perfect Italian. He pointed left. "Those are fine roses!"

He leaned close enough for the bill of his cap to brush the wrought iron. To one side, a curved path led around the fountain past the gazebo to the back of the main house. To the other, Donald could just see a corner of the carriage house, and above it, the one-bedroom apartment that Albino and Paolo shared.

"Grazie, grazie," Albino called back, rising stiffly to his feet. He produced a bandana from his coveralls and used it to pat sweat from the back of his neck as he shuffled toward the gate. "Signore Brown, how are you today?"

"Bené, grazie," Donald answered as Albino selected a heavy key from the ring on his belt and unlocked the gate. "And you? How have you been, Albino?"

"Accusì, accusì," the gardener said, fingers wide as he tilted his head and one hand in unison side to side. "Come. I show you something new."

Donald spent a minute admiring the lemon tree Albino had planted that morning, then leaned in to whisper mischievously, "Where's Paolo?"

"UFFÀ!" Albino said, stiffening his body and loudly puffing his cheeks. He spit into the bushes to show the matter was closed.

Donald heard the library's French doors open and turned in time to see Nina Carhart emerge under the portico. He snatched off his cap as she approached.

Chapter 4

It always surprised Donald how graceful a woman could be.

"My dear boy," Nina Carhart said as she reached for his hand, "it is perfectly acceptable for you to enter my home through the front door." She said that, but he felt more comfortable coming through the garden.

"It's good to see you, Mrs. Carhart."

Her dress caught the light as she moved. Donald had never seen such a color. It reminded him most of a perfectly ripened peach, except that it was shiny. As they walked up the path toward the house, sunlight reflecting from her skirt made the bricks in front of her glow.

"My cousin in London sent two issues of the journal. I read them yesterday, so they're yours. As usual, the writing is a bit stuffy for my taste, but there are some articles you might enjoy."

"Thanks! You're sure you don't want them?"

She laughed. "It wouldn't do to leave copies of the *British Journal of Photography* lying around. My friends would be shocked."

"Is there an article about the new Speed Graphic?"

"If so, I may have missed it, Donald. You know I don't care for the technical side. It's bad enough dealing with chemicals to make my prints."

"When are you going to show me some of your work?"

"Another time, perhaps. Why are you interested in that camera?"

"I have one that needs repair. Jake Miller, one of the *Chronicle* photographers, gave it to me this morning."

"Foots?"

Foots! Donald stumbled, then steadied himself on a post.

"You know him?"

"No, but Elsie does. I've heard her call him 'Foots.' Odd name, don't you think?" Donald opened the library door for his mentor and she rang the housemaid for tea.

"Let me show you something far more interesting than your technical journals," Nina said, moving toward one of the bookcases that lined three sides of the library. Each wall of books had its own ladder that rolled smoothly left or right on a rail in the floor, and a matching rail attached to the highest shelf. A thick round table sat directly under the chandelier in the center of the room, with a short sofa in an alcove to one side.

After Elsie brought tea and pastries, she remained discretely in the next room, standing within earshot on a footstool and dusting the china cabinet. Briefly, she stretched on tiptoe to reach an upper shelf. Donald studied her trim figure through the open archway.

Was Elsie another of Jake's lady friends? Donald wondered what it would be like to have one of his own. His hand touched the frame of his heavy glasses. Slim chance with these goggles, he thought.

Elsie turned toward the open library door, caught Donald's gaze and smiled. Reflex made him look away. He was sorry at once. She was one of the few girls who paid him any mind. Donald wanted Elsie to know that he noticed her as well, but it was already too late. By the time he looked back, she had moved to another task.

Nina found the book she wanted: a history of famous photographers. "You'll recognize these names from books I've shown you before," she said. "You once favored the old-school artists."

Donald nodded. He finished pushing Elsie from his mind, then began turning pages slowly front to back. Mrs. Carhart wanted him to discover something for himself, and she'd been moving to this point for months.

"Each of these photographs looks like it could be on a museum wall," Donald said.

"Exactly so!" Nina swept her hand over the open book. "These photographers are trying to duplicate paintings. That is what they do in portrait studios, and it is what they do outdoors.

"Yes," Donald said, then reconsidered and disagreed. Some teachers would be angry, but Mrs. Carhart encouraged it.

"What about Mathew Brady's Civil War photographs? Surely you can't say he was trying to duplicate art."

"Yes, I would," she said. "Did you know that Brady and others often altered a scene before photographing it? Remember O'Sullivan's *Harvest of Death*?"

He did. She'd shown him that print—one of her late husband's more gruesome acquisitions—during his last visit. It was said that O'Sullivan had assistants arrange the bodies to improve the composition.

"Now let me show you something else." She opened a new volume to a page marked with a snip of green ribbon. "What do you think of this?"

Velum protected the print. Donald lifted away the thin tissue and studied the black and white photograph before answering. A muscular worker was shoveling coal, his bare arms and back glistened. Sweat streaked the black dust on his white skin. The only light came from the open furnace door. Flames from the firebox lit the lower half of the worker's face, stressing his strong jaw but hiding his eyes. All that showed was his strength.

"I feel like I'm looking at a machine."

"Excellent, Donald! Now you are seeing with your mind, not just your eyes."

She showed him a dozen more prints, each as strong as the first: young girls working in a textile factory; dusty prisoners in a Mississippi chain gang watched by white men on horseback with guns; five coal miners, none more than twelve years old, taking a break for lunch.

Donald turned each page slowly, then froze on one. It was less dramatic but somehow more real than the rest. It showed a country lane raked in morning light. Buggy tracks ran wide nearby and narrow in the distance. Two children, a boy and girl, appeared to be on their way to school. The camera was closer to their bare feet than to their heads.

The children were near enough that their faces were cropped from the top of the frame, leaving viewers to focus only on the books they carried—his bound with a leather strap and hers in a flour sack—and their clothes. They were ragged, but clean. Behind them a thin young woman, small as a twig in the background, watched as they walked away.

Donald forgot he was in the library of an elegant home until its owner spoke. Her voice was soft. Briefly, she touched the back of his hand.

"You see, Donald, none of these are posed. The photographers were documenting life, using their skills to tell a broader story."

"Documenting life," she'd said. Donald thought of that on the trolley ride home. He often saw things as if looking through the viewfinder of a camera, but until recently, his goals were composition and detail: How did the angle of the street fit the frame? Was there a good range of contrast between shadow and light?

"Is that the best you can do?" Nina asked one day after looking through some prints he'd brought for her to see. She began pushing him then, and slowly over the last year, she had changed the way he made pictures.

Chapter 5

Clarence Stokes was repairing the fence when Donald got home. Age had made him more meticulous. Instead of squatting easily on the ground as he used to do, he now began each project by setting out a pair of sawhorses he kept in the stable he called a "garage," even though the Stokes didn't own a car. An old door resting flat on the sawhorses formed a workbench. His tool box sat at a comfortable height on one end, and a broken gate rested in the middle.

"Hi Donny. Fetch me them two boards yonder by the shed."

"Sure, Pa," Donald said, scattering chickens as he trotted across the yard.

"And my handsaw from the garage," Clarence called.

"Here you go," Donald said a minute later. "Ma will be happy to see that fixed."

"Yep," Clarence said, grinning through his moustache. "I'll build up credit for this."

"Did Jake come by?"

"Jus' left a few minutes ago. Says to tell you he's goin' to Galveston this evening and wants you with him. He's comin' at five. Some kind of trouble down there?"

"We're not sure, Pa. Elton Sparks was working on a story, but he didn't come back. Now one of the editors wants Jake to get some photos and to find out what he can about Elton."

"You boys be careful. Galveston's turned mean since the gamblers and whores moved in. Goin' to get worse, too, if Prohibition starts next year. Them crooks will run things for sure."

Donald smiled at the salty wisdom.

"Thanks, Pa, we'll be careful."

"When yer ma and me lived there, things was different. Better, I'd say, even though there was still enough meanness to go around. Did I ever tell you 'bout the time me 'n old man Hammers went ..."

"I remember, Pa. Sorry, but I've got some things to do before Jake gets back."

"Fair 'nough," Clarence said, picking up the broken gate.

Back in his shed, Donald stopped to examine Elton's Speed Graphic, then began taking it apart. He opened his journal and drew two parallel lines below the day's first entry, then wrote *Sunday, mid-afternoon*.

He looked up from the broken camera, thinking again of Galveston. What were his parents doing, exactly eighteen years before? What did they see? Gathering darkness? Punishing rain? Certainly those, but when did they realize it was no ordinary storm? When did they know they were trapped?

Donald shook his head, willing himself back to the task at hand. Inhale ... hold ... exhale ...

Elton's camera was in rough shape, just as Jake described. Donald bent over his journal to begin the list of parts he'd need if the camera could be repaired.

"At least the film holder is intact," he said aloud as he wrote.

"There he goes again, talking to himself," Cletus used to say.

Donald straightened from his workbench and touched a picture of Cletus that was pinned to the wall. He didn't mind the family joke.

Returning to the film holder, Donald eased the half-inch thick wooden frame sideways, removing it from the back of the camera. Springs on each corner snapped the ground glass back in place.

"Good. The clips still work."

The black wooden frame, about the size and thickness of Donald's journal, held two sheets of film, one on each side. Eight identical film holders were in Elton's bag. From the way the dark slides were inserted—black tabs out—Donald knew that both sheets of film from the camera and four sheets in Elton's bag had been exposed. White tabs on the remaining six holders told him that the film inside had not been exposed.

He set the camera aside, pulled back the curtain of his darkroom and checked his pocket watch. Just time enough to process and dry the film.

Two hours later Donald heard Jake's car. He slipped a manila envelope into one of Mrs. Carhart's books and stuffed it deep into his traveling bag. He rinsed the last of the chemical trays, hung his rubber apron on a nail, grabbed his duffel and left.

Clarence was already leaning on the driver's side door, where he and Jake were sharing jokes. Naomi had ham sandwiches and apples ready in paper bags, one each for Donald and Jake. She intercepted Donald.

"Here's your supper, Donny. Do you have your extra pair of glasses and clean underwear?"

"Yes, Ma," he said, hoping Jake had missed that last remark. He kissed Naomi's cheek, waved goodbye to Clarence and hopped into the car.

"So," Jake said as they pulled away, "you got clean underwear?"

Jake eased into the shade of the Rice Hotel, grabbed his camera bag and duffel, then tucked the Sunday *Chronicle* under one arm. He peered across the street, scanning tracks at the Interurban station. He turned to Donald.

"So what about the draft? Will you register Thursday?"

"Sure, didn't you, when it was your turn?"

Jake ignored the question.

"Look," he said, walking toward the station. "That war never should have started in the first place. I voted for Wilson because he said he'd keep us out. Now we're in the thick of it. We've got what Wilson calls the 'Committee for Public Information' telling lies, but all they want is for boys who don't know any better to sign up. Who can you trust?"

"I trust my own feelings," Donald said.

Jake laughed.

"Your feelings? Where did they come from, some speech by a Four-Minute Man? The CPI pays those guys to wave flags and get fellows your age to fight the evil Huns."

"No, Jake, I'm thinking about Cletus. It's not fair he's in France and I'm not there to help him."

People standing on the sidewalk stopped their own conversations, and some began staring with more than curiosity.

"Look, Don, do you really think the whole German race turned evil overnight?"

Three men were following them now, staying close enough to hear.

Donald glanced back nervously. Jake pushed ahead, jaw set. Rather than holding his tongue, Jake's voice rose.

"We're being manipulated by powerful old men."

Jake turned to Donald, stopping to better make his point.

"Boys just like you are in German trenches, shitting their pants and wondering how the hell they got to be in such a mess! The Brits, the French, Canadians and now Americans are doing the same!"

"Slacker!" someone shouted.

"Coward!" a woman called.

Donald adjusted the strap of his duffel and grabbed Jake's arm. Four more idle men—all too old for the draft—drifted in their direction.

"Don, do you really believe everything the CPI says?" Jake growled. "They make trench warfare look like some patriotic game. Get your ass shot off if you want, but I'm staying here. I say the propaganda our side puts out is no better than what the Germans are doing."

Donald eased Jake toward the right track. Under the thin fabric of his summer jacket, Jake's upper arm was a bundle of steel. He shrugged off Donald's grip.

Passengers scrambled for seats, even though the trolley was half full. Donald sat by the window and Jake on the aisle. Donald looked forward, then back. None of others may have had heard Jake's comments on the street, because there were no more angry looks.

"Where are we staying tonight?" Donald asked as the electric car pulled smoothly away on its hundred-minute run to the coast. Jake crossed his leg and let one foot dangle into the aisle, then balanced his hat on his knee. A soothing clack-clack vibrated up from the wheels through the seat.

Running the fingers of both hands through his hair, Jake pressed his head back against the leather seat and sighed.

"I know someone with a spare room," he said, finally calm. "Clara Barnes owns a house near the Strand and rents rooms in her carriage house to a couple of women. We've got the third bedroom."

"We're staying in a house with two women?" Donald whispered.

"Yes," Jake whispered back. "Why?"

"It doesn't seem proper."

"You'll be in no danger."

"That's not what I mean!"

"Don't worry about these girls, they know the ropes. They both work at one of the new clubs along the seawall."

Donald glanced up and down the aisle. No one seemed to hear.

"Club? You mean a restaurant?"

"You might say that. If you know the right people in Galveston, you can get a meal and a side dish—like one of my lady friends. All it takes is cash." Jake leaned back, pleased with his own cleverness and Donald's distress. "And if you're not interested in dessert, you can always drink and gamble. That's what pays the rent."

Donald watched their shadow run flat across the prairie as the trolley crossed the viaduct over the Santa Fe tracks. It seemed to lean forward, like a runner starting a race.

Jake dozed for a while, then turned to his newspaper. "Well look at this," he said, slapping the page with the back of his hand. "Pershing is adding twenty thousand more names to the Army's casualty list. He says they're all 'slight' injuries that were just too trivial to mention before. I'll bet all those wounds weren't trivial to the boys who got them."

"General Pershing must have had a good reason," Donald said. Jake glanced sideways at him, turned the page and continued reading.

On a stretch of dirt road adjacent to the tracks, a man paced the trolley on his Indian Model O light twin. Donald knew the bright red motorcycle from a magazine ad, but he'd never seen one on the road. The lightness of the little two-cylinder made up for its lack of power. He was surprised at the speed. The Indian was keeping up with the trolley, which had to be going at least thirty-five miles per hour.

Dust billowed from the ground, rolled briefly around the rear fender, boiled up and finally drifted away in the air, unable to keep up. The rider raised himself up, knees bent like a jockey, absorbing each new bump with his arms and his legs. Donald watched for more than a mile, imagining himself roaming the county in tall boots, gauntlets, goggles and of course, a dashing leather helmet. Someday, someday.

Jake brought him back.

"Hey, here's Enoch's first story about the labor shortage on the seawall."

It took Donald a few seconds to remember where he was.

"The extension to the fort?"

"That's what Elton was supposed to shoot. I'll get out there tomorrow and ask around." Jake read on. "Says here the project has only half the workers it needs."

"Elton did go to the seawall," Donald said quietly.

"What?"

"There were four exposed sheets in his bag and two more in the camera. I had time to process the negatives before you picked me up."

"What did he get?"

"The first four are what you'd expect; a foreman looking at people pouring concrete. There's a shot of workers around the pile driver and a good angle of the steel forms on the gulf side of the wall."

"And the other two?"

"I'm not sure."

"Let's see," Jake said, stuffing his newspaper in the space between the seats as Donald recovered the envelope from his bag. Jake took all six negatives and moved across to use the west-facing window as a light box.

Each translucent four-by-five-inch celluloid sheet was thin and stiff as an average postcard. Jake checked first to see which side of the film carried the emulsion, then pressed that side to the window glass.

"You can tell who's the foreman," he called. "He's the only one not working."

Donald waited. Jake raised the fifth negative to the glass, leaned closer, then dropped back into his seat. He stared across at Donald. "This wasn't taken at the seawall."

"I know." Donald swung his knees into the aisle and leaned toward Jake. "That's one of two that were still in the camera."

Jake squinted again at the last negative, holding it firmly against the glass. He lowered his voice so that only Donald could hear. "Looks like I was right about Elton having a lady friend in Galveston. I can't tell who she is from this, but she has a nice figure."

Overcome with curiosity, a boy lunged from behind for Donald's side, but his mother held him back.

"I think both shots were taken in the same room," Donald added. He watched as Jake lowered the negative from the window and raised the last one of the set.

"Wow!" Jake said, "Elton sure didn't take these for the newspaper."

"What's a negative?" asked the boy. His mother apologized and tried to pry her son's hands from the back of Donald's seat.

He turned to face the child.

"A photographic negative is what we use to make pictures."

"How does it work?"

Donald heard Jake groan.

"Photographers start with a thin piece of celluloid or glass that's coated on one side with special chemicals. Those chemicals have to always be kept in the dark, because even a little bit of light changes them. You see, the photographic emulsion ... "

"Is that magic?"

Donald smiled, seeing himself in the child. He glanced across the aisle, but Jake was back at the window, intent on the negatives.

"I asked someone that very question once," Donald said. The boy's face brightened. "Yes, it looks like magic, but it's just chemistry. You see, the photographic emulsion contains ... "

"But what does a negative do?" the boy pressed.

Donald sighed. Jake cupped one hand to his ear in mock attention. Donald refused the bait.

"Do you ever put your hand in front of a lamp to make shadow puppets on the wall?"

"Oh, yes!" the boy said, "I make up stories for them!"

"Why are your puppets always dark?"

"Because they block the light?"

"Right. And why is the area around them bright?"

"Because the light from the lamp is shining on the wall?"

"Right again," Donald said. He heard Jake moan, but ignored him.

"Cameras are like that. The film inside a camera remembers what is light and what is dark. The film becomes the negative we use to make prints of our pictures. You see, the photographic emulsion is ..."

"Is there a lamp inside the camera?"

"No." Donald smiled at the boy. "The light comes from outside. Can you remember what a camera looks like?"

"Sort of a box?"

"There's a round piece of glass on the front, like my eyeglasses here." Donald tapped the side of his frames. "That part is the lens. Inside is a mechanism called a shutter, and that determines how much light reaches the emulsion. Then the chemicals ... "

"The shutter, is that what clicks when you push the button?"

"Yes! That sound is the shutter opening and closing very fast to let in a tiny bit of light. If you were a camera, it would be like holding your eyes tightly closed, then suddenly opening and closing them again."

The boy blinked several times.

"Like the shutters on our windows at home!" he said, loud enough for other passengers to hear. Some turned and smiled, although one man huffed and snapped the newspaper he was trying to read.

The boy's eyes opened wide. "And that light shines on the film inside the camera!"

"Exactly so!"

Now the boy was beaming, and so was his mother. "Excuse me," Donald said as he slid into the seat next to Jake.

Chapter 6

It was twilight by the time the Interurban reached the 21st Street station. Despite the cool front, Galveston's humid salt air made it clear that summer was not over. Jake and Donald began walking. Ten minutes later they reached the oyster shell driveway of a two-story carriage house. A tidy Craftsman bungalow stood next door. The structures were joined by a wide arbor that opened onto a large garden behind the main house.

From the driveway, Donald could see what had once been a flower garden. Now the surviving rose and lantana bushes tended themselves, and the remaining beds were given over to vegetables and fruit.

"Clara Barnes rents rooms here," Jake explained as he knocked on the carriage house door. "She lives in the main house and lets tenants use her kitchen." Donald imagined an elderly widow, living off the rent.

"Foots!" squealed the woman who opened the door. "Foots!" called another from down the hall. She waited her turn to hug Jake, then asked, "Who's your friend?"

"Ladies, this is Mister Donald Brown, soon to be the second best news photographer in Houston. Don, meet Miss Rebecca Simpson and Miss Jennifer Lane."

"Nice to meet you, Miss Simpson," Donald said, tipping his cap.

"Please, call me Rebecca."

"Thanks. And nice to meet you, too, Jen ... uh, Miss Lane."

"Jenny is my name," she said, "but at the club they call me Gin."

"Imagine that," Jake said. "Ladies, all I've had to eat tonight is a ham sandwich and an apple. Suppose we head to Black's for some real food. Don, are you going?"

"Thanks. I'll stay here." He was hungry, but the thought of an evening listening to Jake impress his friends left him suddenly tired.

"Ladies, you've got ten minutes." Jake watched admiringly from below as Jenny and Rebecca jiggled to the top of the stairs.

"I thought we came to Galveston to look for Elton," Donald said a bit harshly after the women had closed the doors to their rooms. Jake turned, a faint smile fading from his lips.

"Don, from what I saw in those two negatives, I'm sure now that Elton's just on another binge. Hell, we might find him tonight, passed out in one of the clubs."

"I hope you're right."

"You sure you're not coming with us? You don't know what you're missing. These gals can show you a good time."

"I'll take your word for it. Where's our room?"

"In the back near the bathroom. Take my stuff when you go."

Donald lugged the bags down the hall, dropped Jake's just inside the door, then pressed the button to turn on the electric light. Their room was surprisingly large. A small desk with a two-bulb banker's lamp separated the twin beds. Open windows on three sides allowed a welcome breeze through the screens, although weeds brushed against the one in back.

He set his own bag on the nearest chair and looked around. More lace and frill than necessary, but the room had a comfortable chair and several shelves of books. A thick tome, *Modern Methods on Nursing,* was open on the desk. Beside it, a simple white vase overflowed with holly leaves and freshly cut lantana.

Donald stooped to peer into a photo on the desk. It showed a toddler perched sidesaddle on a pony, a black man in uniform holding the reins. He set his glasses aside and lifted the picture close. The girl, perhaps three years old, wore a white dress with a dark ribbon around her waist and another in her hair. She smiled confidently at the camera, but the groomsman stood in profile, stiff as a hitching post.

Laughter from the front room announced that "Foots" and his friends were about to leave.

"Will you be all right?" Jenny called to Donald. "Clara will be home soon, but we use her kitchen. The back door is open. We all buy food, so help yourself to whatever you find."

More laughter. "Don't wait up, my man," Jake said as he closed the front door.

`Donald savored the silence. He found his glasses, took his journal and a pencil from his bag, then went next door to check the icebox.

"Oh, boy!" he said aloud to the apple pie and milk.

Donald had just taken the last bite of pie when the front door opened, then slammed shut. He chewed quickly so he could swallow and call out, but the intruder spoke first.

"OUCH!" said a female voice, then, "... Ah ... Ah ... OUCH!" He heard something small hit the floor.

"Hello?" he called.

Silence in the front room.

"Hello? Mrs. Barnes?"

"Yes?" Clara said as Donald emerged from the kitchen, using his sleeve to wipe milk from his chin. Clara stood by the umbrella stand, straw hat dangling from the back of her neck and one hair comb lying on the floor. Her arms were pinned behind her, both sleeves tangled in the jacket she'd been wearing over her white blouse.

"Are you the overnight guest?"

"One of them," Donald said. "Jake took Rebecca and Jennifer to get something to eat. I'm Don ... Donald Brown."

"Miss Clara Barnes. Pleased to meet you Mr. Brown."

Hostess and houseguest stood firm; Clara contemplating the athletic man with goggle eyes, and Donald transfixed by the slight, windblown young woman bent double, arms fast behind her as if tied with a rope.

"OUCH!" she cried again, jerking her chin to her chest. A second hair comb thumped to the floor, landing near the first.

"May I help?" Donald said, gathering his wits.

"Please! My neck! Something is sticking me. Will you see if you can find it?"

"Of course!" Donald said, sounding more certain than he felt.

"Here," he said, first removing the hat from her shoulders, then freeing her arms and hanging the jacket and hat on a stand by the door. Clara gathered her hair from her neck and bent forward. Donald moved to her side, arching one arm over the top of her head, the other hovering just above her neck. When Clara flinched, her shoulder pressed briefly against Donald's chest. He caught the scent of lavender.

"Do hurry, Mr. Brown. This really hurts!"

All he saw was a tangle of ruffles and lace.

"Hold still, Miss Barnes," he said, slipping his glasses into his pants pocket. He put his hand on her back, lightly at first, and then with more conviction. He felt the warmth of her skin through the fabric of her blouse. He leaned closer. A wisp of auburn hair brushed his cheek. He felt her breathing. He felt his own.

Donald's vision sharpened as he peered in. Without glasses, his keen eyes following the fibers as easily as others might view a fishing net. He caught a tiny flash of silver.

"I see it!" he said. "Yes, a small pin is caught in the seam of your blouse and collar. It must have dislodged when you tried to remove your jacket."

"I believe you! Just hurry!"

A bit of lace snagged the pin, forcing the point deeper. "Ouch!" she cried again.

Donald hesitated, then without asking, released the top two hooks at the back of her blouse. A trickle of blood marked the spot where the tip of the pin went in. He lifted her collar aside and noticed the gentle arch of the woman's bare neck.

Clara's skin glistened under his hand. Donald eased out the pin and took a few seconds more to work it through the hem and the lace. He left his own hand underneath, a barrier in case the pin slipped. When it was free, Donald used his fingertip to wipe a drop of blood, then let the fabric fall back to Clara's neck.

"There, that should feel better," he said, suddenly aware that he'd been breathing on a stranger's neck, and barely knew her name. Stepping back too quickly, he bumped a chair with the backs of his knees and sat with an awkward thump. He froze, holding the tiny pin at arm's length.

"Here you go. This was the problem."

"Thank you!" he heard her say, but even the short distance between them meant he no longer saw her clearly. A moment before, he could have counted the hairs on her head. Was she smiling? He wasn't sure.

"Are you all right, Mr. Brown?"

He squinted back.

"Oh yes, I just forgot, I mean, wait." he said, first patting the front of his shirt, then each of his pants pockets before finding his glasses. He bent forward, looped the metal arms smoothly behind his ears and twitched his nose to settle the lenses on his face.

"There!" he said, looking up.

Clara giggled.

"Oh! Forgive me!" she said, hand over her mouth. "But those glasses make you look like an owl."

Donald's face reddened as he stood, and Clara quickly changed the subject.

"Are you one of the newspaper photographers?"

"Not yet, but I might be soon. I go with Jake on some of his assignments."

"You're on an assignment?"

"Yes. We're here to document the new section of the seawall, but we also want to learn what happened to Elton Sparks, one of the *Chronicle* photographers. He came down Thursday and we haven't heard from him since. The police are looking for him too."

"Oh, my goodness!"

Donald thought Clara was reacting to his words, but instead, she'd caught her reflection in the mirror behind him.

"Please excuse me for a moment, Mr. Brown."

"Of course!"

Donald turned. Hands clasped behind his back, he rocked slightly heel to toe, pretending to study the parlor as Clara worked to repair her hair. He stifled the urge to hum.

The room was sparsely furnished. A small dining table with six chairs stood near the center, but the most prominent feature was a reading chair and footstool in a corner with five tall windows. A low bookcase extending from the east wall formed a cozy nook. Most of the books were within arm's reach of the chair, and one lay open on the side table.

Clara mumbled something past the hair comb held between her lips.

"Pardon me, Miss Barnes?"

Removing the comb, she said again, "Is your friend in trouble?"

"We're not sure. Jake wants to make some inquiries."

"From what I've heard, he certainly knows who to ask."

"How do you know Jake?" Donald asked, happy she hadn't called him Foots.

She hesitated. "Mainly through Rebecca and Jenny."

Clara fitted the last comb in her hair. Glancing at Donald's shoulders in the mirror, she paused, then gave each of her cheeks a pinch and a pat.

"You may turn now, Mr. Brown," she said. "I'm going to make tea. Would you like some?"

In the kitchen Clara slipped a blue gingham apron over her head and tied it behind her waist. She filled the kettle with water from a pitcher by the sink, placed it on the stove and took a safety match from a metal dispenser hanging on the wall. Clara struck the match on the sandpaper strip and turned one of the four gas valves. Gas hissed as she eased the flame toward the burner, which ignited with a solid thump.

"Where do you live?" she asked, surprised and pleased to see Donald take his own pie plate and empty milk glass from the table to the sink.

"Houston. And you? Have you lived in Galveston long?"

"All my life. My brother and I were both born in this house."

Donald's hand cupped the cool edge of the sink. "So this house survived the storm." He gazed blankly around the kitchen. "Do you remember it?"

"Of course. Today is the anniversary."

Donald shook his head. "You wouldn't know that by reading today's newspaper."

"I've been thinking about it all day. I was four years old, but I still recall every detail. We spent the night here."

"Where are your parents now?"

Clara paused and Donald was sorry he'd asked. The question caught her by surprise. Tears formed as she spoke.

"Miss Barnes, I shouldn't have…"

"No. I'm all right." She took a deep breath and went on. "It was a Saturday, and Papa had gone to meet some friends for lunch. Nobody knew how bad the weather was going to get. When water filled the streets, they stayed in the restaurant."

Clara paused, then straightened her back before continuing. "The men were still there when a printing press fell through from the second floor. It killed Papa and six others."

"Terrible," Donald said weakly, looking down at his hands. He tried to think of what to say next, but the only sound was the kettle water trying to boil.

Clara cleared her throat, gathering strength to finish her story.

"I was young, but I remember him well. Papa taught at the medical school. He read bedtime stories to me and my brother every night. I think that's why I enjoy books so much now."

"Are those your books in the spare room next door?" Donald asked, eager to change the subject.

"Yes, I use that as a study because the afternoon light is so nice. My parents had quite a library before the storm, but almost everything was ruined."

"It's nice of you to share your books with Rebecca and Jenny."

Clara laughed. "They don't read, I'm afraid. They prefer having a good time in the clubs."

She turned to the stove, so her back was to Donald when she spoke next. "We lost Mama last year. Consumption. I think she contracted it working with patients at the hospital."

"I'm sorry, Miss Barnes." Donald's voice was soft.

"Thank you. It's not so bad now. I rent the rooms next door to help pay the bills and keep from being lonesome." She turned back toward Donald, forcing a smile. "My brother is in France. From what the newspapers say, the war may be over in a few months. I hope he'll be home soon."

When the kettle began to whistle Clara turned off the burner. She scooped tea leaves from a jar into a small strainer fitted to the top of a porcelain pot. As she slowly poured steaming water from the kettle through the strainer, the smell of fresh tea filled the room.

"There's a small lemon tree outside that door on your right," Mr. Brown. "They're just beginning to ripen. Would you mind getting one for our tea?"

Clara set out a plate of cookies and filled their cups. She hung her apron by the cupboard, then noticed Donald washing the lemon at the sink. She sat watching as he used his pocketknife to quarter the fruit. He placed the small cutting board and fruit on the table before taking the chair across from hers.

"Are you always so polite, Mr. Brown?"

"What?"

"The lemon."

"The lemon?"

"Yes. Another man would have simply handed it to me."

"I'm sorry. I'm used to helping out at home. I wasn't thinking."

"Please, don't apologize!" She smiled and reached for the sugar bowl, quietly enjoying the way Donald squirmed in his chair.

He added a spoonful of sugar to his own tea and squeezed a slice of fresh lemon, cupping one hand over to avoid spraying the juice. Clara smiled again.

Donald hesitated. "Can you tell me more about your family? About that night?"

"Of course. It helps to talk about it." Clara looked directly at Donald. "Especially today." She turned in her chair toward the parlor, recalling the scene in her mind.

"Mama took me, my brother and our dog upstairs when water reached the front door. Many of our neighbors were here, too. Papa always said that if a bad storm came, this house was the place to be. It's stronger than most, but I still remember watching from the upstairs landing when a big man with an axe chopped a hole in our living room floor. As soon as he broke through, water gushed in."

"Ah," Donald said, "That probably saved your house from floating off the foundation."

"Yes. The storm peaked around midnight. Mama said the water was three feet deep upstairs. I remember the house shaking and I heard debris striking the outside walls, like angry men hammering to get in."

"The noise must have been terrifying."

"Oh yes. But it got worse when the wind died down. That's when we heard people screaming for help. It was dark, but then lightning would make everything bright as day. Suddenly, for a second or two, we'd see them, people and horses and mules and cows, all trying to keep their heads above water. Even as a little girl, I wanted to help, but there was nothing I could do. I still have nightmares about it."

Donald looked toward the window. The curtains lifted slightly in the evening breeze. Clara raised her teaspoon and studied a pattern on the handle. She traced it lightly with her finger.

"The men pulled in more than a dozen people through the upstairs windows. Some didn't even have clothes. Then I heard my mother scream. She wouldn't stop. My uncle said later that a body floated in one window and bumped against her legs in the dark. Someone pushed the body out again. Nobody knew who it was."

Donald shuddered. He reached for a cookie, raised it halfway to his lips, then returned it to the edge of his plate.

"It's hard to talk of these things," Clara said, "but we must, don't you think? Where were you that day, Mr. Brown?"

He sipped his tea, then set the cup gently in its saucer. He gazed out the back window and into the darkened yard. They sat that way for nearly a minute. Clara gently swirled the liquid in her cup and watched the tea leaves settle to the bottom. She was about to ask a different question when Donald spoke.

"I was here. I was nine months old, so I don't remember."

"You were born in Galveston?"

"I don't know." Donald nudged the cookie on his plate, but didn't pick it up. "I was raised as an orphan in Houston. When I was seven or eight, one of the matrons told me all she knew, but it wasn't much. She said a woman left me at Sealy Hospital around midday, before the worst of the storm."

Clara waited for him to continue. His voice sounded far away.

"The woman who left me ... " Donald took a breath and started over. "The woman told the nurse she had a little girl nearby and was afraid she couldn't carry me any more with the streets full of water. She handed me to the nurse and never came back."

Donald removed his glasses and rubbed his eyes. The kitchen blurred, but part of the doctor's letter seemed to hover above the table.

... The poor woman's clothes were soaked through. Her hat and combs were gone, her long hair matted about her face. She was sobbing, trying to explain that she had been caught out when the street cars stopped running ...

After a moment, Donald looked toward Clara. He swept one hand across the table, found his glasses, tipped his head and slipped the loops behind his ears. His eyes focused and once again she was there, head down, her hand clutching a teaspoon.

"I have a photograph of me," he said.

"Oh?" The spoon wavered.

"And a letter written by a doctor on duty that day. He wrote to let his wife know he had survived, and he told her about me. She kept the letter and eventually traced my name to the DePelchin Home in Houston. She wanted me to have it."

Clara leaned forward, elbows on the table, one hand lightly touching her throat.

"The doctor's name was Lealand. He was on duty at the hospital," Donald repeated. "Charles Lealand?" he asked hopefully.

She echoed the name. "Lealand. No, I don't know that name. But my mother could have. She worked at Sealy from 1900 until last year."

Clara refilled their cups, squeezed a few drops of lemon into her tea and glanced at Donald. His face seemed relaxed, even serene. She had heard of children who lost parents in the storm. An orphanage. What could life be like, without a family, and not even knowing who they were?

"We always had clean clothes and plenty to eat," Donald said.

Clara started, as if he had been reading her thoughts.

Donald noticed and smiled. His face relaxed. It was easy to talk about the children's home; the storm was another matter.

"The staff was kind," he continued, "but with so many children to care for, we had to stay on schedule. We rarely did anything out of the ordinary."

"Did you attend school? From your speech, it sounds as if you did."

"Thank you, Miss Barnes. Yes, we all went to school. The matrons were quite strict about that. I didn't do well at first because of my eyes, but then one of the wealthy patrons from the women's guild noticed and made sure I got my first pair of glasses."

"How kind. Who was she?"

"Nina Carhart. Perhaps you've heard of her?"

"No."

"She's often in the society pages, but she prefers to be known for her charity work. After her husband died in 1910, she devoted herself to various causes."

"Did you ever see her again, after she provided your glasses?"

"Oh yes! You might say she became my mentor, even after I went to live with the Stokes. We still talk about books and art, and we share an interest in photography."

"That's delightful, but strange."

"What?"

"For a society woman to be a photographer."

"I never thought of that as strange. Photography seems the most natural thing in the world to me. Mrs. Carhart is a brilliant woman with many interests."

Clara eased her chair from the table and crossed to the cupboard, returning with the cookie jar. "Have another, Mr. Brown?"

He looked down. The one on his plate had disappeared.

"Thank you. That would be great."

"How long did you live at the orphanage?"

"Until 1912, when I was taken in by Clarence and Naomi Stokes." Donald scooped up the last crumbs from his plate. He smiled at Clara. "I want to be on my own soon, but haven't decided just how."

"Are you a professional photographer?"

Donald paused. This was new, a young woman interested in what he had to say.

"Not yet. I repair cameras and build tripods for some of the newsmen, and I take pictures for myself. Jake helped me find a job at the *Chronicle*. I'll probably take it."

"You don't sound happy."

"About the job? No. It's a good one; that's not what I mean. The trouble is that I think it would be grand to be free."

"Free? How so, Mr. Brown?"

"If you work for someone, others tell you what to do and when to come and go. If I'm a newspaper photographer, my editor will tell me what to photograph."

"Still, it sounds like interesting work. Everyone has a boss."

"I'd rather be the one deciding what to shoot."

"Shoot?"

"I'm sorry. Jake says that. I mean, what to photograph."

Clara laughed, leaned back in her chair, closed one eye and made a pistol of her hand. She pointed it about the kitchen. "Shoot is a good word for it. I can see why you say that. Are you shooting tomorrow?"

"Jake's here working on a story about the new extension of the seawall."

"Oh yes, so you said. And you're inquiring about Mr. Sparks."

"Yes, he and Jake are good friends."

The mantle clock in the parlor chimed four sets, then ten single tones in a row.

"Goodness, ten o'clock already. It seemed much earlier. "Am I keeping you up, Miss Barnes?"

"Not at all. There's another cookie here with your name on it."

Donald reddened but grinned as he reached for the jar. "They're delicious! Did you make them yourself?"

"Of course. The nuts came from a tree Mama and I planted after the house was raised to its present grade. The tree is only now beginning to bear pecans. The first of them dropped a few days ago, and I found them before the squirrels did."

Donald was distracted. When Clara's lips smiled, her eyes smiled too. Suddenly he remembered the large book in the carriage house.

"Are you a nurse?"

"Yes. Well, a nurse in training. It takes time to become certified. My classes resume next week at Sealy. They're hard, and sometimes I wonder if I can keep up."

Clara looked across at Donald. He nodded in return.

"I love the work," she continued. "I just hope I can equal my mother's skill. My father taught at the medical school and they met one day when he lectured to her class. Mama earned her certification, but didn't work while Papa was alive. Everyone was needed after the storm, so she volunteered. Nursing soon became her full-time job."

From the kitchen, Donald noticed a small lamp shining at the far end of the parlor. "I'm sure," he said slowly, "your parents would be proud of you."

"Thank you." Clara followed his gaze, then remembered the photograph he had mentioned earlier.

"Your baby picture. Did your mother leave it with the nurse at the hospital?"

"I don't know if the woman who left me was my mother, but yes, the photograph was tucked in my blanket."

Clara sensed that Donald had more to say. She fixed her eyes on the table top and chose her words carefully.

"The picture surely means a great deal to you, Mr. Brown. As a photographer, I suppose you've spent hours studying every detail."

"It looks like someone's home," he said abruptly.

"Excuse me?"

"I mean, it's not a typical portrait from a professional studio. It was taken in an ordinary room."

Clara leaned forward, but continued to gaze at the table while Donald described the print.

"My hand is resting on the arm of a chair. I'm dressed in a baby's white smock, with embroidery on the front. There's a door and striped wallpaper in the background, and books or boxes are leaning against one wall ..."

"Ah!" Clara gripped the table's edge with both hands.

"What's the matter?"

"That image—a baby in a chair—sounds familiar. I may have seen it before."

"What! Where?"

"After the storm, Mama saved photographs that she and others found in the debris."

"Why would ..." Clara raised her hand to stop him.

"My mother was a nurse, so at first light, the morning after the storm, she left me and my brother with our aunt and made her way to the hospital. One poor man she met was clutching a photograph and sobbing. He told Mama it was all he had left of his family. Mama never forgot."

"But you said she collected photographs?"

"Yes. She was walking home that first day, picking her way through the wreckage, when she found a photograph. It was damaged, but not so much that you couldn't see who was in the picture. She remembered the desperate man she'd met in the hospital and brought the photo home."

"Did she recognize anyone in it?"

"I don't think so, but from then on, she watched for pictures. As soon as Mama's friends heard what she was doing, they brought more. Mama numbered each one and wrote down where it was found, who gave it to her and when. She did her best to preserve them, drying the paper prints and cleaning off the mud. I remember seeing batches of them here on this table, spread on dish towels to dry."

"Was your mother able to identify the people?"

"Only a few. And sometimes strangers who learned about her collection would come here. If they recognized a family member and asked for the picture, Mama always gave it to them."

"But she kept the rest?"

"Yes, wait here." Clara hurried upstairs. When she returned, she found Donald pacing the kitchen.

"Here," she said, setting a handsome cherry wood case on the table.

"Wow! My pa—I mean Clarence—would be impressed with the craftsmanship." Donald ran his hand over the lid. The box had recessed hinges and handles made of polished brass. The wood reflected the kitchen's electric lights. "Look," he said, "these joints fit so perfectly that you can hardly see the seam."

"Father Shannon made it," Clara said, resting her hand on the top. "He wanted something to honor all the people he'd lost in his parish."

Clara stood to Donald's right, facing the box. She released a small latch and lifted the lid, which opened silently until it came to rest on two brass supports. Inside were a mix of vertical compartments and trays for different sizes of prints. Clara removed a book from the top tray, opened to the first page, placed her finger along the edge and began reading aloud.

Dear Reader:
September eighth, 1900 began a night of terror from which those of us who survived shall never fully recover. For some of the dead, these few photographs are the only proof they ever lived. Please guard them with all of the loving care they deserve. — Martha Barnes, January 10, 1901

"The only proof," Donald repeated, lightly touching his head.

"Mama made a lot of entries in the first three months," Clara said. "After that, most of the photographs she found were too badly damaged to save."

"Yes, the paper would have deteriorated quickly after it got wet, or the sun would have faded the image."

She handed the journal to Donald. The second page began a sequence of numbered entries. Each was the same: first an image number, then the date and place where it was found, along with the name of the person who found it. Following that, a paragraph—sometimes as much as a page—told anything more that was known about the people in the picture. The last entry, number 324, was made on June 23, 1901.

Clara stood over the box. Two trays were on the table, and she was leafing through a collection of cards in the third tray when she pulled one out.

"Ah, here," she said, examining the card closely.

For a moment, Donald couldn't breathe. On the back he saw the familiar inscription: *b. January 1, 1900.*

"Please," he said.

Clara handed him the photograph. He stared at the date a moment more, then turned the card over in his hands.

Clara lowered herself into the chair beside him.

"Is this the picture you described?"

"Yes," he whispered, "that's me."

Chapter 7

Thirty seconds passed with only the sound of the clock ticking in the parlor. Clara leaned gently toward Donald, waiting.

"So, there were at least two copies," he said, finally looking up and tapping the print against the fingers of one hand. "The card I have in Houston has writing on the front. Other than the number your mother added, this one is blank."

Clara pulled away, amazed to see Donald remove his glasses and study the print like a jeweler inspecting a diamond ring.

"Then what ..." Clara struggled to regain her composure. "What does it mean, the fact that there's a second photograph?"

"I'm not sure. I need more," Donald said, looking with unfocused eyes toward the far wall. "A name, an address; anything would help."

"Do you think your parents took the picture of you? Your father might have written your birth date on the back. Your mother could have written 'Maude Brown's baby' on the front."

Donald turned to face Clara. "If my parents did make this photograph, it means that they probably took more—lots more. Whoever made this image used good equipment and knew how to handle the light. They may have had a darkroom to process the negatives and make prints. In 1900, the negative for a print this size would have been glass."

"Glass," Clara repeated. "I remember. Sometimes Mama and her friends found glass negatives, or pieces of them, but after laying out in the sun a few days, the image was gone."

Donald nodded. He stood and walked around the table, opposite where Clara sat. He rested his palms on the back of a chair, but didn't bother to put on his glasses. It was easier to think when he couldn't see.

"My parents may have taken the picture, but this print is not from a professional studio. If it were, the name of the studio would be printed on the back."

Donald looked toward the box, squinting to see. Frustrated, he retrieved his glasses and pointed to different cards.

"That one is from a portrait studio in Columbus, Ohio. Here's one from Steubenville, Indiana, and that's from a Galveston studio. See? They all have the studio name and fancy artwork on the back." He turned over two prints. "The format is called *carte-de-visite*."

"Yes," Clara said, "we had a box full before the storm. I don't think photographers make them anymore. People nowadays prefer to frame their prints or keep them in books."

Clara pulled more cards from the case, each with similar art. The remaining photos were of poor quality. Most were out of focus and badly composed. She reached across to the picture of Donald, turned the card over, noted the catalog number and began looking for it in the journal.

"Number 47," she said, glancing up. "A low number means that the card was found soon after the storm." Clara found the page and laid the journal flat on the table. Donald walked back around to sit beside her, and their shoulders touched as Clara read aloud. She traced her finger along the edge of an entry that began near the bottom of the page:

No. 47 – found by Henry Booth, Saturday, September 15, 1900, in the upstairs remains of a house.

"The upstairs remains of a house," Donald read again. "Do you know the man who found this picture?"

"Yes! Mr. Booth fixed a broken window for me just last month. He owns a hardware store and makes small repairs for people in the neighborhood." Clara turned the page, where the journal entry continued.

Mr. Booth discovered the photograph when he was with three men searching for victims in the buildings along 12th Street near Avenue J. Mr. Booth said the home was not in its original location. He could not identify the house or its owner.

After an awkward silence, Donald looked back to the table. "This is a lot to think about," he said, placing the photo of himself back on the table. "My parents were probably lost in the storm. I've always wanted to know what happened to them, but I figure after eighteen years, there isn't much hope. Now this. I don't know what to make of it."

"Would you like to talk to Mr. Booth before you go back to Houston?" Clara asked. "I could introduce you. Perhaps tomorrow?"

"Of course. Thank you. I ..." Donald watched as Clara resorted the prints and returned them to their compartments within the box. She glanced up before placing the picture of him in its proper tray. The small journal rested again in the top section. Clara gently closed the lid and slid the latch into place. She smiled at Donald.

"Sleep on it, Mr. Brown. It's late."

Donald slept, but not well. When he heard giggling at the front door he waited, eyes closed, for Jake to enter the room. Jake finally did come in, but only to retrieve his bag. The carriage house was quiet after that, until Donald heard more laughing upstairs.

Chapter 8

Monday, September 9, 1918

Donald woke at sunrise, at first padding around the room in his socks to keep from waking the others. The indoor washroom was a luxury. He brushed his teeth, then shaved, using the straight razor, brush and soap he carried in his duffel along with a small folding camera, extra film and spare glasses.

When he crossed the arbor to the kitchen next door he carried his journal and Mrs. Carhart's book. The parlor had good light and a comfortable chair. After his late night, it might be a while before Jake was ready to go.

As Donald crossed through the kitchen, past the landing of the stairs and into the parlor, he noticed a patch of flooring where the oak was a different shade from the rest of the wood. He went to one knee and lifted back the heavy oriental rug that hid most of the damage. The repair was at least a foot wide and three feet long.

"That's where our neighbor chopped a hole in the floor during the storm," Clara said from the stairs behind him. Donald jumped to his feet, dropping the corner of the rug.

"I'm sorry I startled you, Mr. Brown." she said, heading for the kitchen. "Would you like some coffee?"

Donald followed, laid his books on the table and watched Clara move easily about the kitchen. Her skirt reached only to mid-calf—the new wartime fashion—but her high-necked blouse, black stockings and laced shoes were from an earlier time, probably things her mother had worn. Clara's hair was in a tidy chignon, coiled above the nape of her neck.

A breeze stirred the white lace curtains above the sink, and once more, Donald smelled lavender. From the magnolia tree outside, a mockingbird ran through its repertoire of chirps, twills and tweets.

"Would you mind grinding the coffee?" Clara said, placing the mill and small burlap sack in front of him. Donald scooped a handful of beans.

"I'm sorry for being so curious about your house," he said as he gripped the handle on the side of the wooden box and began turning the crank on top. He raised his voice above the noise of the crunching coffee beans. "I have talked to storm survivors, but I've only been to Galveston twice before. Did you say your house was raised to the new grade level?"

"Yes, the whole end of the island was raised. This house sits a few feet higher than it did before the storm. The land at the seawall is seventeen feet higher."

"That must have been something to see."

"It was. I was still in elementary school when the workers got to our part of town. This house and all of the other buildings to be saved were jacked up on stilts. For blocks and blocks, it looked like every house had spider legs. We still lived here, and there was a catwalk from our porch to the neighbors next door."

"I've seen pictures of barges dredging sand from the bay and pumping it under the houses."

"Every day the mud rose until we could no longer see the piers. The smells and mosquitoes were terrible! For weeks it looked like we were living in a lake. I asked Mama if our house was sinking, but finally, the muck covered the piers and the workmen stopped the pumps. When the ground dried, other workers came and rebuilt our chimney, right on top of the old one."

Clara pulled the drawer from the coffee mill and emptied it into the basket of the enameled pot on the stove. She struck a match, lit the gas flame and adjusted the burner.

As the fresh-brew smell filled the room, she took biscuits from the breadbox and put them to warm in the oven, then set out two plates, two napkins and two knives. She stowed the bag of coffee on a cupboard shelf and returned with two cups.

"Mr. Brown, would you get the butter and cheese from the icebox please?" He didn't mind a bit.

For the next few moments the only sounds in the kitchen were the soft clicks of cups and saucers. The cheese and butter plates, along with the biscuits, passed easily back and forth. Donald extended his cup for more coffee.

"I appreciate your offer to see Mr. Booth today," He said after a sip.

"Certainly. We can go later this morning. When do you have to return to Houston?" Clara stood to begin clearing the table.

"It depends on what we learn about Elton. Jake has permission from his editor to stay at least two days." Donald nodded in the direction of the carriage house. "He's going out to photograph the seawall this morning, so I think our visit with Mr. Booth will be fine."

"Do you know Jake well?"

"We met some years ago, before I went to live with the Stokes. He came to photograph the orphanage, and I couldn't stop watching him work. I thought he was a hero. I'm afraid I made a pest of myself."

Clara laughed. "And Jake didn't mind?"

"No. It surprised me, really. I wore glasses by then, and Jake noticed some of the other children were joking about them. After that, whenever he was nearby, he'd stop and ask for me. Later, when I went to live with the Stokes, he began teaching me photography."

Donald paused, then added, "Jake helped me feel good about myself, and he never made fun of my glasses."

Clara raised her eyebrows and Donald recalled her remark about looking like an owl. He lifted both hands, palms out.

"Oh! I didn't mean anything by that, only that Jake helped me accept the way I am. He said my eyes are a special gift."

"A gift?"

"Once I repaired a camera that Jake thought was too damaged to fix. I took the shutter apart and found a tiny burr on one leaf. It was easy."

Donald hesitated, then decided to bring up something that had been on his mind. "Last night," he said, "you mentioned that you knew Jake through your friends."

"Ah. Well, I think I understand why Jake might be able to learn more about Mr. Sparks than our sheriff can. Rebecca told me once that Jake knows some of the people who run gambling clubs in Galveston. One of them is a cousin."

"Isn't gambling illegal here?"

"It is, but the laws are not enforced. The sheriff ignores them. People say gambling is good for business because it attracts tourists."

"I suppose. Pa—my adopted dad—says that, uh, when … "

Clara, still at the cupboard, turned to face Donald. Soft light filtering through white curtains glowed on the side of her face. Cropped just so, it would have made a beautiful portrait. Donald stared.

"Yes, Mr. Brown? You were saying?"

He forgot.

He struggled for words.

"Um … oh! Do you know Elton?"

"Elton Sparks? I met him a few months ago. He and Jake are quite good friends. They stayed next door and spent most of their time with Rebecca and Jenny."

"Do you know if Jake introduced Elton to anyone else?"

"Probably so. I only hear these things secondhand, but Jenny said Jake hired a jitney for the day and took Elton to see all the clubs."

"That doesn't sound like Jake. He's not one to throw money around."

"He didn't. Rebecca said that when she and Jenny were with them, nobody paid."

"Are you talking about me?" Jake said from the arbor. Even through the screen door, Jake looked like he could use another two hours' sleep instead of the cigarette in his hand. Hinges on the wooden door creaked as he stepped into the kitchen.

"Morning Jake," Clara said a bit stiffly. "Outside with the cigarette."

The screen door creaked, then slammed behind him as Jake stepped back onto the arbor and flicked his lit cigarette into the vegetable garden. The door slammed once more when he came back into the kitchen. He eased his camera bag to the floor.

"I see you've met young Mr. Brown. Is he giving you an earful?"

"Not at all, Jake, and please don't let that door slam again."

How strange to hear someone give Jake orders, Donald thought as Clara went on.

"I was telling Mr. Brown that you came to Galveston with Elton in April. Rebecca and Jenny said the four of you had fun in the clubs."

"Yes, we had fun. Got any more coffee?"

"On the stove," said Clara, staring at Jake, but not moving from her chair. Jake stared back, but he was first to blink. He found a cup, poured his own coffee and sat down. Clara took a sip from hers before speaking.

"Did you find your missing friend last night?"

"Not yet. Jen said Elton has been back a few times since April, but I knew that. I think he's seeing someone he met on our first trip. Rebecca thought so too."

"Any idea who it was?"

"I've been trying to think. We met a lot of people."

Jake reached to take a biscuit from the plate in the center of the table and used Donald's knife to cover it thick with butter. "Got any jam?" he said, chewing as he spoke.

Clara didn't respond.

"My cousin owns three clubs." Jake glanced at Donald and Clara. Seeing no surprise in their expressions, he continued. "He thought I could get him some favorable publicity. On days when there isn't enough real news, newspapers need fillers to take up the blank space. So-and-so having a good time at the club. The so-and-so club has a new singer. Everybody smiling and looking at the camera."

"Free advertising?" Clara asked.

"Nothing's free," Jake said, chewing another biscuit. "Businessmen like my cousin pay good money to advertise in the paper, and they expect something extra in return."

"You call them businessmen, but some are just thugs." Clara said.

"My cousin calls himself a businessman, and so do I," Jake said, shoving the last biscuit into his mouth. "I got the shots he wanted. Elton was just along for the experience."

Clara inhaled to reply, looked toward Donald and changed her mind. He couldn't tell if she wanted to comment on Galveston's new class of entrepreneurs, or the biscuit.

Jake turned to Donald, still chewing, "I've been thinking about those last two pictures from Elton's camera. Why don't you run fetch them?"

Donald wanted to tell Jake to "run fetch them" himself, but knew it would only mean Jake rifling through his bag. Still, it was embarrassing to be ordered around in front of Clara.

Donald excused himself and went to his room. He quickly found the negatives and had just returned to the arbor when he heard Jake and Clara arguing. He couldn't make out all the words, only the loudest.

Jake: "... nothing like that!"

Clara: "... and what then?"

Donald didn't approve of eavesdropping. He thought of Naomi Stokes, hand over the mouthpiece, listening to her neighbors' telephone calls on the new party line. Donald opened the screen door of the guest house and coughed loud enough for Jake and Clara to hear. The argument stopped in mid-sentence. He crossed the arbor and entered the kitchen.

"Here they are," he said, handing over the envelope.

Jake found the two pieces of film that had been in Elton's wrecked camera and held one to the window light.

"You can't tell much from a negative," he explained as if Clara had never seen one before. "You see, the image on a negative is the exact opposite of what you're used to seeing."

Jake glanced toward Donald, then continued. "The emulsion is like a thin coat of paint on one side of the film. Inside a camera, the emulsion remembers every place where light touches it, but the image is reversed. Skies are black and shadows are white."

Donald smiled, then realized Jake wasn't trying to be funny.

Shifting hands and looking purposefully at Clara, Jake held the second negative to the light.

"These were both taken in the same room," he explained. "There's only one person in the picture, and even a blind man could tell she's a woman, especially in this second shot. I'd say Elton and his lady friend were having a private party."

Jake passed a negative to Clara, who took the film, raised it to the light, tilted back her head and studied the image just as Jake had done.

Donald studied only the shape of Clara's neck.

"I see a liquor bottle on the table," she said, "and two glasses. Do you know the room?"

"I can't recognize the woman, not from a negative. We need to make prints."

"No," Donald said, "there's a faster way." Clara and Jake both turned.

"There's a trick." Donald took the negative from Clara and held it level in front of him. The thin celluloid sheet was translucent, but stiff enough to remain flat in his hand.

"We normally look through the shiny side of a negative," Donald explained, first holding the film flat, then flipping it over. "The back side carries the emulsion, so it appears dull compared to the front."

"So what?" Jake said. "That's still a negative whether you look through the front or the back."

"Right, but remember, film contains silver crystals. If you look at the emulsion side and hold it so the light rakes across at a sharp angle, the silver crystals shine. With the light at the right angle, they appear lighter than the clear portions of the negative, so the image reads almost like a print. Watch."

He set his glasses on the table and held the negative flat with the emulsion side up. He raised the negative to eye level, about two inches from the tip of his nose.

Clara imagined Gulliver peering over a Lilliputian landscape.

Donald faced the window and tilted the negative back and forth until he found the right angle. An image appeared that was still black and white, but the dark and light tones were no longer reversed. Jake grabbed the negative from Donald's hands.

"I'll be damned!" he said, trying it for himself. Donald winced at Jake's language. He glanced toward Clara, but without his glasses, couldn't tell if she was annoyed.

"I can see the woman!" Jake said, tilting the negative slowly right and left. He closed one eye. Five seconds later he groaned, first in disbelief and once again—this time much louder—when he recognized the face.

Chapter 9

"If Elton is still alive, he's in serious trouble," Jake said, tossing the negative to the center of the table like a losing hand in poker. "That's not just another club hostess. She and her husband work for my cousin." He leaned against the table, both fists pressing into the edge.

"His name is Benebeota. Everyone calls him Beno. He's one of the Sicilians my cousin hired two years ago. He's not too bright and he doesn't speak much English."

Jake gazed again at the negative. "He's a monster, but he keeps the peace in Sergio's clubs. The whole bunch, maybe six of them, are that way. They're all from the same village near Palermo."

Jake looked up at Donald and Clara, then flicked his hand toward the negatives. "This gal—her name is Maye but people call her 'Maybe'—likes to play. They're a good match."

"It appears you know her well," Clara said flatly.

Jake's eyes narrowed. "Maye is flashy and loud. Her job is to get noticed, so yes, I know who she is."

Jake's voice took a sharp edge. "She changed jobs after she married Beno," he said, "but I suppose the office hours didn't suit her. Elton may have caught her eye when we were here in the spring."

He paused, slowly shaking his head. To Donald's ear, Jake's voice softened as the truth set in.

"The women Elton knows in Houston are different from the ones he met here. Maye likes to flirt, and Elton isn't used to that." Jake looked at Clara, almost pleading. "I knew he was spending more time in Galveston, but I didn't know why."

Clara pushed back from the table with both hands and went to the stove. She returned with the pot of coffee and divided the last of it evenly into the three cups on the table.

"More to eat, anyone?"

"I'm full," Jake said, patting his stomach.

Donald was still hungry, but didn't want to impose. "No thanks," he said. He reached for the negative and studied it again.

Jake went on, shaking his head and speaking almost to himself. "Elton's no gambler. He never would have risked spending time with a married woman, especially one with a husband like Beno." Jake looked toward Clara. "Maye didn't like to wear her wedding ring."

"This looks like a hotel room, not a house," Donald said.

"How do you know?" Clara said.

"I can see the door." Donald pointed with his little finger to a spot on the negative. "There's a notice attached to the center, about eye level. It probably has rules for using the room and the checkout time."

Jake grunted.

"From the angle of the light," Donald said, "I'd say this picture had to be taken at night using only the electric lights in the room."

"What about flash powder?" Clara asked.

"We don't use it indoors, at least not in a small room. Flash powder makes too much smoke, and there's always a chance of fire."

Jake, seeing that Donald was about to hold forth another photography lesson, rested his chin in his hand and rolled his eyes to the ceiling.

Donald ignored him and went on.

"Ordinary electric bulbs don't produce enough light to take the picture with a hand-held camera, so Elton—if that's who made this picture— would have put it on a tripod or a table, then used a long exposure time."

"That bottle looks half-empty," Jake offered. "I doubt if Elton and Maye spent time on the technical details." He scooped the negatives from the table and shoved them back into the envelope.

"I know someone who runs the darkroom at the *Galveston Daily News*. I'll get him to make prints. After I get the seawall shots, we can head for the hotel and show the first picture to the desk clerk." He waved the envelope dramatically. "This could lead us to Elton. Come, Mr. Brown, we have work to do."

Donald glanced at Clara before answering.

"I think I'll stay here, Jake."

Jake stared for a moment, then winked at Donald when Clara looked away.

"Suit yourself, sport. I'll be back in a few hours."

Jake hefted his camera bag and pushed the screen door wide. The door remained open long enough for Jake to step out under the arbor. He paused, searching his coat pocket for a cigarette and match. Slowly, the screen began to move, its long spring gathering leverage against the creaking hinges. Just before the door slammed shut, Jake lifted one heel behind him and caught the frame. He eased it closed with his foot, struck the match on a post and pulled deeply on his cigarette before crunching down the shell driveway toward the street.

Clara smiled, then turned to the sink, wiping her hands on a dish towel.

"Miss Barnes, do you think we could visit Mr. Booth now?" Donald asked.

"I'll be ready in a moment. And please, Mr. Brown, call me Clara."

Chapter 10

Henry Booth was a wiry man with broad shoulders, narrow hips, large ears and just the faintest wisp of hair on his head. He wore a spotless white bib apron over his pressed denim pants and equally crisp white long-sleeved shirt. A yellow pencil perched behind his left ear. He was sweeping the sidewalk in front of Booth's Hardware when Clara and Donald approached.

"Good morning, Mr. Booth," Clara said.

"Well, hello, young lady!" he replied, resting his oversized hands one above the other atop his broom. "How are you today? That was a delicious pie you gave us last week."

"And I appreciate the window you fixed for me."

Henry eyed Donald as if he were a suitor, calling on Clara for the first time.

"Mr. Booth," she said, "I'd like you to meet Donald Brown. He came down from Houston yesterday and wants to ask about a photograph you found after the storm."

"That was a long time ago," he said, visibly relaxing and shaking Donald's hand. "I'll do the best I can. Let's go inside."

Booth's Hardware had the sweet oily smell of red sawdust, a cleaning product that Henry Booth himself scooped from its five-gallon can and swept over the wooden floors each night before going to bed. "Gives me time to think," he tells his wife.

The old floorboards creaked as Donald and Clara followed Henry toward the rear of his store, which he explained had been a bathhouse during the American Civil War.

"I'll be in the office if you need me," Henry called to his clerk, a young man at the counter who was wrapping brown paper around a customer's pound of nails.

"Sure thing, Mr. Booth." The clerk finished tying the package with twine and rang the sale on a huge brass cash register. Its wooden drawer slid out, and a bell echoed throughout the store.

"Has he been with you long, Mr. Booth?"

"No, Clara, just a few weeks. Young men are hard to find these days, with the Army taking 'em so fast. How about you, Donald? You look to be at least eighteen."

"Almost nineteen, sir, and with the lower draft age, I'll register along with everyone else on Thursday. I'm just not sure if they'll take me because of my eyes."

"From what I hear, the Army needs everyone who can still stand."

Clara caught her heel on a raised floorboard and Henry steadied her. "There are quite a few slackers, you know. I'd go myself if I wasn't so old."

"You're much more valuable to us here, Mr. Booth," Clara said quietly, slipping her arm through his and patting his shoulder as they walked. "My brother writes that the trenches are dreadful to live in day after day, although I'm sure you could make yours more comfortable."

Henry laughed. "I could handle the lice and rats, but I don't know what I'd do about the mud."

He stopped at the rear of the store where two low panels extended from the wall to form a space about twelve feet square. A pot-bellied stove with a battered coffee pot on top stood in the center of the back wall. At least two dozen photographs hung without order on the side walls, mostly of men standing behind long stringers of redfish, flounder and trout.

"Grab yourself a seat," Henry said as he settled into his favorite rocker. Donald held a chair for Clara, then pulled up another for himself. The chairs were roughly arranged around the stove, which had the feel of an open hearth. Mesquite and oak kindling rested in a tidy stack just right of the firebox.

"This is your office?" Donald asked, taking his seat. Henry and Clara both smiled.

"My little joke. This is where I do my best work, here, visiting with my fishing friends. Now, what can I do for you?"

"Mr. Brown and I were looking at some of the photos Mama collected after the storm," Clara began as she pulled an envelope from her handbag. "We want to know about this one you found in a house near 12th Street and Avenue J."

"Like I said, that was a long time ago," Henry said, slipping the card from the envelope into his hand. "Cute kid, but I don't recall ..."

"Mama wrote in her journal what you told her at the time. It was September 15, a week after the storm. You were with a group of men searching for victims."

"We were all searching," Henry said. "For the first two weeks, sheriff's deputies grabbed every man who could walk and put him to work of some kind, whether he wanted to or not. The soldiers were here, too, mainly to stop looters. Our first job was just clearing paths so we could get the horses and wagons in."

"You told Mama the house was not in its original location."

"Most houses were just piles of sticks, but others stayed more or less together even after they washed off their foundations. Sometimes half a house would be standing in the middle of the road. You could see all the rooms and furniture, like you were looking at the back of a doll house."

"Do you remember anything at all about the place where you found this photograph, Mr. Booth?" Donald asked.

Clara sat forward in her chair, hands together in her lap, heels hooked on a rung of her chair with only the tips of her shoes touching the floor.

"No," Henry looked briefly at the photograph, "I can't say that I do. There were lots of terrible smells," he added slowly. "Cats and dogs and chickens hanging in the trees, and horses and cows and people dead in the streets. When we dug through the debris, we never knew what we'd find. More than once I'd lift some boards or a door, only to find a bare arm or leg sticking out from underneath. It always made me jump. Every mule cart in town was used to pick up bodies ..."

Henry pinched the bridge of his nose. "Everyone afraid of disease, so we... we burned most of the bodies, and the fires... The fires along the beach lit up the sky every night ... I'm sorry Clara, it's still hard for me to talk about."

"Yes, I'm sorry, Mr. Booth. Those were terrible times. But perhaps you can remember where you might have seen this photograph? In a cupboard, or on a shelf?"

Booth rocked quietly, elbows resting on the arms of the chair and suddenly looking older. He sat with the fingertips of both hands touching just under his chin, not looking at either of his guests. He rocked forward, then stopped. "Why, yes," he said, "It's coming back. A strange chemical smell is what I remember."

Donald's chair creaked as he leaned in.

"The house was sitting in the middle of the street. It was two stories tall, but the back was sheared off and part of the roof was hanging down where the sleeping porch had been. All the windows and doors were gone. Debris piled against it like a snow drift, so high that we just climbed over, straight into the second floor." He hesitated, afraid to be too explicit in front of Clara. Finally, he continued.

"Smells helped us find bodies, so we followed our noses. I remember looking inside a closet in what was left of that house. There was an awful odor, but not the smell of death. When I pried open the closet door, there was nothing inside but a bunch of broken bottles."

"Sir, do you remember the color of those bottles?" Donald asked.

"The color? Why, yes, they were all brown. And where liquid had spilled and dried, the floor was kind of crusty yellow. Soon as I opened that door, the smell made my eyes water and it burned my nose."

"Did you notice anything about the walls, Mr. Booth?"

"What? Yes! The darnedest thing—inside, the walls and ceiling were painted black! Not shiny black, like you might paint furniture—but dull black, like midnight with no moon. There was a table against one wall and shelves, but no place to hang clothes. And one more thing, there was a funny little kerosene lamp with red glass lenses instead of clear."

"A darkroom!" Donald said. "You found a darkroom."

"One of those places they make photographs? Oh, my." Booth sat up, more animated now. He beamed as if he had won a prize.

"Mr. Booth," she asked quickly, "is that where you found this photograph? In the room with the black walls?"

"Hum ... no. Not there. In a bookcase, I think. Yes! I remember being surprised the books were still in the case, and that they hadn't gotten too wet, even though one whole wall of the room was gone. That wall must have come down late, after the worst of the rain. The pictures were on a shelf, stuck between two books."

"*Pictures*, Mr. Booth? There were more than one?"

"Yes, Clara. Three, I think. I gave them all to your ma."

"Why didn't I think of that?" Clara cried, hands trembling as she fumbled with the lock on the front door of her house. Donald finally took the key from her hand and opened the door.

"People often found several photographs together." She dropped the key in her bag and the bag on a nearby chair, then hurried to the foot of the stairs.

"If those pictures are in Mama's collection, they should be numbered in sequence. Wait here!"

Donald stood in the foyer and watched Clara run upstairs, one hand on the rail, the other holding her skirt to the side so she wouldn't trip.

"Here," she said a minute later, handing him the wooden case at the landing. She followed him to the kitchen where the light was best. Donald placed the box on the table. Clara slid the latch and tipped the lid back until it caught silently on its supports, then removed her mother's journal.

"The picture of you is number 47," she said, tracing the list with her thumb and finger down the edge of the page. She flipped a page back, then another. "Numbers 45 and 46 were brought in by someone else, not Mr. Booth." She checked another page. "And 43 was found by my mother."

Clara turned several pages forward.

"I have it!" she said, pointing to one entry. "Mr. Booth found this on September 15, 1900. The same with number 49! The next came four days after, and that photograph was found by someone else."

Donald leaned closer to see the journal. "Did your mother write anything more about these two?"

"She just noted the date, location and time," Clara removed the top two trays. She found numbers 48 and 49 right away.

"Oh, look," she said, handing him the prints.

"Both of these were taken in the same room as the picture of me! That's the same chair, and those are the same books leaning against the wall."

Donald placed the photographs side by side to compare them. One was a simple, straight-on image of a young woman sitting stiffly in a chair with her hands folded in her lap. The other showed a man about the same age with a child.

"Who is the man in the second picture? And the child he's holding, that's not you."

Donald picked up the card in both hands, fingertips on the edges. Clara leaned in, and together they studied the print. A man with a walrus moustache was sitting in the same chair that was used for Donald's baby picture, playfully lifting a young girl into the air. The man himself was smiling at a point just to the right of the camera. The same place I was looking, Donald thought.

"She's about four years old," Clara said. "How old would you say he is?"

"Thirty, maybe, but no more. He could be the child's father."

"And yours!" When Donald didn't respond, Clara thought he hadn't heard what she said.

Donald paused, eyes shifting from one print to the next.

"All three pictures were made on the same afternoon."

Clara looked at Donald, who had removed his glasses. He held the photograph motionless just inches from his eyes. How could anyone have so little feeling, she thought, seeing pictures of his family for the first time?

"Afternoon? How can you be sure?"

"The second and third pictures show more of the room." He tilted the print toward Clara and pointed with the tip of his finger to a clock on a table in the background. Donald closed one eye and pulled the print closer. "The clock is out of focus, but I can still see the position of the hands."

Clara took the print from Donald's hand and stared—numbed by his lack of emotion. He'd been excited to find the prints, but now, holding them in his hands, all he wanted to do was study the details. Who is this person beside me, Clara wanted to know. Instead, she asked about the clock.

"Can you really see the position of the hands? I barely see a clock."

"Yes, I see things most people can't. There are limits, of course," he added as if speaking from a podium. "The light-sensitive chemicals that produced this photograph are just a pattern of lighter or darker grains on the paper, like particles of sand on the beach. If you look close enough, you no longer see a picture, only the individual grains."

Clara squinted back at the print and moved it closer to the window light. "I don't see any grains."

"I do," Donald said.

"So, according to the clock, when was the photograph taken?" Clara heard her voice growing hard. Donald didn't seem to notice.

"This one of the man and the little girl was made around 4:30 in the afternoon. And the print of the woman by herself was taken half an hour later."

"It's a shame there's not a clock showing in the picture of you. It would be interesting to know the time." She meant it as a joke, but instead of laughing, Donald laid all three prints side-by-side on the kitchen table.

"This is the order in which they were taken. First the one of me, then of the man and the girl, and finally the one of the woman."

"How do you know?" Clara felt alone in the room.

"The angle of the shadows," Donald said. "See, they get lower later in the day. The photographer used a single light source, probably two or three large windows along the southwest wall of the house. They must have been covered by thin curtains or a sheet, because the light is diffuse. Did you notice the shadows? If there was direct sunlight on the subject, the shadows would be more harsh."

Clara barely followed his reasoning. More than confused, she was growing angry, but didn't know why.

"I've only looked at photographs as pictures. You read them like books."

Donald agreed. "It's what photographers do." He continued as if teaching a class. "Most people just point their Kodaks and push the button, then wonder why the results are disappointing. To make good pictures, you have to pay attention to the light."

"I thought it was just the quality of the camera." Clara's expression was calm, her voice cool, but under the table, her fists were tight.

"Having a good camera helps," Donald said, "but the eye of the photographer is the main thing."

Clara focused on the prints a moment longer. "You said the windows faced southwest. How do you know *that*?" Her toes began tapping the floor under her chair.

"Again, it's the angle of the light and the time of year. Also, I know these pictures were probably made here in Galveston, where all of the streets conform to the island's northeast to southwest shape rather than a true north-south grid." He pointed to one of the prints. "For this time of day in September, the light had to be coming from the southwest."

Clara turned and gripped Donald's arm. "Donald, Mr. Booth told us where the house was after the storm. It couldn't have floated more than a block without coming apart. Since you know the angle it faced, maybe you can determine its original location!"

"Yes!" Donald said, finally showing some excitement. "We'd need a good map and property records." His shoulders sagged. "But ..."

"But what?"

"All those files were lost in the storm."

That stopped them both short. Clara eased her grip on Donald's arm, and he leaned back in his chair.

They sat quietly, and in the silence Clara's anger returned. It rolled through her mind, gathered steam and exploded into words too suddenly to stop.

"Donald, why are you talking so much about photography?" She waved her hand toward the little row of pictures. "These people are the family you never knew! This woman is probably your mother, but all you can talk about is light and grains and the time of day!"

Startled, Donald turned to Clara, whose cheeks were turning red. He was good at discerning color and tone, even without his glasses. Clara reached past him for one of the prints. She stood suddenly, scraping her chair across the floor. She waved the print beside her face like a fan.

"For all you know, this little girl is your sister! The man holding her is likely your father! I should think you'd be more excited by that than you are about details of the print!"

Donald looked up blankly at Clara's face, too stunned to speak. She stared back, shocked by her own rage at this near stranger, but still searching for a hint of emotion in his eyes.

There was none.

Seconds passed. Clara's anger waned, replaced by understanding. They were close, barely five feet apart, but Donald was only looking toward her, not at her.

"Donald, can you see me at all?"

"Well, no, not very well. I'm sorry. Just a second." He patted the table for his glasses, found them, then slipped the loops behind his ears and forced a smile. "There! Good as new!"

He looked into Clara's eyes. They were blue and moist.

"Are you all right?"

"Yes, yes. I'm sorry for my outburst, but you surprised me. Don't you care who these people are? Why aren't you more excited? We found your family!"

"We can't assume these people are my relatives."

She pointed to the second print. "What about this one? Don't you think that's your mother?"

Donald picked up the print and held it so they both could see. An unsmiling young woman stared back. She wore a simple dark dress with extra fabric around the shoulders and upper arms, as was the fashion in the late 1800s. She wore her hair in a tight bun. The woman appeared to be in her mid-twenties. No necklace or earrings, but there was a handsome ivory cameo pinned just below her lace collar.

"I can't just guess." Donald said, still staring at the face on the card.

"Why not? This seems clear to me. I think it is safe to assume ..."

"NO!" Donald said, thumping his fist on the table. Clara flinched.

He dropped the card next to the others. When he turned to face Clara again, she sat, hands in her lap and eyes wide, waiting for him to go on.

"Clara, I grew up in a children's home, wondering who my parents might have been. Besides the employees, a group of ladies volunteered their time and raised money to support the home. The woman I mentioned before, Nina Carhart, was one of them, and she still helps whenever she can."

"Very nice," Clara said, "but what does ..." Donald lifted his hand to stop her.

"From as early as I can remember, I wondered if one of those ladies was my real mother, quietly keeping an eye on me. I made up stories in my mind. I told myself that she had a secret, some special reason why she couldn't let anyone know I was her son."

"Oh, Donald, I'm sorry." Her hand reached halfway to his, then returned to her lap.

"I know better now, but when I was a boy, still living at the orphanage, the thought consumed me. Whoever smiled at me or was kind in some way, I imagined she was my mother, and for some reason she couldn't tell. In my mind, it became an unspoken secret between us."

Donald shifted in his chair and gazed at his knees. Clara noticed the thumb and first finger of his right hand were just touching, forming a little circle just as they did in the photo of him as a child. Seconds passed before he continued.

"For more than a year, I was convinced it was Mrs. Carhart. I knew it was her and treasured the secret. She was so kind to me, more than any of the others."

"Was she the one who noticed you needed glasses?"

"Yes. She drove me herself to the optometrist in her Cadillac. I remember because it was the first time I'd ever ridden in a motor car, and the first time I'd seen a woman drive. I was so proud that she was my ma, even if she couldn't tell me."

"Were you disappointed to learn she wasn't?"

"Devastated. All of us at the home were orphans, but at least the others knew who their parents had been. I dreamed of finding mine, or at least learning what happened to them. Hope was all I had."

Clara searched Donald's face as he went on.

"A few months after Mrs. Carhart bought my first pair of glasses, I learned more about her life. One day I realized she couldn't have been my mother. After that, I never made the same mistake."

Clara moved again to touch his arm, then stopped. "But you think of her as your friend?"

"Mrs. Carhart took an interest in me. She's a widow and doesn't have any children of her own. Maybe she's just lonesome, but I like to think it's more than that."

Without asking if he wanted some, Clara got up to make tea. It gave her time to consider what Donald had said. After she put the kettle on the stove, she turned and leaned back against the kitchen counter, hands lightly gripping the edge.

"Donald, you seem well-educated. I know people with college degrees who can't express themselves as well. Is Mrs. Carhart responsible for that?"

"Oh, thank you, yes," Donald said, finally looking up. "She's been like a guide, a tutor or a coach. All three, actually. When I was eleven, she got permission from the orphanage to have me visit her home for dinner once a week, always on a Thursday. Her driver would pick me up. I guess you'd say that she taught me manners: how to eat, how to dress, how to behave in polite company, that sort of thing."

"Just the two of you for dinner?"

"No, there were always others, usually creative people such as artists, authors and musicians. She has many interesting friends and she travels a lot. Her mother lives with her, so she's there, too, whenever I visit. When I first started going to her dinners, the best thing was that no one treated me like a child."

Clara poured two cups of tea, set them on the table and returned with two slices of pecan pie. Donald, suddenly hungry, was learning that Clara was a wonderful cook. He picked up a fork, then did something Mrs. Carhart had taught him never to do. He spoke with his mouth full.

"The weekly visits continued even after I left the orphanage and went to live with the Stokes. I don't go for dinner as often these days—she's traveling more—but sometimes I'm invited to her home on Saturday or Sunday afternoon."

Clara studied Donald over the rim of her cup. The strain had left his voice when he began talking of his lady friend.

"What do you and Mrs. Carhart talk about?" she pressed, surprised at her own curiosity. Donald thought for a moment.

"She has traveled all over the world. Sometimes we discuss places she visited with her husband. She picks books for me to read from her library and we talk about them later. We even share an interest in photography, although I've never seen any of her prints." Donald sipped his tea, then continued. "Mrs. Carhart and the Stokes are the closest thing I have to a real family."

Clara smiled. "Maybe better. Some families don't get along as well."

"Yes, and Jake's been a good friend, although my ma—I mean Naomi—thinks he's a bad influence."

Clara laughed and covered her mouth with the back of her hand to keep from losing a morsel of pie. "Oh yes, I can see how she might."

Chapter 11

Jake tugged the strap of his camera bag, checked the traffic on Mechanic Street and crossed to the entrance of the *Galveston Daily News*. He skipped up the steps two at a time and pulled open the heavy wood and glass door. Five minutes later a reluctant editor agreed to make enlargements of the six negatives from Elton's camera.

"But keep it quiet for now," Jake said. "If there's a story here, I'll make sure you get it first."

"Two hours," his friend said, turning for the darkroom.

Outside again, Jake headed down 21st Street. At Broadway he caught the trolley to the beach. He crossed the wide boulevard and stood briefly on the seawall, looking down at the sand and waves some twenty feet below. He shaded his eyes and scanned to the southwest, following the curve of the shore. In the distance, Murdoch's Pier and the Galvez Hotel. Nearby, pelicans glided over the water, like a squadron of Spads or Nieuports on patrol.

Jake inhaled, drawing strength from the moist salt air. Swinging his bag to the opposite shoulder, he began walking northeast up the beach. Ten minutes later he reached the spot where seawall construction was underway—or would have been if it weren't for all the police.

Three officers stood atop the last completed section, a solid wedge of concrete long as a locomotive and tall as a two-story house. Jake knew the dimensions by heart. The flat top was five feet wide. The backside, facing inland, formed a vertical slab sixteen feet tall. The ocean side arched gracefully to the sand, where granite boulders protected the wall's wide base from the heaviest waves. The foundation rested on piles driven forty feet into the ground.

Thick wood and steel forms were in place to pour foundations for two more sections. Activity normally continued around the clock, so it was odd to see men idle in the middle of the day.

A dozen African and Mexican workers lounged in the shade of a rail car, enjoying the unexpected rest. Their foreman, a beefy white man with thick forearms, paced back and forth at the top of the incomplete wall, stopping occasionally to yell in the police captain's face. At the base of the wall, other officers did their best to keep interested locals away.

One burly cop looked vaguely familiar, like a lineman Jake might have faced when Galveston Ball played his own Houston High. The policeman's nose had once been badly broken. Jake kept quiet about the possible football connection, in case he had done the damage himself.

"What's going on?" Jake said.

"Who are you?" the officer barked instead of answering outright.

Jake gritted his teeth, but managed to control his temper. "Reporter and photographer for the *Houston Chronicle*, sir. What happened here?"

The policeman hesitated, then offered a tidbit.

"A guy saw someone dumped in the fresh concrete Thursday night. Didn't bother to let us know until yesterday."

"Here? Shit!"

"Yeah. And since then, more concrete has been poured. Now the boss says he's not going to bust up a week's worth of work just because of what someone thinks they saw in the dark."

Jake wiped his mouth with the back of his hand. Color drained from his face.

"Hey fella, you sick?

"No, officer ..."

"You know somethin' 'bout this?" The policemen turned slowly, suddenly interested. He squared his shoulders to Jake, who struggled to stay calm.

"No! I ... I just think it's terrible. Buried in concrete. What a way to die! Are you sure that happened?"

The cop turned back toward the seawall.

"Naw, that's what they're arguing about. Foreman says the guy on the phone was probably drunk. The sergeant thinks so, too, because he answered the call. The whole thing could be a hoax."

"Look, off-ee-sir," someone yelled, deliberately slurring the word.

Jake looked up, following the policeman's gaze. The foreman's voice carried easily above the wind.

"This section of the wall—from Sixth Street all the way to Fort San Jacinto—is a *federal* project," he railed. "We're already behind schedule because we can't get enough men to work on it, and we're not about to break up this concrete on the word of some drunk!"

Frenzied seagulls working the surf squawked in response. A young couple strolled by, more interested in each other than the birds or the argument raging high above them. Watching the couple gave Jake time to think. He turned back to the policeman.

"What did this guy, what's his name, the drunk, say about the body?"

"You really a reporter?"

"Yes, sir!" Jake pulled a thin notebook and pencil from a vest pocket and held them like an eager student, ready to record every word.

The policeman studied Jake, then looked around for guidance and found none.

"I don't know ..." he began. Jake didn't respond. His gaze fell instead on the huge cement mixer. Only the pot was rotating, keeping the cement inside from sticking to its walls. The tumbling slurry made an angry growl, enhanced by the shape of the drum.

Annoyed, the officer's eyes hardened on Jake.

"You look familiar, did you ever play ... "

"No, officer. No sir, I don't think so. You must have me confused with someone else."

After a skeptical pause, the policeman went on.

"Well, like I said, this drunk called claiming there's someone in the seawall. The sergeant didn't believe him."

Jake wrote the words "drunk" and "called Sunday" in his notebook. It galled him to be so polite, but he needed facts. He still hoped Elton was safe somewhere with his Galveston lady friend.

He had to be.

"Why did you come out if you didn't believe the man on the phone?"

"Sarge said the drunk's story got better as he told it," the policeman laughed. "The call lasted maybe ten minutes because the guy was so hard to understand. He refused to come in but swore that he saw someone dumped into the concrete."

"What are the police doing?" Jake had to be careful, the big cop was growing impatient.

"What do you think? Sarge filed a report. Today we're investigating."

On cue, the foreman's voice rose, but Jake didn't look up.

"Do you mind if I take pictures, officer … ?"

"Bunsen. Officer Carrol Bunsen. No reason not to, I suppose." Bunsen shifted his weight from one foot to the other, hiked his uniform pants and sucked in his stomach.

"How about one of me?" Bunsen turned his head in profile, which only drew attention to his mangled nose.

Jake didn't like wasting film, but he took a quick photograph.

"Thanks, officer Bunsen, you've been a big help."

"Carrol Bunsen. Two Rs, one L."

"Thanks again," Jake said, making a show of correcting the spelling in his book.

Jake took more photographs of the derrick, the pile driver and the wooden crane. For the final shot, he positioned himself to make sure the background included the idle crew, and the rail cars filled with crushed granite, cement, pilings, reinforced steel and what the workers called "riprap," the massive granite boulders used to line the base of the seawall.

He looked up at the last completed section. The call to the police station had to be a prank.

To save time, Jake hired a jitney. His prints would be ready soon, and he needed a break from walking. He dropped his bag on the rear seat of the open Ford and climbed in front next to the driver.

The man hunched behind the wheel reminded Jake of his own father, a quiet, gentle soul that everyone pushed around. "A weakling with a kind heart," people said.

"Where to?" the driver asked.

"Murdoch's."

"Sure thing."

Jake judged the driver to be about his own age, perhaps a little more, yet he had the haggard look of someone with too much responsibility. A family man, Jake thought. No life for me.

"Were you living here during the storm three years ago?"

"I was, sir," the driver said. He sat up straighter.

Jake realized the man wanted to talk. No one ever asked or cared what weak men thought. He saw it often enough as a boy, watching others ignore his dad.

"I guess all the effort to build the seawall and raise the land was worth it," Jake said.

"You're right about that." The driver glanced over his shoulder at Jake. "Fewer people died, and we didn't have as much flooding. Folks say the storm in '15 was even stronger than the one in 1900." He checked again to seeing if Jake was still listening.

"What did you do when it hit?"

"My wife was terrified, so we went to her sister's house in Houston. When we came home, we didn't find a drop of water in our house. Lucky for us, with two little ones and another on the way."

The driver made a smooth U-turn in front of Murdoch's Pier, stopping at the point where Tremont Street met Seawall Boulevard.

"Only a handful of tourists here now," he offered, turning his head toward Jake and resting both wrists on the top edge of the steering wheel. "But you should have seen it on Labor Day. That whole weekend, you could hardly move for all the bicycles and buggies and cars."

Jake retrieved his camera bag and handed the driver fifty cents—twice the normal fare—and told him to keep the change. "For your kids," Jake said as he closed the door.

For my dad, Jake thought as he walked away.

He bought a nickel's worth of peanuts from a vendor on the boardwalk, then waited for several buggies and a bicycle to pass. On any other visit to Galveston, he'd be wondering who to ask to dinner, but with Elton still missing, Jake was increasingly annoyed and worried.

He smiled. Well, last night had been all right. He shook his head. Elton would turn up. He had to. A shout from behind made him jump.

"Read all about the World Series!" a boy in knickers yelled to people passing by. Jake turned. He bought Monday's *Galveston Daily News* for a nickel and gave the young proprietor an extra nickel for himself.

"Thank you!" said the newsboy, two fingers touching the bill of his cap. He pocketed the coins and grabbed another paper from his stack, raising it over his head. "World Series news from Fenway Park! Cubs on the defense! Babe Ruth pitching today for Boston!"

Jake tucked the paper under the flap of his camera bag and began walking. A block up Tremont Street he boarded the trolley, found a seat and rested his arm on the open window as the car began to move. What to make of a drunken claim that there's a body sealed forever inside the concrete seawall?

Elton?

Impossible.

The trolley's overhead wires flashed and popped each time they touched. Every few seconds, the powerful arc sent glowing specks of metal floating through the air. Jake flinched when a particularly large one drifted through the window and landed on his sleeve.

Chapter 12

Clara broke the silence first. "Not much to it," she said, touching the photograph. "Just a woman staring at the camera. Is there anything about this one you can be certain about?"

Donald laid his upper arms flat on the table, hands together with his fingers interlaced. He leaned over until his chest rested on the edge of the table, his head turning slowly from one image to the next, analyzing each with a fresh eye.

"I think the picture of me, and the one with the man and the child were made by the same photographer, but this one of the woman was made by someone else."

"Really! How could you possibly know?"

"It's the photographer's style," he said. "See how the other two are so animated? In each of them, the subject is reacting to someone who is in the room, but not in the frame. I'm looking just to the right of the camera, and so is the man holding the girl."

"I see," Clara said, "but ..."

"My guess is that someone was leaning out from behind the camera, waiting for exactly the right moment. The photographer caught me just as I started to smile. In the shot of the little girl, they tripped the shutter when the child reached the highest point, right before the man lowered her again."

"You seem so sure."

"It's how I would have taken the pictures myself. I can almost feel my hand on the shutter release, waiting and watching, maybe trying to get the sitter to react, but always waiting for the right moment. It's the difference between simply recording an image and making a good picture."

Donald edged the photograph of the woman aside. "Whoever took the picture of me and this man with the little girl would not have been happy with such a boring result. They would have tried for something more candid."

Clara smiled at Donald's certainty. "I never looked at photographs that way before. It's as if the photographer is telling a story."

"Exactly, Clara, exactly so."

A thump on the arbor porch made them both jump. "Looks like I missed lunch." Jake said, swinging open the screen door, but catching it before it slammed. He dropped his camera bag on the floor and took an empty chair beside it, sighing heavily as he sat.

"What's all this?" he said, waving his free hand toward the open chest and pictures on the kitchen table.

"We found a new photograph of Donald," Clara said.

"I've seen that one before," Jake said, turning toward Donald. "You brought it from Houston?"

"No, that's a duplicate of mine. See, there's no writing on the bottom."

Jake picked up the card. "Well, I'll be damned. Where did …"

"Later," Donald said, glancing at Clara and slipping his glasses back on. "Did you get Elton's prints?"

"Yes, and I went to the seawall. I have some news."

"About Elton?"

"I hope not. Police were there, just where Elton was photographing last week. I talked to one of them. He said someone claims there's a body in the cement."

Clara gasped. "Not Elton?"

Jake shook his head. "I don't know. The police don't know. A guy said he saw someone fall or get pushed in sometime Thursday night or early Friday morning. He didn't telephone the police until yesterday. The sergeant who took the call said the man was slurring his words. The police figure he might have drinking for days. Anyway, he called the station to report it, but they didn't really believe him."

"But they checked anyway?" Clara said.

"That's what they were doing when I got there. The foreman says he's not about to break up eight hundred tons of concrete on the word of some drunk."

Jake shifted in his chair and began digging through his camera bag. He put Monday's newspaper on the table, and next to it an envelope with six fresh 8x10 prints. He paused, then spoke.

"Um, Clara, I was rude this morning."

"Rude?" Clara said in mock surprise. She spread one hand across her chest in a fair imitation of Mary Pickford in *Poor Little Rich Girl*. Her eyes fluttered. "Why, Mr. Miller!"

"Make fun if you want, I deserve it."

"You're worried about Elton. I understand." Clara stood, briefly resting a hand on Jake's shoulder. "You didn't miss lunch. How about some soup and fresh bread?"

"Yes!" Donald and Jake said in one voice.

"You should open a restaurant." Jake added.

"I'm afraid nurses are needed now more than cooks," Clara said. "The soldiers' ward is already full, and more are coming every day. I'm worried that so many have the flu."

Jake grew quiet, and Clara knew not to go on. Once she had called him a slacker for avoiding the draft. Now she wasn't sure. So many men had left for adventure and glory. Now they were coming home, horribly damaged and old beyond their years.

"Let's see Elton's pictures," she said to clear the air.

Donald spread the six prints on the table. It was much easier to read the black and white enlargements than it had been to squint at smaller negatives. Jake pointed to one of Elton's seawall shots.

"This is where I was today, only now, these steel forms have been removed and this is a solid wedge of concrete sixteen feet tall."

Jake drew his finger to the right across the photograph and tapped twice on the wood and steel framework. "This part of the seawall—where the body's supposed to be—is finished and the crew has moved farther up the beach. Tonight they'll begin pouring concrete for the next section."

"These pieces are huge!" Clara said. "You don't realize it until you see workers nearby."

"And here are the two prints of Maye," Jake said. "She looks like she's had a few drinks."

"Especially standing there in her underwear," Donald added. Clara and Jake laughed. Donald snatched off his glasses and put the print close to his eyes, which only set them laughing more.

"Say, Don, you don't need to study her figure that closely," Jake said.

"That's not it," Donald said, his cheeks turning red. "I missed something before."

Clara, still smiling, put a pot on the stove, lit the burner and adjusted the fire to low heat. She took a Mason jar of soup from the pantry and twisted the lid, which made a pleasing pop as the rubber seal released the vacuum inside. She poured her stock into the pot, then chopped two small potatoes from the garden and added the bite-sized pieces as filler. Clara then placed three empty soup bowls on the table and sat, just as Donald looked up from the print.

"Here! When we were looking at the negatives this morning, I thought this was a picture hanging on the wall, but it's a mirror." Donald pointed with his index finger. "That's Elton's reflection."

"Let's see," Jake said.

"This one, too." Donald slid the second print toward Clara. "This is Elton, and I can see his Speed Graphic sitting on a small table."

Jake dropped the print he was holding, and exhaled loudly.

"I'm beginning to see what happened. That's probably Elton's hotel room. Maye must have gone there while Beno was still at the club. He got suspicious and followed her."

Jake stopped abruptly. "My cousin told me once that even the other Sicilians are afraid of Beno."

Clara returned to the stove to stir the soup and adjust the flame.

"I need to talk to Sergio," Jake said.

"Your cousin?" she asked.

"On my mother's side. He's older than me, but we played together as kids. He opened a restaurant here and was doing fine until Houston deepened its own port and took customers away from Galveston."

"Is that when your cousin expanded his menu?"

"If you're talking about the gambling and the women, yes. He's a trying to survive. He had to change with the times."

Clara pointed a long wooden spoon toward the newspaper at Jake's elbow. "Last month a customer in one of Sergio's clubs was badly beaten and left out on the beach. It's a miracle he survived. And there was the shooting last April. That time a man from Houston died."

"Sergio didn't have anything to do with that."

"Perhaps not, but some of the owners, including Sergio, are getting bad reputations,"

Clara opened the breadbox and removed the loaf she'd made the day before. She sliced it in half, put the knife and half loaf on the table, then returned to the icebox.

"This will keep you going until the soup is ready," she said, placing the butter dish next to the bread.

Donald enjoyed watching her move about the kitchen, a fact not lost on Jake.

Clara stirred the soup, tasted it, then added pepper and a few leaves of fresh basil. She stirred and tasted again. Satisfied, she laid the spoon across the lid of the Mason jar. She wrapped the remaining half loaf of bread in a clean dish towel and put it in the breadbox, then turned, leaning back against the kitchen counter. She looked directly at Jake.

"Galveston is changing," she said. "Most people talk about police payoffs like they're a normal part of business. Scandal isn't shocking any more. Even the few honest politicians say the city needs the money that the clubs are bringing in."

"Maybe so," Jake said. "But I've got to ask Sergio about Elton. I'm going to his club this afternoon."

"I'll go with you," Donald said.

Chapter 13

"Strange to be without my camera bag," Jake said. "Do you at least have your Autographic?"

"Always," Donald said, patting a slight bulge on the inside pocket of his summer jacket.

"Where is Sergio's club?"

"Near Murdoch's Pier. Maye could be there, too."

"Is that where Rebecca and Jen work?"

"No, they're at one of the fancier casinos up the street. The club owner has a driver bring them to work in the evening, then take them home just before sunup, if they come home at all."

Donald pondered the arrangement until he noticed that Jake seemed amused. He let his fingertips bump along the pickets of a fence as they walked. The day was still warm, but the sun would be down in another hour and the humidity wasn't too bad. Wind from the northwest. Should be a nice evening.

"Jake, how did you get a deferment?" Donald said at last. "The draft board would have hauled you in as a slacker if you didn't register when it was your turn."

"Did I mention that I'm the sole support for my elderly parents?" Jake sighed. "It's a constant burden for me."

Donald bit his tongue.

Sergio's Flamingo Room offered reasonable food, liquor and dancing, plus non-stop gambling in the back. The club's unadvertised services depended on the customer's budget. Those with cash were welcome.

A thin man wearing a tuxedo—a new employee since Jake had last been to the club—stopped them just inside the door. His waxed hair and moustache appeared to be painted on. He slowly enunciated each word.

"Do you have a reservation?"

"It's still early, pal, and your place is half full," Jake said.

The man in the tuxedo stiffened. He glanced briefly toward the bar and raised one hand. Donald squirmed, wishing Jake would relax.

"Still, sir, we require ..."

"We're here to see Sergio."

"Whom should I say ..."

"His cousin. And hurry."

"Wait here."

Tuxedo stepped first toward a beefy man sitting on a stool at the bar. He leaned close to speak, covering his mouth with his hand.

The fellow at the bar had no neck that Donald could see, only a pair of chins sagging over his collar and tie. Wide shoulders met at the sides of his head just below the ears. His upper arms stretched the fabric of his evening coat like enormous links of pork sausage. A fleshy lower lip nearly touched his wide nostrils, but for all that, his small dark eyes were the most frightening. They never left Donald and Jake.

"We've been waiting a long time," Donald murmured. He wished Jake had been more agreeable, and was relieved when Tuxedo returned.

"Mr. Leone will see you now. Follow me." The hulk at the end of the bar slowly returned to his drink.

Tuxedo led them toward the back. Donald surveyed the dining area. Privacy booths lined the wall. Only a few tables were occupied. A noisy family filled one, the children being fed an early dinner after a day at the beach.

Donald and Jake followed Tuxedo down a wide hall, through the kitchen and into a smaller passage that had no windows or doors. He stopped before a blank panel and knocked. Donald heard two sets of footsteps on the other side before the panel opened silently into a large, windowless office. A man motioned them in, then flicked two fingers. Tuxedo nodded and backed out the door.

"Mio cugino!" Sergio said, hugging Jake with one arm and thumping him loudly on the back. Sergio's free hand held a cigar aloft. A lone cigarette smoldered in the ashtray, but there was no one else in the room.

"How have you been?" Sergio said, finally releasing Jake.

"Still standing," Jake said, stepping back. Sergio laughed.

Donald compared the two men. No one would guess they were related, or that Sergio's family was Sicilian. Jake's mother was Italian, but his father was German stock. Sergio was the taller of the two. Donald guessed they weighed about the same. While Jake was considered handsome, Sergio could pass for a movie star.

"What brings you back, cousin?" Sergio asked. He smiled broadly.

"Don't you know?"

"Perhaps. But first, who is your friend?"

"Sergio, meet Donald Brown. Don, this is my cousin, Sergio Leone."

"Nice to meet you, Mr. Leone."

"Sergio, per favore!"

"Grazie, Sergio, piacere," Donald said, shaking hands.

"Ah, your friend speaks a little Italian!"

"Just enough to be trouble. Look, Serg, I need to ask about Beno."

"Piano, piano, cousin! Slowly, slowly. Would you like a drink?"

Sergio stepped toward the built-in bar, but Jake grabbed his arm. Sergio's smile vanished.

"Per favore, cousin," he said, "what do you need to know?"

"A friend of mine is missing. I think Beno knows where he is."

Sergio smoothed the sleeve of his jacket, then spoke. "Your friend? The photographer from Houston?"

"His name is Elton Sparks."

"Mr. Sparks is a very foolish man."

"Why do you say that?"

"He was spending time with the wife of Beno."

"I was afraid of that."

"Beno found out. This is a town of 40,000 people, but there are few secrets."

"Do you know what happened?"

Sergio shrugged. "I have heard about it." He stepped behind his desk, casually sweeping his hand toward the guest chairs.

"Beno was here Thursday night," Sergio offered. "One of the customers asked for him. They talked, then Beno left quickly."

"You saw this?"

"I was told."

"Do you know where he went?

"To a hotel." Sergio looked to Donald, then back at Jake.

"It's all right," Jake said. "Don is helping me."

Sergio leaned back in his chair, drew thoughtfully on his cigar, opened his mouth and let smoke drift toward the ceiling.

"Beno was unhappy to see his wife with Mr. Sparks, and I'm sure Mr. Sparks was surprised to learn that the lady was Beno's wife." Sergio regarded the end of his cigar, then tapped the ashes into a crystal tray.

"It was an unfortunate mistake for your friend. Beno did not react well. He was unkind to his wife, but she was used to his ways. I heard that he left Mr. Sparks at the beach, perhaps to think about what he had done."

Jake leaned forward, gripping the front of Sergio's desk.

"The beach? Do you know where?"

"The new section of the seawall."

"And Beno? Where is he now?"

Sergio sighed. "I do not know. No one has seen him since that night."

Jake hustled Donald down the Flamingo Room's broad stairs and onto the street. "We need to call Clara," he said.

"Why?" Donald stepped in front of Jake, one hand flat against Jake's chest. "Why?" he asked again.

"Beno knows I was the one who introduced Maye to Elton, and he knows that with Elton missing, sooner or later I'd come looking for him."

Jake started to move, but Donald pushed back.

"But Clara?"

"Look," Jake said, shaking off Donald's hand, "where Beno comes from, revenge is a sport. He knows I'm in town and where I stay. He might go there looking for me."

Donald turned away. He slapped automatically at a mosquito, but didn't bother wiping the blood from his cheek. He darted between a Ford and a passing buggy to the phone booth in front of Murdoch's Pier, then tugged at the door before noticing the man inside.

When Jake trotted up, Donald confronted him again.

"Do you think he would hurt Clara?"

"Beno can't control his anger."

The earlier fear and confusion Donald had seen in Jake was back. He turned and rapped on the telephone booth glass, but the man inside only scowled.

"Beno's crazy," Jake said, half to himself. "If he killed Elton, he's probably looking for me."

"And you're sure he knows where you stay?"

"Yes."

The door of the booth began to open. Donald jerked the handle to hustle the man out. He started to protest, saw the look in Donald's eyes and ducked away.

Donald opened his journal to the place where he'd written Clara's number, pressed the book open and wedged it with an elbow against the inside of the booth. He snatched the receiver from its holder, rang the operator and waited for her to place the call.

"Give me a nickel!" he shouted to Jake.

Chapter 14

Clara looked up from her textbook to admire the back garden in twilight. It was so different from the days when she and Mama tended it together.

"Victory gardens," the newspapers called them now, encouraging the home folks to do their part. Fewer flowers, more vegetables and fruit. The only sad area—Clara could just see it from where she sat—was the dense tangle of oleanders and weeds behind the carriage house. There had been no time in the hectic year since Mama died to clean them out, and no extra money to hire it done. The longer it went, the worse it got, Clara knew. She rubbed her eyes, sipped her tea and returned to her book.

The view of Clara's house from the alley was different. A tidy yard. A few rows of beans. A window. A woman sitting alone at a desk. With the window open, one could even hear the telephone ring, but to know what was said, it was necessary to get much closer. Fortunately, the fading light made that easy.

"Hello?" Clara said into the mouthpiece as she held the heavy receiver to her ear. "Yes, this is Clara. Oh, Donald! Is everything all right?"

She transferred the receiver to her other ear as Donald gave a quick account of the meeting with Sergio. Donald's voice sounded tinny and far away, like one of Mr. Edison's talking machines.

"There's a chance Beno is looking for Jake," Donald said. "From Sergio's description he's a wild man. Seeing his wife with another man made him worse. Sergio said Beno beat her." Donald paused. "And Jake thinks Elton is dead."

The words didn't make sense. A woman beaten? Elton dead? A wild man loose? Her fingers tightened around the phone's mouthpiece, in part to hold herself up.

"And you think he's coming here?"

"Jake is afraid he might."

Clara glanced behind her into the comfortable room where she'd been reading, in the house where she grew up. She felt trapped.

"Will you be back soon?"

"We're at Murdoch's now, but we'll be there in twenty minutes."

"I'll be waiting."

"Clara? "

"Yes."

"Do you have a gun?"

"Are you that worried?"

"Jake is. He said to ask you."

"There's one upstairs. Mother taught me to use it, but it has been a few years."

"Please get it and keep it with you until we return. We can talk then."

The one-sided conversation told the listener in the garden all he needed to know. This was indeed the right house, and Jake would be home soon. He eased himself toward the kitchen door.

It took a minute for Clara to find the firearm, wrapped as it was in a leftover yard of blue velvet and high on a shelf behind two hat boxes.

The old Webley service revolver was heavy in her hands. She unwrapped it quickly, remembering the day her father brought it home after a trip to England. On a lark, Clara and her mother had used the last of the ammunition shooting at cans on an empty stretch of beach two years before. They hadn't bothered to buy more.

"So, Mr. Webley," Clara said, hefting the revolver with both hands, "like most men, you are completely useless, but unless I drop you on my foot, at least no one will get hurt."

She was halfway down the stairs when she heard the first sound. Jennifer and Rebecca were at work, and she wasn't expecting anyone else. She steadied her hand on the banister and waited. The creaking screen door—another thing she meant to fix—told her someone was inside. She raised the revolver with both hands, steadying herself by leaning against the wall.

"Where are all the damned jitneys?" Jake yelled to Donald as they ran to catch the 21st Street trolley. It took another twelve minutes to reach the Avenue C terminal. They jumped from the trolley while it was still rolling and ran the remaining blocks to Clara's house.

"All the lights are on," Donald said, puffing hard as they raced up the shell drive toward the arbor. Jake stumbled, caught himself on one of the arbor posts, and was right behind as Donald flung open the screen door. The biggest revolver he'd ever seen was on the kitchen table, and he heard moaning from the next room.

"Jake! Donald! Hurry, I'm in here."

Clara was down, knees to one side. Donald didn't recognize the other figure on the floor. His left eye was swollen shut and a deep bruise spread across his jaw. His upper lip formed a grotesque sneer. His head rested in Clara's lap.

"Elton!" Jake said, dropping beside them.

Elton moaned again as Clara squeezed water from a dish towel and laid the damp cloth across his forehead.

"He came in while I was upstairs," she said.

Jake touched the blood on Elton's shirt.

"Did you shoot him?"

"Of course not! But seeing the gun probably sapped what little energy he had left. He just collapsed."

Elton's jacket was torn at the shoulder. He still had shoes, but his trousers were ripped, exposing raw flesh on both bloody knees. His hands and face were covered with scratches and mosquito bites.

"He has at least one broken rib," Clara said, "but I don't think there is anything worse. These injuries are several days old. If he had internal bleeding, he would have died by now. I think his worst problems are hunger and dehydration. And he's badly bruised. Donald, would you bring a fresh dish towel?"

"Of course."

"And please put a kettle of water on the stove."

"Right," he said, happy for something to do.

"Jake, could you and Donald carry Elton upstairs? I need to give him a bath. He can stay in my room tonight."

"Give him a bath?" Donald called from the kitchen sink, water from the kettle now dripping on his shoes.

"Don't worry, I've done this before."

For the next ten minutes, Jake and Donald stayed with Elton at the foot of the stairs, placing a pillow under his head after Clara left to prepare the room. When she returned, Donald was intrigued to see her gathering bandages, ointments and creams.

"How do we carry him upstairs?" Jake called as Clara passed by.

"He shouldn't be jostled any more than necessary."

"The dining chairs have tall backs," Donald offered. "We could have him sit, tilt the chair back, then carry him up. It would be almost as good as a stretcher."

"Excellent," Clara said. "Jake, please bring one of the chairs."

Donald saw a flicker of surprise, but Jake recovered quickly and went for the chair.

"How did you do that?" Donald whispered to Clara. "Jake never fetches anything when I'm around."

Clara winked.

The two men eased Elton to a sitting position, then grasped the chair on both sides and gently tilted it back. They paused for a deep breath.

"Here we go," Jake said.

Upstairs, Donald and Jake helped Elton from the chair. He was just conscious enough to sit on the edge of the single bed, which Clara had carefully covered with towels. Donald slipped off the remains of Elton's shoes and socks.

Clara directed as they removed the rest of Elton's clothes, leaving only his BVDs. She began to sponge off the accumulated sweat, filth and dried blood. She was very deliberate, yet gentle, Donald thought. He helped by handing her fresh towels.

"Let's see if he can drink some water," Clara said. "And there's leftover soup in the icebox. You can heat that."

"I'll get it," Jake said, already turning from the room.

Clara smiled at Donald. "And would you mind gathering Elton's clothes and leaving them in the mud room? I'll wash them later and see what can be salvaged. For now, just put some water in a pan and soak his shirt; that will help remove the blood stain."

"Sure," Donald said, arms already full of dirty clothes.

"And Donald, please make sure Jake gets the soup hot."

Elton mumbled something, but his mouth was too swollen to talk.

Jake and Donald, returning to Clara's room about the same time, were surprised to see Elton dressed in men's pajamas, the last of his underwear laying on the floor beside the bed. They stood for a moment, mouths open, Donald holding a glass of water, and Jake, a bowl of hot soup.

"You may take over now," Clara said, gathering towels from the bed and Elton's BVDs from the floor. She paused, looking from Donald to Jake and back again. "They were my father's pajamas," she explained, certain that was not what they wanted to know.

With his good eye, Elton watched Clara go.

"Sip this," Jake said a moment later. He slipped one hand behind Elton's head and held the glass to his mouth.

"Don, Clara left a bottle of pills for him on the night stand. Let me have a couple."

Donald unscrewed the metal cap and shook two Bayer Tablets of Aspirin into his hand. A doctor had ordered the same after Clarence fell from the ladder a year before. "The miracle drug," it was called.

"Here you go."

"Take these," Jake said, pressing the pills into Elton's mouth and raising the glass again.

Elton's lips refused to close on the glass, and water dribbled down his chin. Jake caught it with a handkerchief before it reached Elton's pajamas.

"And how about some soup while it's still hot?"

"Yeth. Tan ... tank you."

"Save it," Jake said, offering a spoonful of soup. "Finish this and get some rest. We can talk in the morning."

Chapter 15

Tuesday, September 10, 1918

Clara slept late. It was nearly 10 a.m. before she checked once more on her patient and came downstairs. Her back ached from spending the night fully clothed on the couch. Elton was sleeping deeply and didn't stir when Clara touched her hand to his forehead. The last time she'd seen such bruises, the patient had been kicked by his mule.

She smelled coffee and was surprised to find Jake alone at the kitchen table with Tuesday's *Galveston Daily News* spread before him. Staring out the kitchen window, Jake didn't notice her at first.

"Where's Donald?" she asked, taking the chair across from his.

"Oh! Good morning. Don's out back. When you told him last night that Elton might have been hiding in the weeds behind the carriage house, he decided to clear them out."

"How kind!" Clara glanced toward the window. Through the magnolia leaves she could see Donald's bare torso, his arms swinging her grandfather's old scythe with some skill.

"I made coffee. Would you like some?"

Clara turned toward the stove.

"No," Jake said, lifting one hand. "I'll get it. Keep your seat. I imagine you had a rough night with Elton."

"He slept straight through, but I did check him every hour or so."

She swallowed a laugh when Jake picked a cup and saucer that didn't match, and instead of the small sugar bowl, he brought the whole tin.

"Milk in your coffee?"

"Yes, please."

Jake took a full quart bottle from the icebox and set it on the table.

"The ice man came early this morning," he said, "so the milk is good and cold."

"I was afraid he wouldn't come until this afternoon. Sometimes he uses his new delivery truck, but it isn't as reliable as his mules."

Jake laughed, but Clara could see his thoughts were not on their conversation.

"Elton will be all right. A few good meals and rest are all he needs," she said, stirring her coffee with the soup spoon Jake provided.

"I know. You were very good with him." He stopped.

"Are you still worried about Beno?"

"Yes. And it bothers me that my cousin had something to do with Elton's beating."

"Do you think Sergio knows more than he told you?"

"I'm sure of it."

"Good morning," Donald said, opening the screen door into the kitchen. Clara noticed the hinges no longer squeaked.

"Donald! Thank you for clearing the weeds! It was a big mess back there."

"There's more to do, but it looks better now." Donald fastened the top two buttons of his shirt and tucked the shirttail into his pants. "I hope you don't mind. There were tools in your shed. I trimmed the oleanders and cut the weeds that were growing through the bricks. Did you know you have a nice little patio?"

Clara laughed. "Yes, my brother Henry laid it after the house was raised to the new grade. Mama asked a carpenter friend to make a couple of Westport chairs she'd seen in a magazine. We loved sitting there in the evenings. Of course the trees were still saplings, but the garden was so lovely. Mama and I gathered fresh flowers for the house every week."

"Your vegetables look well-tended," Donald said, gesturing over his shoulder with his thumb.

"I planted a victory garden like everyone else, but the vegetables need so much attention that I don't have time for the flower beds and the patio. With Mama gone and my brother in France, I'm afraid the weeds took over. I'd like to see the work you did. Were you ..."

"Don is a handy fellow," Jake said, already tired of the conversation.

Clara looked at Jake, then back to Donald.

"Donald, Jake thinks his cousin knows more about Elton than he told you yesterday."

"Oh?" Donald said, washing his hands at the sink and drying them on his pants.

"Yes. Sergio has changed in the last few years. It struck me yesterday how different he is from when we were kids. Now I don't know ..."

Jake stopped short. He spread the fingers of both hands and moved them slowly across the newspaper in front of him. "Draft Registration Day, September 12," he read out loud.

"Did you notice the fresh cigarette butt in Sergio's ashtray?" Donald asked, refusing to let Jake off. He took the chair at one end of the table. "I think someone else was in the room just before we came. And what a strange door! If you didn't know where to look, you wouldn't see it at all."

"I missed the cigarette," Jake admitted. "Sergio probably keeps a bodyguard now. It wouldn't surprise me if someone was behind another door, listening to everything we said."

When Donald recalled Sergio's hired thug in the bar, his right hand twitched. He covered it with his left hand, pretending to have an itch.

"Would you like some coffee?" Clara asked, rising from her chair to face him.

"I'll have some of this milk, thanks."

She turned toward the cupboard for a glass.

"Are you two going over there again?"

"Yes, this afternoon," Jake answered. "I have to know if Beno is looking for me or not. Don, I'd feel better if you stayed here with Elton and Clara."

Clara returned with an empty glass and a full plate of cookies.

"If you insist," Donald said, reaching for the bottle of milk.

Jake was restless as he pieced together what he knew. Going to the police would be useless. If he accused Beno of beating Elton, they'd say he had it coming for being caught with Beno's wife.

He was sitting alone on Clara's front porch swing when the Beacon Club's Buick pulled into the shell driveway with Jennifer and Rebecca in back. They waited while the uniformed driver walked around to open the door. It was clear the women were dog-tired, with none of the glitter they'd had when the car picked them up twelve hours before.

"Good morning ladies," Jake said, touching the brim of his hat. "Unusually late night?"

"Three oil men from Houston were in town and they needed to get rid of some money," Rebecca said.

"We helped them," Jennifer added, laying one outstretched arm casually over Jake's shoulder, "but now I could sleep for a week."

"We did so well for the club that we have tonight off," Rebecca added. "We earned it."

Jake could smell the whisky on her breath, and watched as the two club hostesses wobbled toward their rooms in the carriage house.

"We found Elton," Jake called to their backs. Both women stopped and turned. Rebecca spoke first.

"Is there any news about Maye?"

"No, why?"

"We heard Beno knocked her around. He's done it before, but this time nobody knows where she is."

"Beno's wife is missing?"

"Yes, since last Thursday."

"Sergio told me Beno had been rough with her, but that she was going to be all right. He must not have known she was missing."

"Jake, believe me, everyone knows."

"Show me what you've done in the garden," Clara said when Donald had finished his milk and third cookie.

"You bet." Donald held open the screen door for Clara.

"And you fixed the hinges," she said.

"They just needed oil. I found some in the shed."

Even with the carriage house covering part of the land, Clara still had a generous back yard. She briefly took Donald's hand to step down from the arbor onto the brick path that led past her victory garden toward the rear picket fence. As they passed the last row of okra, Clara could see the freshly-cleared space near the back of the property. She left Donald's side and skipped ahead onto the patio.

"Oh, Donald, this is better than I remembered!" She whirled slowly with her arms wide to take it all in. "And you found the Westport chairs!"

"They were overgrown with weeds. I didn't see them when I first came out. Here, Clara, have a seat."

Donald pulled up the second chair and sat beside her, with a view of the gardens and rear of Clara's house. He'd trimmed the oleanders into a high arch that left dappled shadows on the red brick at their feet and shaded the two sitters from the late-morning sun. A male blue jay darted away into the pecan tree and began scolding the intruders.

"This is wonderful," Clara said, easing farther back in her chair and pointing her toes toward the yard. She rolled her fingertips over the wide, flat arms of the chair. "Just wait until you see the light at sunset."

Seeing the joy in her face, Donald was sure it couldn't be any better. The moment passed when he heard footsteps on the garden path, just before Jake rounded the back corner.

"Ah, there you are," he said. "Jen and Rebecca are back. With news. If anyone is in the seawall, I know who it is."

"Who?" Clara and Donald said together.

"Maye." Jake took a deep breath. "She's been missing since Thursday. Beno could have dragged her to the same place he dumped Elton. I think he wanted to kill them both, but Elton got away."

"Oh dear." Clara said through the fingers of both hands.

Jake turned and headed for the driveway. "I've got to talk to Sergio," he said.

"Wait," Donald called. "It's broad daylight. There are people on the streets. Beno's not likely to cause a disturbance now. Let's go together."

He turned to Clara. "Do you need help with Elton?"

"Go," she said, "I'll be fine."

Chapter 16

"Elton's back, that's what counts."

"Did you let Mr. Foley know?" Donald said.

"I sent a telegram first thing this morning."

Walking to the trolley gave both of them time to think, but Jake was surprised he couldn't concentrate on Beno.

"Are you afraid of your cousin?" Donald asked suddenly.

"No. But, I didn't like what I saw yesterday."

"You've known Sergio all your life. You said he's changed."

"I still think of him the way he was ten years ago, when he took over his family's restaurants in Houston. I was glad to see him expand so quickly, then open a place here in Galveston. I want to be like that."

"You want to open a restaurant?"

"No, I just want to do more than earn a salary. When Sergio started, he was as poor as me. Now look at him! He owns three successful clubs. All the people who work for him call him 'Mr. Leone,' and say 'Yes, sir!' Hell, he's even got a driver, while I'm still wearing out my shoes hustling newspapers."

"You're doing all right, Jake." This was fresh, Donald thought, Jake questioning himself. "Sergio sounds like a go-getter. Some people are just that way. It doesn't mean you have to be like him."

"I don't want to be *like* him, Don, I just want to be *rich*. Don't you?"

"Never thought of it. I can't imagine being rich."

"Oh, come on, Don, aren't there things you want? A car, maybe? Nice clothes? A house?"

"Someday, I suppose. Right now I'm learning my way around. I'm happy enough."

Jake rested his hand on Donald's shoulder as they matched strides. "My boy," he said, "you have got a lot to learn."

Jake and Donald paused for several buggies and a motor car, then crossed the street and entered the Flamingo. Donald's eyes went straight to the bar where the rat-eyed man had sat watching them the night before. He was relieved to find the stool empty.

A lone bartender was polishing glasses and hanging them one by one in the overhead rack. In the dining room, chairs normally filled with patrons were still upside down on the tables. Donald's hand twitched. He inhaled deeply to calm himself, but the damp smell of tobacco and stale beer felt like a warning to keep out.

"This sure doesn't look like it did last night," Jake said. He braced one hand on the wall and leaned around a corner to peer deeper into the bar. The bartender ignored him.

"At least I don't see Tuxedo and his watchdog," Jake added, looking across the room. "With all the electric lights on, this place is not so fancy."

"Candles and soft music make a lot of difference," Sergio said.

Donald jumped. Sergio smiled with his mouth but not his eyes.

"Were you looking for me?"

"We found Elton," Jake said, "or rather, he found us."

"Bene, molto bene," Sergio said. "And he is well?"

"Not well, but he'll survive. Beno was pretty rough on him."

"Your friend is very stupid."

"I'm sure he didn't understand the situation, Sergio." Jake braced himself. "We just heard that Beno's wife disappeared the same time as Elton."

"No," Sergio said, "Maye is here. Do you want to see her?"

Jake was lost for words, so Donald answered for him.

"Please, yes, we'd like to see her."

"Certainly. This way."

Sergio led them from the bar to one of the privacy booths. In cold climates, the tall sides and heavy drapes across the open end kept customers warm. In Sergio's club, they kept conversations from being overheard. Sergio stopped in front of the last booth, its curtain half drawn.

"Maye?" Sergio said gently, "You have visitors."

Maye's knee-length silk dress revealed more than Donald had ever seen of a grown woman's legs. They were crossed, and her left thigh showed a bit of the garter and yellow ribbon that Donald suspected held up her stockings. She made no effort to cover herself when Jake spoke.

"Maye? Do you remember me? It's Jake."

"Foots? Sure. Have a seat." She patted the cushion beside her, but slid only a few inches deeper into the booth.

"I'll leave you," Sergio said. "Maye, call me if you need anything."

Sergio made a move to go, then turned back to Jake. He gave him a quick open-handed pat on the cheek. "Everything is fine, cousin. Have the bartender show you to my office when you finish."

Jake nodded, then pulled away the curtain. The brass rings slid easily on the overhead rod. He sat next to Maye. She turned her head to the rear of the booth and held one hand toward the bright room.

"Too much light," she said. "Pull the curtain back."

"There," Jake said, giving the drapery two quick tugs until the booth was completely enclosed. The brass rings clicked. Like everything else in the room, the fabric reeked of tobacco and beer. In the dim light, Maye turned back to face Donald across the table. She rested her hand on Jake's knee.

"Who is this handsome fellow?" she asked, tipping her cigarette toward Donald.

"This is my friend, Don Brown," Jake said. "Don, this is Mrs. Maybelle Benebeota."

"Don't mention that bastard's name!" she spat, jabbing the stub of her cigarette as if to punish the ash tray.

Only once had Donald seen a lady smoking in public. He'd never heard one swear, and he had never seen a woman with a black eye.

"Pleased, uh, I mean, nice to meet you ..."

"My friends call me Maye."

"Nice to meet you, Maye."

Maye stared for a moment at Donald's thick glasses, then turned to search her purse for a fresh smoke.

"Foots," she said, raising the cigarette to her lips, "ask Ruben to bring me a gin fizz. Order anything you want. Sergio is buying."

Jake pulled the curtain aside just enough to get the attention of the man behind the bar, then drew it closed it again. Maye smiled at Donald. She nudged her ankle against the side of his calf and left it there. Donald felt sweat trickle down his back and wished he could remove his jacket. At least the ceiling fans were on. There was a polite knock at the end of the booth and Jake slid the curtain aside once more to address Ruben.

"Another fizz for the lady," Jake said. "And I'll have a beer. Do you have *Southern Select?*"

"Certainly. We have all the local beers on tap, and several others in cans."

"The *Select* for me. Don, how about you?" Jake pulled back the curtain a few inches more so Donald could see the bartender.

Donald was about to order his favorite, a *Triple-X* cream soda, when Maye spoke up, jabbing her unlit cigarette across the table.

"Is this boy old enough to drink?"

"A *Southern Select* for me, too," Donald heard himself say, "and a shaker of salt."

"Very good," said the bartender.

Jake winked at Donald as he snapped the curtain closed. He turned to light Maye's cigarette, cupping his hands around the match. She held her own hand over his a few seconds longer than it took to get the light. She inhaled deeply, then tilted her head back to exhale. With the last of her air, she rounded her lips and puffed.

Donald watched, open mouthed, as a perfect smoke ring drifted toward the ceiling. Under the table, Maye's ankle felt warm against his leg.

Another quiet knock. Ruben was back with a tray of drinks and bowl of salted nuts. Jake used the shaker to sprinkle salt around the rim of his glass. Donald did the same with his own, as he'd seen Clarence do many times.

Before taking the first sip, Jake raised his glass high over the center of the table.

"Well, as the Tommies say, cheers!"

"Cheers," said Donald.

"Cheers," said Maye, clinking her highball glass to theirs. "But tell me, Foots, what would you know about Tommies?" Maye, grinning now, raised her glass again. "To all slackers!"

"Cut it out, Maye."

She took another sip, then leaned hard against Jake's shoulder, studying him over the rim of her glass. Donald fought to keep his eyes from her cleavage. It was an interesting term, cleavage, and purely abstract until now.

"Did Beno do this to you?" Jake said, lifting his little finger from his glass toward Maye's black eye.

"The evil bastard—may he rot in hell." Maye sat up. She paused to pick a bit of fresh tobacco from between her lips, examined it briefly, then flicked it toward the rear of the booth. A stain matching the color of her lips already coated one end of her smoke.

"Yes, he did this. Your friend was in town and I went to see him. Nice boy. Just a friendly visit. We had a couple of drinks before that ape kicked in the door. I thought your friend was going to wet himself."

"You didn't tell Elton about Beno?"

"I forgot."

"What happened then?"

"I screamed. The dumb bastard hit me, then he started on your friend. When he saw the camera, he kicked that around, too. I yelled for Elton to run."

"Did he?" Donald said, no longer able to keep silent.

"Yes. The window was open, but we were on the third floor, too high to jump. He made it to the fire escape, then the Great Ape chased him down the stairs."

"Do you know what he did with Elton?" Jake demanded.

"Hell no! By then, people down the hall were shouting and I could hear the night clerk taking the stairs two at a time. I grabbed my dress and shoes and headed for the window." At that, Maye recalled another detail and laughed.

"Oh, this is rich! For some reason I stuffed your friend's camera in his bag and took it with me, but when I got to the bottom of the fire escape, I couldn't remember why I had it. Too much gin. Anyway, I tossed it behind some garbage cans and ran."

"Where did you go, Maye?" Jake looked grim.

"My face hurt pretty bad where that dago bastard hit me. A friend of mine lives a block from the hotel. She took me in." Maye drained the last of her drink and shook the empty glass in front of Jake.

"Not yet, Maye," he said. "Where's Beno?"

"You don't know?"

"Tell me."

Maye laughed, harder than before, and finally hard enough to start a rasping cough. She lifted her hand from Jake's leg and began patting her ample chest. It took a moment for Maye to recover. The same with Donald, but for other reasons.

"That dumb sorry bastard will never hurt me again!"

"What do you mean?" Jake said, grabbing her forearm as Maye fell into another laughing fit. Donald heard rushing footsteps.

"Beno's part of the seawall now!"

Sergio jerked back the curtain, filling the booth with light. Jake and Donald both flinched, too stunned by Maye's words to speak. Donald took a long sip of beer as he studied Sergio, leaving a thin layer of foam on his upper lip. Seconds passed. The only sound was Maye's coughing laugh. She was convulsing now, and slapping the table with her free hand. Tears washed black eyeliner into streaks down both cheeks.

She hiccupped. Sergio's timing had been grand.

"Ruben, please bring Maye another drink," Sergio called calmly across the empty room. To Jake he said more quietly, "Cousin, come with me." He glanced at Donald. "And your friend."

Sergio ushered Donald and Jake into the dead-end hall and touched his hand to a section of the wall. The panel door opened silently. This time, others were in the room. Donald recognized one as the hulking man who had watched them the night before. Another stepped behind Donald and Jake, between them and the door. Donald glanced back.

"We need no introductions here," Sergio said. "Jake, Donald, please sit." As they complied, Sergio casually opened the upper right drawer of his desk, glanced down, gently closed it again and remained standing behind his desk.

"Serg, what is going on?" Jake said.

Sergio selected a fresh hand-rolled Tampa Robusto from the humidor on his desk. He studied the cigar's torpedo shape before clipping the head and slipping a full two inches of it into his mouth to moisten the outer leaf. The monster on his left produced a safety match, but Sergio declined the light. He clamped the unlit cigar in his mouth, preferring for now just to chew.

Sergio finally sat. He looked briefly at Donald's thick glasses, then turned to Jake.

"Forgive me, cousin, but this is a serious matter. I need for you to understand."

The bodyguards stood as still as a pair of granite lions. Sergio rested his elbows on the arms of the chair, fingertips together beneath his chin.

Donald waited for someone to speak. His mouth was dry. He needed to pee.

Inhale ... hold ... exhale ...

Jake returned his cousin's stare, but Sergio spoke first. He gestured with his cigar toward the guards.

"These gentlemen work for me," he explained. "Several of their friends as well. In a business like mine, it is comforting to have them around. I don't want any trouble. It's bad for business. These men make sure there is no trouble. Do you understand?"

"Of course," Jake said, "But what happened to ..."

"To Beno? He became the trouble. He grew loud. He pushed customers around. As a responsible proprietor, I had to let him go. He is no longer an employee."

Sergio's words lingered in the air. He leaned back, stopping only when the chair's heavy springs reached the far end of their range. Sergio held that position, like a stone loaded in a slingshot. Donald thought it best to keep quiet, but Jake had something to say.

"You can't just kill people, Sergio."

Sergio sprang forward, both hands slapping hard on the edge of his desk. Donald would have jumped up were it not for the meaty hand that instantly grabbed his shoulder, pinning him to the chair. Just as fast, Sergio's anger was under control and the guard eased his grip. Donald wanted to rub his shoulder, but was afraid to move. He knew there'd be a bruise.

Sergio spoke slowly, as if addressing a child.

"I did not say that Beno is dead. I merely said he is no longer an employee. He has probably left the island to find another job. Look for him if you want, you will not find him here."

"But Maye said ..."

"For all her charms, Maye lives in fantasy. She cannot be trusted to know or tell the truth."

Jake was silent. Sergio turned to Donald. "Does this make sense to you, young man?

Sergio's face let Donald know there was only one correct answer.

"Yes, sir."

Sergio turned back to Jake.

"This matter with my employee does not concern you, cousin Jake. Elton Sparks had an unfortunate accident, but he will be all right. That is the important thing. Maye is a pretty woman with an empty head. She imagines things that did not happen. Have I made myself clear?"

Donald studied the thick man at Sergio's right. His twin was behind Donald and Jake, close enough for them to smell the garlic on his breath. Once more, sweat made Donald's one good shirt stick to his back. This would make a great entry for his journal, if he ever got to write in it again. Seconds more passed in silence. Donald forgot to breathe.

Finally, Jake slapped both hands to his knees. "Well, Sergio, that makes sense. You're right, your employee problems are none of my business. All I know is that Elton is safe. I'm sure he will be more careful with his next lady friend."

Sergio smiled, stood and extended his hand. "Excellent. Please come to see me the next time you are in town. We have more business to discuss."

"I will. Ciao, Sergio."

"Ciao, cousin."

A minute later, Donald and Jake were on the street, blinking in the late afternoon sun.

"What made you back down from Sergio?"

"Consider it a tactical retreat." Jake said. "I figured Sergio was right. It was smart to let Beno go."

"You don't believe Maye?"

"Look, she could be right. A lot of people must have known Sergio wanted to get rid of Beno. What happened to Maye and Elton could have been the last straw. Maybe that drunk's call to the police wasn't a joke. After all, Beno made a lot of enemies here." Jake looked hard at Donald. "Nobody saw anything. Nobody cares. Beno won't be missed."

They walked another block before Jake spoke, anticipating the next question. "My cousin and the other club owners have an agreement with the police. It's not hard for them to look the other way."

"Why?" Donald asked, but he was beginning to see for himself. What Jake said next was no surprise.

"It's good for business. The clubs bring in plenty of money, and the owners make sure the police, judges and politicians get their share. People overlook things when their incomes depend on it."

"Life isn't as simple as our teachers made it seem in school."

Jake threw his arm around Donald's shoulders as they walked. He lifted Donald's cap and patted him on the head.

"Now you're catching on."

Chapter 17

"Elton's awake," Clara called as soon as she heard the front door open. Donald and Jake took the stairs two at a time, Jake first to the top. When they reached Clara's room, Elton was sitting up, three pillows at his back, sipping hot tea. She had shaved him, brushed his teeth and combed his hair. If not for the purple bruise covering most of his left jaw, he looked fine. The swelling around his eye and the mosquito welts had gone down.

"Elton has quite a story to tell," Clara said. "I took notes so he wouldn't have to repeat everything."

"Tank ou," Elton said with what passed for a smile. He coughed hard, immediately groaned and wrapped one arm around his left side. Clara took the cup from his shaking hand.

"Are you going to bandage his ribs?" Donald asked.

"We can't do much," she explained. "If we wrap his torso, it will be harder for him to breathe. A bandage could also make the bone mend in the wrong position. Elton's body will heal better without our help. The real danger is that the broken rib could have punctured a lung, but I'm convinced it has not." She smiled at Elton and patted his hand. "He'll be sore for a while, but good as new in a few weeks."

"You gave us a scare," Jake said, sliding a chair next to the bed. Donald did the same, placing his chair closer to Clara's.

"What did you learn at the club?" she asked Donald.

"Quite a bit," he said. "For one thing, we talked to Maye. She'd been staying with a friend since last Thursday."

Jake turned to Elton. "What were you thinking? She's a married woman!"

"Ah din ... know that," Elton said, speaking slowly and swallowing between words so he wouldn't cough again. "She ... din ... tell ... me."

Clara turned to the nightstand, where she had a small pan of hot water on a dish towel. Inside the pan sat a clear glass bottle with a cork stopper. She retrieved the bottle, wiped it dry with a cloth, removed the cork and poured a tablespoon of warm syrup. It smelled of lemon. She held it to Elton's lips, cupping her hand under his chin to catch any drops.

"What's that?" Donald asked.

"Mother's cough remedy. It's a mix of herbs, honey, lemon juice and bourbon. Elton had a slight fever, so I added a little Aspirin powder to this batch."

"Ish good," Elton said, "but ... she won't ... give me ... as much ... as I want."

"It's the whiskey he's after," Jake said, patting Elton's head. "Now I know he'll survive."

Donald turned to Clara. "What did he tell you?"

"You were right about the hotel room," she said. "Beno kicked in the door soon after Elton took that second photo of Maye. He said Beno was like a rogue elephant, bellowing in Italian and kicking the furniture. Maye screamed, so Beno hit her, then went after Elton. Maye told Elton to run, but Beno got to him first. That's what happened to Elton's jaw. Then Beno threw him across the room, and that may be when he broke his rib, but Elton got out of the window and onto the fire escape before Beno caught him again."

"Quick for a big man," Elton added, again swallowing between words. The cough remedy improved his speech. "It surprised me."

Clara continued the story.

"Beno drug him to the alley, but Elton doesn't remember anything more until he woke up in the dunes behind the seawall. It was dark, but there were electric lights around the construction site. At first, Elton didn't know where he was."

"Did you see any workers?" Jake asked. "There should have been a night crew."

"No," Elton said before Clara stopped him. She picked up the story again, referring briefly to her notes.

"Elton saw several large men on the top of the seawall, next to a wooden enclosure that had been constructed over the pilings. The men were in suits. There was a scuffle, then Elton saw one of the men topple into the concrete form."

"Sounded ... like someone ... dropped a big rock ... onto gravel," Elton said.

"Wet concrete," Donald said. "What happened then?"

Elton started to speak again, but Clara put her hand on his arm.

"Elton said he could hear the man cursing from inside the wooden form, even over the noise of the cement mixer. The men on top rolled the machine on its rails to the edge and tipped the mouth of the mixer over the form. Elton said it looked like a huge pot of batter being poured into a cake pan."

"After ... after a while ... the yelling stopped," Elton said. "But the men ... on top ... kept pouring ... "

"It went on for another ten minutes." Clara said, again checking her notes. "Then the men climbed down from the seawall. A short time later the night crew returned."

"Elton, did the men look around for you?" Jake's voice sounded urgent.

"How did you get away?" Donald added.

Elton looked first at Jake. "I don't ... think so." He turned slightly to Donald. "I waited ... I guess ... until ... about 4 a.m. Not sure. I lost ... my watch." He held up his empty left wrist as proof. Clara picked up the story from there.

"Elton told me that before the sun came up, he found a fishing shack a quarter mile up the beach from the construction area. There was enough food and water for him to hide there until Sunday. That's when he risked calling the police station."

"I couldn't ... talk ... very well ... before that," Elton said. "I don't think ... the officer ... on the phone ... believed me ... when I told him ... somebody was ... "

"They thought you were drunk," Jake said. "The police were out there, but they're not going to do anything more."

Clara shuddered and Donald put his hand lightly on her back.

"We thought either you or Maye were in the seawall," Donald explained. "Now we're pretty sure it's Beno."

"But ... why ... ?"

"Beno was a problem," Jake said. "Sergio told me he fired him when he heard about you and Maye. I think Beno's enemies took over from there."

"Elton was afraid they were looking for him," Clara said. "After he regained his voice enough to make the phone call, he returned to the fishing shack."

"I ... ran out ... out of food ... yesterday."

"Yes," Clara added, filling in for Elton. "He ran out of food and water, but he thought you'd be looking for him and guessed that you might come here."

Jake nodded as Clara continued. "He walked all the way to the bay side of the island, then kept near the shore, trying to avoid people. He hid behind the carriage house until he was sure he had the right place." She put her notes on the night stand and looked up.

"Elton was outside the window when Donald called, then he entered through the kitchen. He was injured and exhausted, so when I appeared on the stairs with Papa's Webley, it was too much. He fainted."

Elton slowly raised his hands and spread them wide in front of his chest. "Big ... damn ... gun," he said.

Chapter 18

Clara and Donald gathered the soiled pillowcases and towels to take downstairs. Neither spoke until Clara began piling the linens into a large wicker basket in the mud room. Rather than leave the rumpled mess showing, she spread one white towel neatly over the top.

"What are your plans now?" she asked, tucking the edges of towel into the basket.

"I need to return to Houston to register Thursday for the draft," Donald said. "Thanks to you, Elton's much better. I talked to Jake. If it's all right, we'd like to stay here until tomorrow afternoon."

"Certainly. By then I'll know if Elton is out of danger. He can stay until he's ready to travel. With your help," she added thoughtfully, "he could stay in the carriage house. It would be nice to sleep in my own bed again."

"Of course. We can move him this evening."

Clara touched her stomach. "Donald, are you hungry? I haven't had anything since you and Jake left this morning. Let me see what's in the pantry."

"I'm starving, but I don't want you to cook. Do you know a good restaurant?"

Clara smiled in relief. She needed a rest. "Oh, yes. Do you like enchiladas?"

"Sure."

"There's a wonderful Mexican restaurant nearby. Give me a minute."

Donald smiled as Clara left for the washroom. He climbed the stairs and found Jake sitting with Elton, who was drifting in and out of sleep.

"How's he doing?"

"Still a little fever, I think, but not as much pain as last night."

"Jake, what are enchiladas?"

"Mexican hot dogs, but you eat them with a knife and fork."

"Thanks. Clara and I are going to get some. You want to go?"

"No. You're on your own. Enjoy yourselves."

Donald was happy to have Clara to himself, but worried what they might talk about. He'd never invited a woman to lunch – or to anything for that matter. He waved goodbye to Elton, who looked back through half-closed eyes and raised one hand from the sheet.

When Donald returned downstairs, Clara was by the door, pinning her hat in place. She started to take her mother's parasol, then decided to leave it in the umbrella stand.

"Ready," she said, smoothing the front of her dress.

"Wait."

"What?"

"Your collar is twisted."

Clara glanced in the mirror, adjusted herself and turned back in mock civility. "Why, thank you, Mr. Brown."

"Certainly, Miss Barnes." Donald bowed deeply, gesturing like the gentleman comic in a vaudeville play.

The restaurant was a ten-minute walk from Clara's house, and Donald enjoyed the chance to see more of her neighborhood. Most homes in this part of town, she explained, had survived the 1900 storm.

"Water from the gulf side pushed everything this way, until the debris wall itself formed a barrier that protected the core of the city."

"And your house?"

"The gulf-side wall formed at N Street, but to the northeast, it was much closer. John Sealy Hospital was barely a block inside." She slipped her arm through Donald's as they walked.

Mrs. Carhart spoke in Donald's mind: "Walk tall, my boy. Back straight, chest high. Be proud of yourself." Her words never made more sense.

Donald studied the two-story wooden building as they approached the restaurant. The corner entrance included three steps up to the front door. Even from the street, the restaurant smelled of fresh tortillas, salsa and spiced avocado. Donald held open the door.

"Mama loved this," Clara said as they entered. "We ate here at least once a week, but now I don't often come by myself. Blanca is the owner, and ..."

Blanca herself interrupted Clara with a hug and kisses on both cheeks. "It has been too long," she said, now gripping Clara's shoulders and inspecting her at arm's length. Blanca released her and turned to face Donald. "And you have brought a handsome young man!"

"Donald, this lady who is trying her best to embarrass me is Blanca Alvarez, a good friend and fabulous cook. Blanca, meet Donald Brown, a journalist who is visiting from Houston."

"A journalist! How exciting."

Donald felt his cheeks warm. He'd never heard himself described as such, but he liked the sound of it.

"Pleased to meet you, Miss Alvarez."

"Mrs.," she corrected. "My husband is the genius, he says, who keeps our business alive. At least he leaves me alone to run my kitchen. Please, have a seat. I'll send someone to take your order."

Blanca directed them to a table near a pair of windows that overlooked a row of young magnolia trees along Market Street. It was mid-afternoon. Only a handful of other patrons were in the restaurant. Donald heard the clatter of luncheon dishes being washed as Blanca retreated through double swinging doors at the far end of the room.

Clara hung her shawl and handbag on a nearby stand. Donald placed his cap on the hook beside them, then held her chair as she sat. He faced her across the table set for two. Suddenly lost for words, Donald looked up to study the exceptionally high ceiling, then the ornate stairway to his right. Without thinking, he began to scratch the inside of his right arm through the fabric of his jacket and shirt. He would have been more comfortable in the simple denim pants and workman's shirt he typically wore.

"Blanca and her family live upstairs," Clara said. "This was once a private home, but the banker who owned it left Galveston after the 1900 storm. Blanca and her husband restored the building and turned it into a restaurant."

"I like it," was all Donald thought to say. He tapped his foot. He gripped his left wrist, slowly rotating it back and forth in his hand. He rubbed his lower back against the back of his chair. He was relieved to see the waiter finally approach.

"We'll both have enchiladas," Clara said before Donald could speak.

"Good choice," the waiter said. "And what would you like to drink?"

"A *Triple-X* cream soda for me, please," Clara said, turning to wait for Donald.

Donald grinned. "Same here."

Blanca was known for her cooking, but not her speed. Donald and Clara found themselves sipping their cream sodas slowly, with plenty of time to talk.

"Donald, are you certain you want to register for the draft on Thursday?"

"I don't have a choice."

"Of course. Are you worried about being sent to fight?"

"Sure. I know war is not so heroic as the Four-Minute Men claim, but I don't want to be a slacker."

"Slacker," Clara said, shaking her head. "I hate that term, and I'm ashamed that I've used it myself."

"When?"

"Last year, after President Wilson asked for a declaration of war. I felt patriotic, like everyone else. We believed it would be easy."

"I know. The papers said Kaiser Wilhelm would surrender as soon as Americans joined the fight."

"And now it's September, seventeen months later. Who knows how much longer it will last?" Clara twisted her dinner napkin in her hands, saw what she was doing and stopped. She leaned close, speaking softly as if to share a secret.

"I'm worried about my brother. In his letters, he sounds discouraged. I've read awful things about the trenches, and at the hospital, I've seen some of the young men who've come back. Their families hardly recognize them."

Donald yielded to yet another urge to scratch his arm.

Clara noticed.

"Roll up your sleeve."

"What?"

"Just roll up your sleeve."

He unbuttoned his cuff and rolled his shirt sleeve to the elbow, folding the last of it back over his light summer jacket. Clara took his wrist in both hands and rotated his forearm until it was flat on the table, inside facing up. She moved his arm closer to the window light.

"Poison ivy."

Donald looked. A pink rash had spread from his wrist to the crook of his arm. Tiny blisters were already forming in spots.

"Roll up your other sleeve."

"But..."

"Roll up your sleeve."

Donald complied, revealing a matching set of blisters on his left arm.

"You got it this morning, clearing the weeds from my back patio."

She rotated both forearms for a better look. "I'm so sorry. Does your back itch?"

"Yes, a little." Now that she mentioned it, his back itched a lot.

"How about around your waist?"

Yes, there, too, Donald thought. "No," is what he said to Clara.

"You've got a good dose. We need to get something on this soon." Now in full nursing mode, she looked clinically at Donald's face. Without asking permission, she lightly touched his chin to move his head right to left. Satisfied, she then pushed his chin back until all Donald could see was the rotating electric fan above their table.

"Good, no rash on your face or neck."

"Excuse me," the waiter said, balancing a tray with two steaming plates of food on one arm.

Donald couldn't recall when the conversations around them stopped. Now he was painfully aware that he was sitting in the quiet restaurant with his sleeves rolled above his elbows, and that the woman across from him was holding his chin in the air as if she were examining a fresh avocado. The moment seemed longer than it could have possibly been.

Clara released his chin, leaned back and began clearing space on the table. Donald fumbled with the buttons on his cuffs. Something made him look to the far end of the room, where Blanca stood between the swinging doors. Their eyes met. She retreated quickly into her kitchen.

Enchiladas were different from what Jake had described. Still, the warm aroma of soft flour tortillas, beef, onions and melted cheese made Donald's mouth water. He watched Clara use her knife and fork to cut a bite, which she dabbed in chili sauce before eating. Donald did the same.

"Delicious!" he said as he chewed.

"Really?"

"Best enchiladas I've ever had."

"Save room for sopapillas," Clara said. "You like them, don't you?"

"Of course," Donald said, hoping that sopapillas were some sort of dessert.

Chapter 19

"Do your arms still itch?" Clara asked as they walked back from the restaurant toward her house. Donald had been trying to forget, thinking instead of the warm afternoon light and the weight of Clara's arm on his.

Yes, he itched. His forearms itched, his back itched, and now, in the last half hour, a wide band around his waist. He was beginning to itch from the inside out.

"Oh, it's not bad," he said.

"Well, I have something that will make you feel better; another of Mama's remedies. My brother used to get poison ivy all the time."

"Maybe we could do that first when we get home."

"Of course," she said, smiling and momentarily squeezing his arm to her side. He noticed they were naturally in step, their heels landing as one on the concrete sidewalk, making sounds that filled the open space under the canopy of young trees.

"This is a great time of day to photograph," he said. "Evenings and mornings have the best light."

Clara sidestepped a small stone. "So it makes a difference, the time of day?"

"Oh yes, just look at the light!"

The sun was at a low angle to their right. Shafts of gold filtered through the leaves, like hundreds of small spotlights on the wide porches of the homes to their left.

"Let me take your picture."

"Here?"

"No better place. Do you mind?"

"No, but ..."

"Stand by this fence," Donald said before Clara changed her mind. He pulled his folding camera from his jacket pocket. He pressed a small silver button near the hand strap on one end, allowing the bellows and lens to fold out smartly. He snapped them in place and rotated the viewfinder for a vertical shot, then noted the number 6 in the small round window on the camera's back.

Clara squared off, facing Donald, with one hand resting on the low picket fence to her right.

"No, turn your back to me, as if you were walking away."

She gave a quizzical look, but did as he directed.

"Now turn back to me a little bit. There. A bit more. Look over your right shoulder, as if you had just stopped walking and turned to look back at me. Yes, keep your left hand on the fence."

"Where shall I look?"

"Into this little hole," he said, pointing to the camera lens.

Clara laughed as Donald became someone else. Now she could only see the top of his cap, with his elbows straight out from his sides. He peered down, squinting into what he'd called the "viewfinder," looking, she supposed, until he found the view he wanted.

This went on for a while, Donald dancing back and forth on the sidewalk, momentarily lifting his head, looking at her then beyond, and finally down into the camera again. She heard a click.

"One more!" he said without looking up. He turned a knob several turns to advance the film, then glanced at the back of the camera before returning to the viewfinder. Another click.

"Now look that way," he said, pointing across the street. Clara did as she was told, a smile forming dimples on her cheeks.

"Just one more. Look toward the tops of the trees across the street." Another click and Donald advanced the film to the number 8.

"You took so many!" she said after he announced the end of the roll.

"Only five," he said. "This camera gets ten shots to a roll."

As he talked, Donald turned the film advance knob several times more until he heard, and his fingers felt, that he had wound the full roll on its spool. Pulling the same knob out from the camera body allowed the back of the camera to pop open. He removed the exposed spool of film, which looked to Clara like a tight yellow roll about three inches wide. The end of the roll had an adhesive tab that Donald licked and pressed to the paper, holding it a few seconds to give the glue time to stick. He then slipped the spool into his left pants pocket, and from his right, produced a fresh roll of film.

"Always take several pictures," Donald explained, barely looking down as he loaded the new roll into the camera and advanced it to the number 1. "If you take more shots, one is bound to be better than the rest."

He refolded the little camera and tucked it back into his jacket. Normally, he'd write the subject, date and time in his journal, but this time he knew he wouldn't forget.

"Don, let's move Elton to the carriage house," Jake said as soon as Donald and Clara returned home. He was in the kitchen, making sandwiches from items he'd found in the icebox and pantry.

"Elton can wait," Clara said, shaking her head at the mess Jake had made of the bread. "Donald, if you'd care to wash up, I'll make a poultice. Scrub the affected areas with soap and warm water. There are clean towels and wash cloths in the hall closet next door. Leave your shirt off when you finish. Wait in your room and I'll be over in half an hour."

Jake watched Donald go, looked back to Clara, but asked no questions. Clara fished under the counter until she found a battered pot that was clearly no longer for cooking. She took a box of *Arm and Hammer* baking soda from the shelf next to the pantry and set it next to the sink.

"Poison ivy," Clara explained to Jake. She slipped her apron over her head and tied it behind her back, then started water heating on the stove. She took the paring knife from Jake's hand and laid it on the counter, then pulled a long knife from the drawer and cut four even slices from what remained of the loaf of bread. After trading the bread knife for the smaller paring knife, Clara took a small basket she kept by the back door and went into the garden to cut some aloe vera leaves. She returned with tomatoes, a late-season cucumber and fresh leaf lettuce.

"Elton might like this in his sandwich," she told Jake, setting the butter beside him.

"Thanks."

Jake watched Clara rinse the tomatoes and cucumber. She cut them into neat slices and left them along with several leaves of lettuce on a small plate.

"Elton is much better today," he said. "I think we can take him home tomorrow or Thursday."

"A business man from Dallas has the room next week, but Elton is welcome to stay until then. He should be strong enough to travel on his own by the weekend."

"How about Don?"

"This poultice I'm making will keep him comfortable and make the rash heal faster. He'll be fine in a week or so, but he can leave any time."

In the washroom of the carriage house, Donald stripped off his shirt, leaving it to hang upside down from his pants, sleeves brushing the floor. He surveyed the damage to his body, using the wall mirror and a hand mirror to check his back, then scrubbed his skin as Clara prescribed. He was surprised that the sink had two valves. Mrs. Carhart's home had hot running water, of course, but not many others he knew.

The rash was more pronounced now than it had been in Blanca's restaurant. A fresh wave of embarrassment swept over him when he recalled the look on her face as she watched from across the room.

"That's done," Mrs. Carhart said in Donald's mind. "You can't do anything now, so put it out of your mind."

"You weren't there to see it," Donald said aloud.

"Yes, but I have been there, dear boy. Believe me, I have been there myself."

"What do you think of this mess?" Donald asked, turning back to face the wall mirror.

"Not all bad things come to harm."

"What does that mean?" he asked, but Mrs. Carhart didn't reply.

"Donald, are you alone?" Clara called from down the hall.

"Oh! Ah! Hello, Clara, I didn't know you were there. I'll be right out."

"I thought I heard you talking to someone."

"Just myself," Donald said.

"You might as well stay there when you finish. The washroom is as good a place as any to apply this poultice."

Donald dried himself with a clean towel and opened the door. Clara glanced around the small space, but didn't ask again about the one-sided conversation she had heard through the door.

"Stand here," she said, "this is best applied while it's still warm."

Clara dipped her bare hand into the pasty green poultice in the pan.

"This should stop the itching right away," she said, spreading the warm goo evenly around his waist.

"Raise your arms and turn around." Donald did as he was told, and she continued rubbing the soothing paste on his back.

"Now your arms."

He held his arms out toward Clara, the affected side of his forearms facing up.

"There," she said at last, wiping her hands on a towel. "Leave your shirt off and don't lie down or sit back on the furniture until this dries. Give it half an hour to soak into your skin. Just stay in your room if you like. I'll mix another batch tomorrow, but this is enough to reduce the itching and make the rash heal faster."

Clara's touch had already done more for Donald than any poultice. She smiled and returned to her kitchen, leaving him alone in the carriage house, except for Jennifer and Rebecca who were still sleeping in their rooms upstairs.

"You might as well wash your shirt," Mrs. Carhart said.

"Right," Donald mumbled to the mirror. "Make good use of time, there's never enough of it to go around."

He filled the sink with warm water and used bar soap to create suds. He pulled the shirt from where it hung around his waist, dipped it in the sudsy water, then squeezed with his fingers over and over to force water through the fabric. A minute later he drained the sink, refilled it with fresh water and repeated the process until suds no longer appeared. He wrung out as much water as possible, then hung the shirt on the towel rack to dry.

Back in his room, Donald pondered his next move. Thirty minutes, Clara said, before the poultice soaked in. Half an hour before he could lie down or even put on a clean shirt. He looked toward the bookcase for something to read.

The number of textbooks and medical journals did not surprise him.

What did was the variety on the other shelves: a collection of John Ruskin's political essays, three Jules Verne novels, even a theatre play, *Cyrano de Bergerac* by Edmond Rostand. The bright red cover caught his eye. *Cyrano* sounded familiar. He remembered it was something Mrs. Carhart said he should read. That would be a first for him, reading a play instead of one of her history texts.

He let his fingertips bump lightly along the tops of the other volumes, pausing at some, tipping out others, then dropping to the next shelf down. He stopped at a biography of Clara Barton. Everyone knew her as the famous Civil War nurse and founder of the American Red Cross. He remembered his teachers telling stories of Barton's life, and how news of her death in April, 1912 was quickly overshadowed by the horror that the great ocean liner *Titanic* had gone down.

A small envelope marked the center of the book. It was from Barton herself, addressed to Martha Barnes, Clara's mother. Knowing that most people would consider it snooping, yet hoping that Clara wouldn't mind, he pulled out a single handwritten sheet of Red Cross stationery.

Galveston, December 10, 1900
My dearest Martha,

Now that the immediate suffering from this terrible storm has abated and I am preparing to return to Washington, I want to tell you how much your friendship has meant to me over these last three months. Your darling little girl charmed us as well, and I was most honored to learn that you had named her after me.

Thank you, dear Martha, for your tireless assistance. I wish you the best in your career, for you are an excellent nurse. I have recommended that you be given a permanent position at the hospital. Please keep in touch, and now and then, give little Clara an extra hug for me.

Very truly yours,
Clara Barton, President, Am. Nat. Red Cross

Donald read the note again, then slipped it back into the envelope. He promised himself to tell Clara that he'd seen it.

"Oops!" someone called from the hall. Donald turned, now conscious of his bare feet and shirtless torso, which was covered with patches of green paste. A young woman stood in the doorway looking equally startled. It took a moment for her to recognize him.

"Hello, Jennifer," Donald said.

Like him, she was shoeless, although stockings still covered her feet. She was wrapped in a long quilted robe, face bare of makeup, and brown hair flowing over her shoulders. She clutched a towel and a handful of toiletries.

"I didn't know anyone was in the house," she said. "Do you need in there?" She nodded towards the washroom. She looked again at Donald, stepped back and pulled her robe tight under her chin. "What's that all over your arms and waist?"

"Poison ivy. Clara applied a poultice, and I'm letting it dry before I put on a clean shirt."

"Are you contagious?"

"No, Jenny, I just itch."

She grimaced, but eased the grip on her collar and turned toward the washroom door.

"Well, I won't be long."

"Long" is a relative term, Donald learned. Water thundered into the large claw-foot tub for the first ten minutes, followed by splashing. That's when Jenny began to sing.

"Daisy, Daisy, give me your answer do ..."

Donald eased his bedroom door closed to give her more privacy, and to prevent Rebecca from seeing him shirtless if she came downstairs as well. Jenny's voice carried through, increasing in volume as she turned the bath water on once more. She drew out words, adding syllables at random. The noise came easily down the hall. For the next half hour, Jenny favored the chorus above all.

"... I'm half ca-RA-zy, all for the love of YOUUUU! It won't be a stylish MAR-riage, I can't afford a CAR-riage, but you'll look SWEET upon the SEAT, of a bicycle built for TWOOOO!"

Chapter 20

Donald watched a light rain fall until darkness settled in, obscuring his view of the garden. He clicked on the electric banker's lamp. Jennifer had finished her bath and gone upstairs a few minutes before, so it felt safe to venture out. He returned to the steamy bathroom to retrieve his wet shirt from the towel rack.

Jennifer's wet stockings—she'd washed them in the sink as Donald had done with his shirt—hung from the same rack. As carefully as possible, he removed his shirt, but one of the stockings fell to the floor. He was just returning it to the bar when Jake peeked in.

"Not your size, pal," Jake said. "Besides, they look better on the ladies."

Donald laughed. Sometimes that was all you could do.

"This poultice is dry enough for me to put on a shirt now. Should we try to move Elton?"

"That's why I came to get you. Let's put him in our room."

"Where will you sleep?"

Jake rolled his eyes to the ceiling. "Oh, I'll find someplace."

Donald hung his wet shirt over the back of the wooden desk chair and placed it near the electric lamp. He pulled a clean work shirt from his bag, then followed Jake next door. Moving Elton was easy. He was strong enough to walk downstairs by himself, although Jake went first to catch him in case he fell. Donald and Clara followed with extra pillows and a light blanket.

"Would you like some soup, Jake? I made it earlier for Elton."

"No thanks, Clara. We've all had a long day. I'm ready for bed."

Personally, Donald could do with something sweet. The sopapillas he'd had earlier were delicious, but the little Mexican pastries were mostly air.

The men helped Elton settle in, while Clara stayed behind in the main house changing the sheets on her bed. Smoothing the fresh linens, she was tempted to turn in early, but figured that Donald would like a snack before going to bed. She enjoyed their kitchen visits, and besides, a glass of milk would help her sleep. She'd only been down a few minutes when Donald returned.

"Elton's already asleep," he said. "We tucked him in, and it was like turning out a light."

"Would you like some cookies and milk?"

Donald grinned and sat in the nearest chair.

"Are you still returning to Houston tomorrow afternoon?" Clara asked as she set out their snack. "You're welcome to stay longer. My classes don't resume until next week."

"Thank you." Donald faced Clara. "I don't even know if I can pass the physical with these eyes, but, ..."

"Yes?"

"I guess I'm restless to get on with my life. I've never been anywhere or done anything special. Maybe the Army is the push I need. Does that make sense?"

"Will you let me know what happens?"

"If the Army takes me or not? Sure, if you'd like."

"I would."

They grew quiet after that. Clara ate a cookie. Donald had two. Outside the open window, dozens of tiny chirping frogs, encouraged by the recent rain, called for each other in the garden.

Elton was dreaming when Donald returned to their room, perhaps yelling in his own mind, but the sounds he made were nothing more than quiet squeaks and moans. Donald stopped in the bathroom to brush his teeth, then returned to the room. He could tell that Clara had just been there, probably to check on Elton. He smelled her lavender perfume.

To keep from turning on the electric light, Donald lit a candle he found on the bookcase and placed it near the base of the green desk lamp.

He stripped to his BVDs, put on his nightshirt and crawled into bed. He reached for the copy of *Cyrano*, but it was gone from the shelf. He laid on his back and stared at the ceiling instead.

The candle's flame, sometimes still, sometimes flickering in its holder, cast a shadow of the green glass lamp shade on the ceiling. Without his glasses, the shadow seemed more alive than it would have been to a person with sharp vision. Normal eyes would have seen the crisp edges of the lamp shade on the ceiling and the shadow of its brass neck against the wall. To Donald it was a huge soft capsule, glowing pale green where candlelight filtered through the glass shade.

With each flicker, the capsule bounced side to side, like the shoulders of a huge drunken man lurching down the street. He moved, but not toward Donald or away. The man on the ceiling, swaying back and forth, was only marking time.

Donald began weighing the choices he needed to make—or those that would be made for him—in the next few days. He'd never been more than fifty miles from home. Now, after a few weeks of training, he could be on a troop ship heading for France. What if he didn't register for the draft, or lied to the draft board as he suspected Jake had done? In that case, he'd forever be called a slacker, by others and more importantly, by himself.

He closed his eyes, but voices entered Donald's half-conscious mind as though he and his twin were debating what to do.

"What if I register and the Army doesn't accept me?"

"Mr. Booth said the draft board wanted anybody who could still stand."

"I'm fit enough, except for my eyes. Some boys memorize the eye chart just to get in."

"No. If they want me as I am, fine, but I won't lie."

"All right. But what will you do if the Army doesn't take you?"

"I'll accept the *Chronicle* job."

"And watch while other guys go to war while you're safe at home?"

"If the Army doesn't want me, I'll find something useful to do here. You don't have to carry a gun to help win a war."

"We'll see," Donald said aloud.

"Hey Don, you awake?" Donald hadn't noticed that Elton was no longer talking in his sleep.

"Sorry if I woke you."

"Not at all. I was dreaming about that night on the beach. I'm glad to be awake."

"You sound better."

"The swelling in my jaw has gone down. The aspirin and Clara's remedies helped."

They were quiet for a while, Elton thinking about his recent past and Donald about his near future. The flickering candle light, its faint green shadows on the ceiling, the humid salt air and sounds of the frogs outside in the garden made them both feel like they were sitting around a campfire. Questions that might not have aired in daylight came easily in the dark.

"Elton?"

"Yeah?"

"Did you register for the draft?"

"Sure. Didn't Jake tell you?"

"No, what?"

"I took my physical last month. I report to Camp Logan next week."

Donald propped himself on one elbow and looked over. Without glasses he couldn't make out his friend's features, but in the candle light he could tell that Elton was still gazing at the ceiling.

"No, Jake didn't say anything. I thought your asthma would keep you out."

"It might have in the beginning, but they need more men now. Besides, the asthma attacks don't come as often as before. The recruiter said I should be proud to serve my country. He said I could be in France by November."

"Are you scared?" Donald blurted.

Elton waited to speak. Donald laid back on his pillow to watch the shadows on the ceiling. A breeze picked up, momentarily lifting out the curtains on his side of the room and sucking them against the screen beside Elton. When the curtains relaxed, Elton answered.

"Yes."

"You're scared?"

"I guess I am."

The floorboards above them creaked. They heard voices, but Donald and Elton couldn't tell which of the girls' rooms Jake was in.

"Elton?"

"Yeah?"

"Jake said he introduced you to Maye."

"Sure. I met a lot of women when we came to Galveston a few months ago."

"When you took pictures of the clubs?"

"Jake photographed the clubs. He brought me along to meet women."

"Why?"

"I told him I'd never had a lady friend, and he said it was time."

"So it was all Jake's idea?"

"I was interested, but yes, he suggested it. He said ladies in Galveston were different from the ones I knew in Houston." Elton laughed, then hugged his broken rib. "Jake was right," he said between groans.

Donald thought back. Sitting around the kitchen table Monday morning—hard to believe it was only the day before—Jake sounded surprised that Elton was spending time with Maye. Now Donald wondered if Jake had known all along. Jake pushed Elton, perhaps not to Maye herself, but toward women like her.

"Did Jake know you were seeing Maye?"

"It never came up. He knew I was visiting someone here, but he didn't know who."

"Did he encourage you?"

"Oh, yeah. I think Jake enjoyed it. He said it was time for me to be a man, especially if I was going into the Army."

Accidently or not, Donald thought, Elton nearly died because of Jake.

"What did you think about it?"

"I didn't want to go without ever having been with a woman."

A gust of wind made the curtains flap and the candle go out. Donald patted the nightstand for his glasses. The rain clouds were gone, replaced by stars and a half moon. Its pale blue light filled the room. Donald lowered the window and looked back across the garden toward the house. The electric light on Clara's desk was on, and she was sitting near the window, reading a book with a bright red cover.

Chapter 21

Wednesday, September 11, 1918

He woke, as always, with the first light of day. Elton snored in the adjacent bed, but otherwise slept soundly. Donald slipped on his glasses, sat on the edge of his bed and reached out to pull back one side of the white lace curtain. The morning was overcast and cool. Dew hung on the leaves nearest the screen.

He let the curtain fall and rubbed sleep from his eyes.

Wednesday.

Just three days in Galveston. What a whirlwind: meeting Clara, finding Elton, Sergio's cold threats, Maye's figure—don't think of that now—and Beno, most likely, in the seawall.

And then, the photographs! Three of them. A duplicate of his baby picture and two more, all made in the same room. Photographs of a man, a little girl and a young woman—his family? Did everyone die in the storm?

"Humph," Elton said in his sleep. As he rolled over, the last of his covers slipped to the floor. Donald retrieved them and placed the sheet and blanket back over his friend. By the time he gathered his toothbrush and straight razor, Elton was snoring again and Donald was eager to get next door.

"Good morning," Clara said, "you're just in time to grind the coffee."

The early clouds were gone. Clara had tied the curtains back, and now her white cotton blouse glowed in the morning light. This is beautiful, Donald thought as he crossed the kitchen to retrieve the coffee mill and bag of beans from the pantry. Simply beautiful.

"Did you sleep well?" he asked.

"I'm afraid I read too late. Do you know the play, *Cyrano de Bergerac?*"

"By Edmond Rostand? I've been meaning to read it."

"I'm surprised you know of it at all."

"One of Mrs. Carhart's suggestions," he called over the noisy coffee grinder. "It's a play about a soldier with a big nose."

Clara laughed. "Right, but there's more to it than that. You'll like it."

Donald smelled fresh rolls in the oven.

"Eggs?" she asked.

"Yes, thanks."

He tapped the wooden sides of the mill and pulled the drawer from its base, leaving it on the counter beside the coffee pot. Next to it, Clara's garden basket already held fresh tomatoes, a cucumber and several apples.

"I didn't see an apple tree in your yard."

"Anything I don't grow myself, one of my neighbors will have. Almost everyone has a garden and a few chickens. We share everything, and sell what we can't eat ourselves. Mr. Lowman even keeps bees, so we often have fresh honey. He left a jar by the back door just this morning."

Donald heard glass clinking behind him. He turned quickly, startled to see a thin middle-aged man standing at the screen door. His white uniform hung on his meager frame like a scarecrow. No telling how long he'd had been there, just watching.

"Morning, Miss Clara" the man said, Adam's apple bobbing up and down. "Two quarts t'day?"

Now the fellow couldn't stand still. He shifted instead on bowed legs, one foot to the other, as if desperate for a bathroom. The bottles in his wire carton clinked each time he moved.

"Hello, Claude. Make it three. We have extra guests this week."

Claude touched the black patent leather bill of his white hat, opened the screen door and quick-stepped across the kitchen to the icebox. He added three quart bottles of milk and took the two clean empties Clara had left by the door.

"Thanks, Claude. See you Friday."

Claude risked another peek at Donald, bobbed his head, mumbled "g'bye" and left.

Donald followed as far as the screen door. He watched Claude's narrow shoulders swaying back and forth as he scurried down the shell driveway. Claude loaded his empties on a side rack of his wagon and returned the full bottles to the large icebox bolted to the bed. Finally, he turned to his waiting mule. Stroking the animal's nose seemed to help the milkman relax, and the mule seemed not to mind.

"So this is what Mrs. Carhart meant," Donald thought. She had been teaching him lately about photographs that tell complex stories. "Picture essays," she called them. Claude had a story, but how could he approach such a shy man without terrifying him?

Clara noticed Donald's intense gaze. She came to stand beside him, watching from the window as the wagon pulled away.

"Claude is a simple man," she said. "It makes him nervous when anything is different from what he's used to. Seeing you here confused him."

"I understand," Donald said.

"Are you hungry?"

"What can I do to help?"

"Do you mind washing the fruit in the basket? You could slice the tomatoes and the cucumber. Knives are in the middle drawer and there's a cutting board on the counter."

The first knife Donald took was dull. He brushed his thumb lightly across a second blade, then a third, but every one was dull. He pulled the drawer out farther and found a whetstone in the back. Clara watched as he set the stone on the counter and expertly sharpened one of the knives. He rinsed the blade and dried it, then quickly turned the first tomato into six neat slices.

"I'm afraid I'm not good with a whetstone," Clara said. "I didn't know that knife cut so well."

Donald liked the way they worked together; she at the stove, he at the cutting board. Close, but not in each other's way. They anticipated each other's moves. Clara handed him two banana peppers and a squash as Donald reached for a small bowl. A minute later, she emptied the chopped peppers and squash into the raw eggs in her large measuring cup. He got the butter from the icebox and set it beside her. She dropped a spoonful into the mix, added pepper, then stirred and poured it all into the skillet on low heat.

"These will be ready in a few minutes if you'd like to get the biscuits from the oven."

Donald had them on the table, along with the butter and two kinds of preserves, just as Clara came with the steaming platter of scrambled eggs.

"Elton told me something last night that bothers me," Donald said halfway through their meal. "Jake brought him to Galveston last April expressly to meet women like Maye."

Clara sipped her coffee before answering. "That doesn't surprise me. Do you think Jake feels responsible for what happened?"

"He acts troubled, but I don't know why."

"Troubled?"

"I don't know how well you know him, but Jake never doubts himself. He's the most confident person I've ever met. When he offers an opinion, it's always a pronouncement. No discussion. No exchange of ideas. He just tells you the way things are, and that's it."

"But now?"

"Pass the butter, please. Thanks. Now? I think this business with Elton has shaken Jake's confidence. Maybe he does feel responsible. He might see his cousin differently as well. Could be Jake is wondering about things he never questioned before."

"I remember when he came with Elton in April. Elton was like a boy at his first carnival. Jake was the big brother, showing him around. More coffee?"

Clara went to the stove, returned with the pot and refilled their cups.

"Donald," she said, placing the pot back on the stove and turning off the burner. "I need to do some laundry now, but before you leave today, I'd like to talk to you more about the photographs we found in Mama's collection."

"I'd like that very much. It's still early. I'll help with the laundry. Would you like to go to the beach this afternoon?"

"Did the mysterious Mrs. Carhart teach you to wash clothes as well?"

Donald laughed. "No, Ma taught me that." He began running water in the sink. "I'll wash, you dry, then we'll start the laundry."

Clara kept a large tub and wringer outside under the arbor. Donald carried it into the back yard, near the clothes line, and set the heavy tub on the small concrete slab that had been poured for that purpose. Next to the legs of the tub, on the side with the clothes wringer, he placed the low table that Clara said they'd need.

"There's a bucket in the mud room and a rain barrel in the yard," she called through the open kitchen window.

Donald opened the tap, and rain water filled the bucket. Clara's indoor plumbing used city water, but all of it was piped in from the mainland. Many houses kept rain barrels as a backup. Donald poured water into the larger tub. He was just filling the second bucket when Clara came with a kettle of hot water, adding that to the tub along with a cup of Rinso powered soap.

"When I'm here alone, I have to leave the tub where it was. This is much more convenient."

Donald hooked his thumbs in his belt, lowered his voice and did his best vaudeville cowboy accent.

"Why, glad to be of help, ma'am."

Jake watched from the carriage house window as Donald and Clara hung the last of the wet sheets on the clothesline. He turned back to Elton to continue his thought.

"Well, that's your decision."

"I'd like to stay a couple more days here in Galveston. By Saturday or Sunday I'll be strong enough to come back to Houston on my own."

"Then Don and I are going back tonight," Jake glanced out the window again, "if I can pry Mr. Brown away from Miss Barnes."

Elton laughed and immediately paid the price. He breathed hard and hugged his sides.

"At least let me buy you some clothes. The things you were wearing Monday night were just rags."

"That would help," Elton said, still favoring his broken rib. "Thanks."

"Nothing to it, pal."

Elton turned his head to see the full clothesline. Donald and Clara had gone inside. Elton was still looking toward the garden when he spoke.

"Jake?"

"Yeah?"

"I'm sorry."

"What do you mean?"

Elton turned to face Jake.

"I made a mess of things."

"No, you didn't."

"Yes. All the trouble now, between you and your cousin. Maye's hurt. I even got her husband killed."

"You didn't do anything. Beno got himself killed."

"You wanted me to have some fun, something to remember before I went into the Army."

"Aw, you're just ..."

"No, Jake, you don't understand. I wanted it too. But I wanted more than that. I wanted to be like you."

"Stop it, El." Jake looked away.

"It's true, Jake. You're a magnet for women."

"It doesn't mean anything, El. It's just for fun. I don't care about any of them. Believe me, you don't want to be like me."

"How can you be with a woman and not care about her?"

"Come on. Are you telling me that you really liked Maye?"

"I didn't have anything to compare it to, Jake. She was the first one who paid attention to me. She's wild, but yeah. I cared for her. Maybe I liked her just because she liked me. I'm not used to that."

"From the pictures you took, I'd say you were getting used to Maye pretty fast."

"What about Rebecca? Don't you care about her? Gosh, Jake, you spent two of the last three nights with her."

"Only one," Jake corrected. "I spent the first night with Jenny."

"Wow. I'm impressed."

"Don't be. It doesn't mean a thing."

Elton eased back on his pillow, hands behind his head, staring at the ceiling. Jake studied the floor between his feet.

"How can that be?"

Jake was quiet so long that Elton thought he was ignoring the question. When Jake spoke, Elton almost didn't recognize his voice.

"Look, El, I'm going to tell you something I don't want you to repeat, not to Don or anyone."

"All right."

"I'm not kidding."

"I won't tell."

Jake sat forward on the side of the extra bed, facing Elton, elbows resting on his knees. He looked down at his own hands before going on.

"Even in high school, I could see that girls liked me more than the other guys. I liked them too, but none of them meant anything special. Maybe that's what attracted them, I don't know. Maybe they're interested in me now because I don't go crazy the way other fellows do. Men become idiots around women. I don't, and that's because I simply don't care. For me, women are just playmates."

"But how can you ..."

Jake held up one hand. "Let me finish. I never thought about it much, and certainly never told anybody. This isn't easy for me."

"Go ahead, Jake, it's just between you and me."

"I've been thinking these last couple of days. Thinking a lot. Worrying about you, seeing Clara again, and seeing her with Don."

"Clara? What does she have to do with it?"

"When I first met her, it was a couple of years ago ..."

"Yeah?"

"Well, she's a pretty woman and I thought I'd like to know her better."

"Like Rebecca or Jenny?"

Jake looked up. "Yeah, like that. Anyway, I invited her to dinner once or twice. I found excuses to come to Galveston. We spent time walking on the beach and even went to a few flicks. She really likes those moving pictures."

"What happened?"

"Well, I figured that all the time I spent with her entitled me to some extra privileges."

"Yeah?"

"She didn't think so."

"What happened?"

"I got pretty mad, but so did she. I wasn't used to that."

"You get along now."

"Yeah, but now it's only a business arrangement. She has rooms to

144

rent, and I like coming to Galveston."

"Then it's not a problem for either of you."

"Not for her, I'm sure."

Elton looked across from his bed toward the man who'd helped him survive all the schoolyard bullies, the man who had gotten him a job when no one else was hiring, and the man who had decided it was time for Elton to learn about the "weaker" sex.

Jake didn't look up again. He kept his elbows on his knees, hands limp, but now he was tapping both feet, like someone anxious to talk before he lost the will.

"You know me, El. I've always been good at looking out for myself. I like being in control, running the show. But these last three days have been rough. I was worried sick about you—hell, we all were—but it's more than that. I know now that I'm responsible for what happened to you."

"Naw, Jake, I did this on my own."

Jake's head shot up and he locked on Elton's eyes.

"No, you didn't. I pushed you. I wanted you to have a woman, any woman, the way I do. I didn't stop to think you might be different from me. Maybe you couldn't just have your fun and forget it."

"So what, Jake? So we're different. Everyone is different."

"There's more. Seeing Clara with Don—I don't know what will happen between them, but the two of them together, that's real."

"Real?"

"Did you see them in the yard just now? They were washing the damn sheets and towels, but the way they laughed and carried on, you'd think they were at a picnic. That's what I mean. That's real."

"I don't understand why you're upset. Do you still have feelings for Clara?"

"No, Elton, I've never loved any woman, but I can see that Don does, and somehow, I envy him."

Chapter 22

The trolley stopped near Murdoch's Pier and the new Crystal Palace. The popular tourist destinations were busy for a Wednesday afternoon, but the day had turned beautiful, so Clara and Donald were not surprised. Like dozens of other couples, they chose to walk along the seawall, where they could enjoy the beach view without getting sand in their shoes.

"Electric Park was just over there," Clara said, pointing as they walked. "I wish you could have seen it."

"I did," Donald said. "Naomi and Clarence brought me to Galveston soon after they took me in. Cletus, too. He's their son. That must have been about three years before the park closed."

"Then you saw it at its best. I'm afraid Electric Park fell on hard times. The last hurricane took all that was left."

"We came here on the Interurban, right up to this entrance," Donald said. He and Clara stopped in front of two squat but massive pillars just across the street from the Crystal Palace. He touched the stone lightly, as if comforting an old friend.

"And I remember these markers, because of the way they affected my new family." He quietly read the inscriptions, which commemorated the 1900 storm and construction of the first seawall.

"Naomi and Clarence lived on 19th street, a few blocks from the gulf side of the island. They have a photo of Cletus and his dad on the front porch. Cletus was just a toddler then. I don't know how they saved the picture. They lost the house and everything else in the storm."

"They were lucky to survive."

"That's what Pa says, luckier than most. They moved to Houston and started over."

Clara noticed a poster across the street in front of the Crystal Palace. She squeezed Donald's upper arm.

"Donald, do you like moving pictures?"

"Sure!" He looked in the direction of Clara's gaze. There were several posters in a row. He read one of the titles, which was big and bold.

"*To Hell with the Kaiser*? You really want to see that?"

Clara laughed. "No! I mean *The Soap Girl* with Gladys Leslie. I read about it in the paper, it's only showing today."

"Let's go," Donald said, "if we can make it across the street in one piece!"

Clara slipped her arm in Donald's as they waited for enough space between the buggies, motor cars and bicycles to open up. For safety, they chose instead to use the walkway across Seawall Boulevard. It led right to the second story entrance of the Crystal Palace.

"The next show starts in half an hour," Donald said, tucking two tickets and fifty cents change from a dollar into his pocket. He wasn't sure about Gladys Leslie, but he was happy to see that the second feature was a Keystone Cops comedy, *Saved by Wireless*.

Donald bought two nickel cups of ice cream from a kiosk on the wide veranda. He and Clara stood eating them with flat wooden spoons as they looked out to sea. The quickening breeze moved a loose curl that had fallen to the side of Clara's face. Donald fought the urge to touch it. She spoke.

"Donald, I've been thinking about your family."

"Naomi and Clarence?"

"No, your natural parents. When we found those photographs, it brought back all my memories of the storm and the terrible days after."

"I'm sorry."

"No, don't be. I mean it might be possible, even after all these years, to find out more about what happened to them."

"But how? Eighteen years ..."

"I have some ideas. Do you mind if I continue looking after you return to Houston?"

"I'd be grateful, but how?"

"I'll start with Mama's collection. There are more than three hundred photographs in the box, but we only looked at a few. I remember you were certain that whoever took the photograph of you had good equipment and knew how to use it."

"Yes. How does that help?"

"Donald, you said you recognized the photographer's style."

"Yes?"

"What if the same person took some of the other pictures in the box? If they did, you might learn more about the photographer."

Donald looked deeply into Clara's eyes, and she focused as closely on his. He spoke first. "That's an excellent idea."

He wanted to say much more.

The Soap Girl was just as Donald expected. Piano music began even before the curtains parted and the flickering Vitagraph logo appeared. Soon, the image of a young woman filled the screen, long curls hanging down on her shoulders. Her eyelashes fluttered as she gazed up and away toward her unobtainable goal. Words on the screen revealed that she was Marjorie Sanford, lovely heiress to a laundry detergent and cosmetic soap fortune, who longs to be accepted into high society.

"Gladys Leslie is my favorite actress," Clara whispered.

The piano player, hidden in an alcove near the foot of the stage, played louder. Early on, Marjorie meet the man she would likely fall in love with. That's when Donald lost interest in the story, but he enjoyed the lighting and photography. He reshot individual scenes in his mind, imagining how he would have done them better.

Piano music told the audience something exciting was about to happen. The beautiful young Marjorie appeared in a bathtub, up to her neck in luxurious soap bubbles. That scene was well done, Donald thought.

"I knew she was going to fall in love with the press agent," Clara said after the last reel ended and the piano music stopped. Before Donald could respond, the electric house lights came up, and a uniformed man stepped onto the stage. He raised his hands to quiet the audience. A second officer was standing stage right, arms front, right hand holding his left wrist.

"Ladies and gentlemen," the first man urged, "before we begin the second feature today, I invite you to listen to a few words from Captain

Russell Talbot, a brave man who has just returned from the fighting in France."

The audience broke into applause with scattered cheers and whistles. Four-Minute Men speeches were popular. Captain Talbot stepped forward in his crisp dress uniform, complete with kid gloves and rows of combat decorations over half his chest. He waited for the applause to taper off, then swept his right hand slowly left to right.

"My fellow citizens, as you sit here today in this beautiful theater, in the safety of this fair city, enjoying the bounties of our great nation, I ask you to remember the tens of thousands of people in France and Belgium—people just like yourselves—who at this very moment suffer as slaves under Prussian domination!"

There were several boos and hisses from the audience.

"I ask you now, what is it that keeps the same thing from happening here? What prevents the Prussians from dominating our land, killing our people and defiling our women, as they are doing now all across Europe?"

More than a few in the audience gasped at the image of defiled women. More boos and hisses. Clara leaned closer to Donald and gripped his arm. Captain Talbot continued, sweeping again with his right arm, index finger toward the ceiling to stress his point.

"I will tell you. It is our brave men at the front! Men like you, and you and you." As he spoke, the captain pointed to several young men closest to the stage.

"Won't you join them? If you do not fight the Huns in Europe, you will someday fight them here in America! Here, on the streets of Galveston! I urge you now, this very minute, to add your name to the roll! Who will join us?"

"I will!" a young man shouted from the second row.

A second man stood, then a third.

"So will I!"

"And I!"

The applause lasted a full minute before Captain Talbot, wiping tears from his eyes on his uniform sleeve, bade the audience to be silent. He directed the three young men to an Army recruiter at a small folding desk beside the piano player, who began pounding out *Stars and Stripes Forever*.

Donald and Clara left the theater at the end of the second feature. The Keystone Cops two-reel comedy had helped temper the emotions Captain Talbot stirred. To their right, small groups of men and women gathered around the young men who had just signed up. Everyone cheered them on.

Donald felt Clara shudder as they passed the last group. He patted her hand, which she had looped under his arm.

"You're thinking of your brother?"

"Yes."

"And I worry about Cletus. Naomi and Clarence haven't gotten any letters from him lately."

"I'm still receiving letters from Henry, but he sounds different."

"Ma says the same about Cletus."

Donald guided Clara outside and onto the large veranda fronting the theater. The salt air was refreshing. She stopped at the railing and reached into her bag for a handkerchief. He rested his hand on her back. Clara spoke so softly that Donald barely understood what she said next.

"Donald, did you see the captain's left arm?"

"I noticed that he didn't move it."

Clara turned to face him. She put one hand flat against Donald's chest, patting lightly with her fingers spread. She stared at the back of her hand a few seconds more before she could speak. Donald leaned closer to hear.

"That was a wooden prosthesis," she whispered, looking up. "Captain Talbot didn't have a left arm."

Chapter 23

Jake sat on Clara's front porch swing, pushing slowly with his heels back and forth. It would be dark soon. Foley said to be back in the office Thursday morning, so that meant leaving Galveston in the next few hours. Nothing left to do here anyway, he thought. Elton is recovering and I've got the photos I came to get. Even Donald had ...

"Where's your friend?"

"Oh, hi, Rebecca, I didn't hear you walk up. Don and Clara went to the seawall. They'll be back soon. Have a seat." He stopped rocking the swing and patted the slats of the space beside him.

"You looked deep in thought," Rebecca said, gathering her skirt. "Good thoughts, I hope."

"Only the best."

Rebecca's skin glowed in the warm afternoon light. Jake studied her profile with a photographer's eye, something he rarely did. Rebecca fit Gibson's popular illustrations of the ideal woman: slender waist, ample bosom, full lips, and a narrow, slightly upturned nose. She promoted the look with the delicate use of rouge and lip color, which she brushed on sparingly.

How different from Maye, Jake thought. Maye uses cosmetics like a printer uses ink. He started the swing moving again and lifted his arm over its back, behind Rebecca's shoulders.

"When do you leave for work?"

"The car will be here in an hour. Jenny's getting ready now."

"Don and I are going back to Houston tonight."

"I guessed that. I'm sorry you can't stay longer."

"I'll be back soon."

"Maybe I could come to Houston sometime. I'd love to see the newspaper office where you work."

Jake eased his arm from Rebecca's shoulders, pretended to scratch his head, then rested his hands in his lap.

"That would be nice, Rebecca."

Donald and Clara walked along the seawall from 23rd Street to 30th and back again. They didn't talk any more about the war, although it was on both their minds. They stopped instead at a soda fountain and ordered hot dogs. Real ones this time, Donald thought.

"And two *Triple-X* cream sodas," he said to the man behind the counter. They took their food and drinks to a small round table near the front window that faced the boulevard. The traffic was continuous.

"More automobiles every day," Clara said, shaking her head. "Do you remember the first one you saw?"

"No. By the time I was old enough to notice, they were common in Houston."

"I remember seeing my first motor car," she said, "not so much the machine, but how it scared the horses and mules."

"Nowadays there must be more automobiles than buggies. Draymen are learning to drive trucks and livery stables are going out of business. Even the trolley lines are suffering because of motor cars. People would rather drive themselves."

"But cars are so noisy, and the smells take your breath away."

"Not Mrs. Carhart's Cadillac."

"Oh?"

"Yes, sometimes she drives it herself." Donald grinned at Clara. "The chauffeur doesn't approve. He told me it embarrasses him to be a passenger in the front seat with her at the wheel. It's worse because he wears a uniform, so everyone notices."

Donald held the straw steady and sipped his cream soda without lifting the glass. Another couple came in and sat at the adjacent table near the Coca-Cola sign. Everyone wanted a window seat.

"Mrs. Carhart began driving by herself after Cadillac offered electric starters. She bought one of the first models with that feature."

"I like her already," Clara said. "Tell me, who are her friends?" She took another bite of her hot dog and waited. Donald looked at Clara, lightly touched the corner of his own mouth, and she quickly wiped a dab of mustard from hers.

"From what I see, Mrs. Carhart spends most of her time on charity projects. Her Ladies Guild still supports the orphanage where I lived as a kid. She also works for the Women's Suffrage movement, and against the Anti-Saloon League."

"So Mrs. Carhart is against Prohibition?"

"She says Congress can't legislate morality. She claims that banning liquor will create more problems than it solves. Lately she's been traveling a lot, but doesn't talk about that."

"What an intriguing woman." Clara sipped her cream soda and looked outside.

"Occasionally she invites me to dinner parties," Donald added. "I think she selects people who would be good for me to know. In her own way, she's teaching all the time."

Clara laughed and pointed out the window, where a man was chasing his straw boater down the street.

"People are losing their hats in this wind."

"Don't worry, it will die down in time for the mosquitoes to come out."

"Stop it," Clara laughed. "Finish telling me about the dinner parties. What do you remember most?"

Donald sipped his soda thoughtfully before answering. "What do I remember most? I'd say it was a dinner last year. There were nine of us altogether, including Mrs. Carhart and her mother. One guest was a publisher, I think." Donald began counting on his fingers.

"Yes. And there was a musician and two writers. Dr. Covington was guest of honor."

"Benjamin J. Covington?"

"Do you know him?"

"I know his work. The Army Medical Corps is testing his formula to help flu victims. And I know he plans to expand his clinic into a proper Negro hospital after the war."

"One thing he said has stayed with me," Donald said. "A writer there asked about his childhood. Dr. Covington said he was 'born in the sixth year of freedom.' Those were his exact words, and that impressed me the most. Just think, Clara, how it would be to mark your own family history as either before or after the time your parents were slaves."

Jake remained on the swing with Rebecca until it was clear that neither of them had more to discuss. He stood, taking a moment to stretch after the swing bumped to a stop on the backs of his knees.

"Well, I'd better pack my things. Don and Clara will be home before you know it."

Jake walked with Rebecca back to the carriage house and retrieved his duffel from her room. They kissed briefly at the top of stairs. He turned and started down.

"Let me know the next time you're in town," she called to his back.

"I will."

The door to Donald's room was open. Elton was asleep with a book upside down on his chest. Jake picked it up and thumbed the first few pages. *Private Pete* was the personal account of a young Canadian soldier, injured early in the Great War, now telling his story to the world. Across from the title page, a photo showed Harold Pete himself, grinning despite his injuries. He carried a large folding camera in one hand. For a moment, Elton's face, then Donald's, replaced Pete's on the page. Jake snapped the book closed and laid it flat on the desk near Elton's bed.

"Hey, Jake," Elton said, eyes half closed.

"How are you feeling, pal?"

"Much better, thanks. Still groggy, but Clara says that's normal."

"Did you see? I bought you something to wear."

"Thanks, Jake, I'll pay you back when we get home."

"Don't mention it; I owe you that much at least."

"I'm too tired to argue. Thanks for the new duds."

Jake tossed his duffel on the empty bed. He rifled through to the bottom before deciding the clothes on his back were the cleanest he had.

"You need anything before I go?"

"No, Jake, I'm all right."

"How about cash? I'll leave you five bucks. That's enough to get you home."

Elton's voice wavered. "You're always watching out for me. I don't know what ..."

Jake stiffened. "No, El, you really don't know what!" He turned toward Elton, fists clenched. The words came stronger than he intended. When he saw the hurt in Elton's eyes, Jake softened his voice and relaxed his fists.

"Don't you see, El? If it hadn't been for me, you wouldn't be laying here now, busted up. It's all my fault."

Chapter 24

"Let's get inside before we're eaten alive." Donald flicked a mosquito from his ear and took Clara's hand as they skipped up the front steps. They found Jake and Elton in the kitchen, eating chunks of buttered bread, and downing the last of the soup. A blackened pot was soaking in the sink.

"Sorry about that," Jake said, jerking his head toward the sink. Clara checked the damage, then laughed. She poured out the cold water, added a spoonful of Rinso and refilled the pot, leaving suds flowing over the top.

"That's all right, boys. A little charcoal adds flavor to the soup."

"I left the rent and extra money for food in an envelope on your desk. Let me know if it's not enough."

"Thanks, Jake, I'm sure it's fine."

"I'll be ready in a few minutes, Don." Jake stood, taking Elton's elbow to help him from the table. Donald retrieved his bag from the carriage house and was happy to see Clara waiting when he returned.

"I almost forgot this." She handed Donald one of his work shirts, clean and folded neatly as the day Sears mailed it to his house.

"Thanks."

"And here is more ointment for your rash. Apply this when you get home. There's enough here for three days."

"Great." Donald tucked the Mason jar toward the center of his bag and placed the folded denim shirt on top.

"And you might enjoy this while you're waiting for the poultice to dry." She held a book with a bright red cover. "*Cyrano* is one of my favorite plays. I've read it several times. Let me know what you think."

"Thanks, Clara. I'll bring it back to you soon."

She smiled. "I hoped you'd say that."

They stood for a moment, each still holding a corner of the book. Neither wanted to let go.

"Clara, I ..."

The screen door slammed. Heavy footsteps echoed through the kitchen into the parlor.

"Hey, there you are," Jake said. "Come on, Don. If we miss the seven o'clock train, we'll be cooling our heels for an hour at the station."

Donald stared up at Jake as he tucked the book into his duffel, then turned back to Clara.

"Well, goodbye. Thanks for everything."

"Goodbye, Donald. Goodbye Jake. Don't worry about Elton; I'll have him on the four o'clock to Houston this Sunday."

"You'd better run," the cashier said. The metal bars of the ticket window made him look like a chicken in a cage.

Jake and Donald shouldered their bags, jogged again across the platform and boarded as the conductor was closing the doors.

"Close!" Jake panted, crossing his legs and dropping his hat on his knee.

Donald settled into the leather seat, moving right and left several times to scratch the rash on his lower back. He looked forward to more of Clara's poultice when he got home.

As the trolley crossed the causeway over West Bay, Donald glimpsed the single light of a fishing boat motoring slowly toward its berth. He crossed his arms and settled back into the corner of his seat. The window glass felt cool against his cheek. His eyelids grew heavy as the car sped north through the night, clicking rhythmically over the rails that stretched on and on, straight across the open prairie.

"Hell of a trip, eh, Don?"

Startled awake, Donald fought to get his bearings. He wished Jake wouldn't talk that way in public. He sat up straighter in the seat before answering.

"Yeah, things turned out all right, considering how bad they could have been." He stretched his arms over his head and yawned. What seemed like a blink had been a good forty minutes. Jake wanted to talk, so nap time was over.

"So you're going through with it? You're signing up with the draft board tomorrow?"

"Sure, Jake, first thing in the morning."

"What will your folks think?"

"Pa will be proud. Ma will worry."

"Do you wonder what basic training is like?"

"Can't be much fun." Donald said, still struggling to wake up.

"The first weeks of football practice weren't much fun either."

That woke Donald. He leaned forward in his seat and studied Jake's profile in the trolley's dim light.

"You're not thinking about joining! After all you said about the war?"

"Just thinking."

"What about your invalid parents?"

"Mom has her bridge and garden clubs. Dad plays golf four times a week when he's not hunting or fishing with his buddies. They're fine."

"Did your folks ever ask why you weren't already in the Army?"

"They think I've got flat feet."

Donald leaned back in his seat and sighed. "I wonder how they got that idea."

The back gate opened smoothly when Donald lifted the latch. Bosco loped to Donald's side, first licking his hand and then his face when Donald leaned down. There were no lights inside the house, so Donald went straight to his shed in the back yard. Feeling his way through the darkened room, he found the box of safety matches and lit the kerosene lamp near his bed. Bosco whined at the screen door. Donald invited him in, folded an old blanket on the floor, and Bosco settled in for the night.

Naomi had been there. She'd left a towel by his wash basin, clean underwear folded on the bed, and a fresh shirt hanging on the length of baling wire that served as Donald's corner closet.

People say dogs don't snore, but Bosco did. It was good to be home.

Chapter 25

Thursday, September 12, 1918

Donald liked chickens. He liked eggs. But that rooster, that wretched rooster, he could do without. Most nights, the hateful thing perched on a fencepost just outside the shed. The window was usually open for air, so when the bird began crowing half an hour before sunup, it was like a bugle call from ten feet away.

A bugle call. Draft registration day.

How long before I wake up to a bugle every day, he thought. If the Army does need all the men it can get, I could be at Camp Logan in a couple of weeks. What then? At least the camp is nearby. I could walk home in half an hour—if I ever got a pass.

The rooster crowed again.

"Oh boy," Donald said without joy.

He rubbed his eyes. Camp Logan. A year ago Clarence Stokes was one of the thousands of craftsmen who rebuilt the old National Guard camp deep in the woods west of Houston. In less than a month, thirty thousand recruits were training there.

Every night, Clarence would sit exhausted at the dinner table, telling Naomi and Donald one new story after another.

"Furious work," he'd say. "Men swarmin' all over the place. Why, we built a whole darn mess hall in two days! The whole thing!" Then, at some point in the meal, Clarence would lower his voice, shake his head and say, "I never seen the like."

Donald felt Bosco's warm fur against his feet. The old dog blinked sleepily toward the window, then at Donald. He stood, stretched his front legs, shoulders low, rump and tail high in the air, then jumped to the floor, nails clicking wood as he padded to the screen door. He nosed it open and stepped into the yard, looking for a new place to pee.

"Life is simple enough for you," Donald called as he watched the dog go. "Eat, sleep, chase squirrels, take a dump now and then. What more could you want?"

Bosco was too busy to respond.

Sunlight slowly filled the room. It was hopeless trying to sleep, so Donald snapped the covers back and sat on the edge of the bed. He felt his forearms, wrists, and then his waist. Clara's poultice had worked. The poison ivy rash still itched, but it wasn't bad. He reached for the jar and applied more of the greenish goo, lightly this time, so it would dry faster.

Donald brushed his teeth and used cold water and bar soap to shave. He spent another few minutes unpacking his bag, stacking dirty clothes on the chair by the door. He put the shirt Clara had washed in the drawer with his clean underwear and socks. It was so beautifully folded, he hated to hang it up.

Electric lights went on in the house. Bosco bounded up the steps to the kitchen door and waited, nose pressed to the screen, his tail wagging hard. Naomi opened the door, patted the dog's head and slipped a morsel of food in his mouth before refilling his water dish.

"I'm back," Donald called from the shed. "I'll be over in a few minutes, Ma."

"I'll have the coffee on."

Donald filled his wash basin from the pitcher and again splashed water on his face to wake up. That's when he recalled the tone in Naomi's voice. Not as cheerful as she usually was, especially after Donald had been away for several days. He rushed to dress.

"Did you and Jake have a good trip?" Naomi said as Donald entered the kitchen. She crossed the room to hug him. He'd never seen her looking so sad.

"We found Elton. He's all right."

"I'm glad."

"What about Cletus? Any news?"

Naomi nodded toward the table, but didn't look that way herself.

Donald stepped over and reached for an envelope. It had been sent from a military hospital in England.

"I don't even know where Essex is on the map." Naomi's voice caught and she put her hand over her mouth. Tears filled her eyes. Donald opened the envelope and unfolded the letter, which had clearly been read many times.

Sobraon Barracks Military Hospital
Colchester Garrison, Essex, U.K.
3 August, 1918

Dear Mr. and Mrs. Stokes,
I am writing on behalf of your son, Cletus, who is convalescing here at Colchester. Cletus asked me to let you know that he is well and will be returning to the States as soon as he is stronger and transport can be arranged.

Your son's outfit was attacked with nerve gas two weeks ago. Some of his American comrades died and many were injured, since the attack occurred at night and the men in the trenches had little warning. Cletus has suffered lung and eye injuries. He cannot see from either eye, although the doctors here say that it is not uncommon for men to recover some or all of their vision. We pray that is so for your son. His lung injuries could also improve over time.

I know that you will wish to write to Cletus, but he is here for only another two weeks at most. By the time you get this letter, he will likely be at a transport center or on a troopship home. I am sorry that we have no more detailed information at this time.

Cletus is in good spirits and sends his love to you and to his brother, Donald.

Sincerely yours,
Gladys Hansford, VAD
British Red Cross, Sobraon

Donald turned the letter over and back again in his hands, although he knew there was nothing more on the other side. He looked at Naomi, who still had one hand over her mouth, eyes open wide. Donald crossed the small kitchen and hugged her.

"That was written more than a month ago," Naomi said between quick, deep breaths. "It came yesterday."

"It will be all right. Cletus will be home soon."

At that, she broke down, shoulders heaving. "My boy is blind!" she sobbed, hugging Donald as if he was a life preserver, and she, about to drown.

"Here, Ma." With one hand, Donald reached for the back of a chair, pulled it away from the table and slid it to Naomi's side. After a moment she sat, legs to the side, steadying herself with one hand on the back of the chair, the other clutching a handkerchief to her nose.

"I reckon you seen the letter," Clarence said from the hall.

"Hi, Pa. Yeah, I saw it. How are you doing?"

"Fair-to-middlin' I suppose." He dropped into his chair by the window, leaving one knee bent and his gimpy leg straight. He hadn't shaved. "I'm thankful Cletus is still alive, but it's sure goin' to be rough on him, tryin' to get a job if he can't see. How will he support himself now?"

"Papa, we just have to help him out," Naomi said. "And I'm sure Donny will help, too." Naomi patted Donald's hand, then pressed it with both hands to her wet cheek.

"Of course, Ma."

Still holding Naomi's hand, he struggled to think. For the last few days, his world had been expanding. Now it was closing back in.

Donald left his folks' kitchen after breakfast, Clarence washing dishes while Naomi dried. Later he saw her tossing table scraps to the chickens from her old cookie sheet.

Registration day.

Yesterday in Galveston, and then riding home on the Interurban last night, Donald had begun to see himself as part of the cause. A soldier in uniform, marching with thousands of others to the front, brave men trusting each other with their lives. Yes, men were dying. Others were coming home sick and injured and worse. But his world was small and the war was big. War consumed everything.

Donald dropped to his hands and knees, fishing under his bed until he found the poster. He unrolled it on his bed.

"I want YOU for the U.S. Army!" Uncle Sam still called.

"Let's see if you do or not!" he said to the poster. The registration form lay on top, edges curled from being rolled inside. Donald flattened it on his desk and found a pencil. Ten minutes later he was walking quickly down Dennis Street toward Main.

The line at the recruiter's office was already out the door. A pair of fresh-faced junior officers sat at separate desks inside. A third recruiter moved up and down the lines, completing forms for those who couldn't read.

"NEXT!"

Donald stepped forward and handed the lieutenant his form. The man didn't look up.

"You Donald Brown?"

"Yes, sir," Donald said to the top of the man's head.

"This your correct address?"

"Yes, sir."

The recruiter pounded a rubber stamp on an ink pad, then again on a piece of paper. He scribbled the date and looked up. "Here you g ..."

The lieutenant peered at Donald's thick glasses before handing over the card. "Here you go. Expect something in the mail in a few days. That will tell you when to take your physical."

"That soon, sir?"

"Could be. NEXT!"

Donald moved aside. Another young man took his place. Sooner than he expected, he was back on the street, reading the little card in his hand:

REGISTRATION CERTIFICATE
To whom it may concern:
In accordance with the proclamation of
the President of the United States ...

After all the worry, it was done. Printed there, right under the eagle and the shield, was Donald's name and registration number. This card proved that he, Donald Brown, was no slacker. Yes, sir! You see here? Donald Brown is registered for military service!

Surprised and relieved, he tucked the card in his wallet. He stopped by the post office, dropped a postcard in the mail slot and walked home.

Clarence was outside when he got there, replacing a length of chicken wire that had worked loose from the wooden fence.

"So, you done it?"

"Yeah, I registered for the draft."

"Well, your ma won't like it, 'specially after the news 'bout Cletus, but I reckon there was nothin' you could do. Paper says there was more slacker raids just yesterday. Personally, I'm proud my two boys is standin' up for their country. Don't seem right to shirk your duty."

"I knew you'd feel that way, Pa."

"Women just see things different from men."

Clarence dug to the bottom of his wooden tool box for more staples. He put two between his lips and held a third between the thumb and forefinger of his left hand. He nodded his head toward the fence.

"Here, Donny, pull this here wire taut," he mumbled past the staples.

Donald reached over Clarence and tugged with both hands, stretching the chicken wire flat against one of the posts.

Clarence set the staple over a length of wire, tapped lightly, then hammered the staple into the fence with two perfect blows. He reached lower on the fence post and repeated the process twice more, taking the staples each time from between his lips.

"There, that ought to do it. Your ma found a couple of her chickens strollin' down Albany yesterday, and she throwed a fit. To hear her tell it, you'd think I let them damn birds out of the yard on purpose."

Donald helped Clarence take down his temporary workbench and put away his tools. He stayed in the garage as Clarence used an oily rag to wipe the sweat from the hammer, wire cutter and pliers he'd used.

"Pa?"

"Yeah, son?"

"Are you happy being married?"

Clarence put down the pliers. "Happy? What makes you ask that?"

"Just wondering. What's it like to be married as long as you and Ma?"

Clarence considered that a serious question and gave it some thought before answering.

"Well, Donny, I suppose we're like most married folks. When we was your age, we called it 'love.' After Cletus was born, we got down to serious business, raisin' that little boy. And when the storm came in 1900, all hell broke loose. Them next few years we worked like a pair of draft mules to build this house and start over."

"How about now, Pa, are you happy?"

"Now? Well, now we're older. Things has settled down. You and Cletus is grown. Like most couples our age, we just take turns gettin' in the way and aggravatin' each other."

"So, you're not happy being married?"

Clarence smiled and turned back to his tools.

"Donny, don't get me wrong. I couldn't live without that woman."

Chapter 26

Naomi watched Clarence and Donald from the kitchen window. She loved the easy way they talked. She'd grown comfortable in her life. On good days—and there were many—she considered herself lucky. Yesterday, after the Essex letter turned up in the mail, the day turned bad. Things could be worse, of course. At least Cletus was alive and he'd be home soon. No telling what would happen after that. She turned from the window, wiping flour from her hands to the sides of her apron.

"Any milk left?" Donald called through the screen door. Clarence was right behind.

"Plenty."

The kitchen smelled warm and moist and sweet. Donald headed straight for the cookie jar. It was empty.

"There's a fresh batch just out of the oven," Naomi said over her shoulder when she heard the lid of the cookie jar clink. "Give them a minute to cool."

Clarence returned from the icebox with fresh milk for Donald and buttermilk for himself. Clarence broke chunks of cornbread into his glass, then filled it to the brim. He used a teaspoon to stir the soggy lumps into a yellow slurry that clouded the inside of the glass. A sharp, sick smell of milk gone bad assaulted Donald's nose. He finally had to look away.

"How can you eat that stuff, Pa?"

"You don't know what you're missin' boy." Clarence stirred again, spooned another mouthful and answered as he chewed. "Cornbread and buttermilk is one of the seven wonders of the world."

At the counter, Naomi smiled. My boys, my boys, she thought.

Donald spent the rest of Thursday in his shed, first processing negatives from the last few days in Galveston, then printing them.

"I brought you fresh towels," Naomi called as she opened the screen door.

"Hi, Ma. I'll be right out."

She knew not to touch the black curtain that served as a darkroom door. Instead, Naomi turned to the black-and-white prints drying on a short length of twine strung between nails across a corner of the room. She reached for the spectacles dangling from a thin chain around her neck, pinched the lightweight frames onto her nose and tilted her head back. She gently touched the bottom of one print to angle it toward the light.

"Sweet children. Where did you take these pictures?"

"In front of Jake's rent house. I think they live across the street. Those prints are for the family."

Naomi adjusted her spectacles to look at the next set.

"And who is this pretty young lady?"

"Just someone I met in Galveston."

Donald drew the darkroom curtain aside and stepped out with two more paper prints in a white porcelain tray. Different shots of Clara.

"Excuse me, Ma."

Donald placed the wet prints against a sheet of glass, then used a squeegee to remove most of the water. He attached the prints to his drying line with clothespins. Naomi stepped up for a better look.

"She has a sweet smile," Naomi said. "What's her name?"

"Clara Barnes. She's a student nurse. Jake and I rented a room in her guest house for three nights."

"Is she married?"

"No, Ma."

Naomi turned, looking at Donald over the tops of her readers. "Is she one of Jake's lady friends?"

"No, Ma, he just rents a room from her when he goes to Galveston."

"Where are her folks?"

Donald returned to the darkroom, pulled the curtain closed and began lightly massaging the back of his neck.

"Dr. Barnes died in the 1900 storm. He was with some men in a restaurant when a printing press fell through from the second floor."

"Oh my! I remember reading that at the time. What about her mother?"

"Martha Barnes was a nurse who worked at John Sealy Hospital. She got sick and passed away last year."

"Any other family?"

"Clara's brother Henry is in France. He's in the Signal Corps, same as Cletus."

"I see."

"Ma?"

"Yes?"

"I like her a lot."

Naomi smiled. "Yes, Donny, I guessed that."

The telephone was ringing when Naomi went back to the house. Clarence, who could sleep through a hurricane, was taking a nap.

"Hello?"

"Mrs. Stokes?"

"Yes?" The line was surprisingly clear.

"Hello, Naomi, this is Nina Carhart. Is Donald there?"

"He's back from Galveston, but he's working in the darkroom now."

"Well, don't disturb him. Could you give him a message, please?"

"Certainly."

"I'm having a luncheon this Saturday. It's very important. There are some people in town that I would like for Donald to meet."

"That's very kind of you, Nina, I'll give him the message. What time?"

"Noon will be fine. Thanks, Naomi."

"Thank you, Nina."

After Mrs. Carhart hung up, Naomi waited, hand over the mouthpiece of the telephone, for the click that would tell her someone had been listening on the party line. None this time, although she half hoped there would be.

Naomi hung the earpiece back on its hook. She always felt strange calling the famous Mrs. Carhart by her first name, but Nina insisted. Naomi imagined the distinguished and handsome Governor Hobby, or the lovely and gracious Miss Hogg saying "Nina" this and "Nina" that over tea, but not the likes of Naomi Stokes, a carpenter's wife who lived next door to former slaves in Houston's Fourth Ward.

For a society lady, Nina Carhart was certainly down to earth.

Chapter 27

Saturday, September 14, 1918

"Hello, Mr. Hanson." Donald pointed over his shoulder with his thumb. "How are they selling?"

"I could sell more if you'd just make them faster," the store owner told him. "My customers like your tripods better than the ones I get from New York." He pointed to the window display. "That's the last one I have in stock. Can you bring me three more?"

"Sure thing. How about Wednesday morning?"

"Perfect. What can I do for you today?"

Although he was a good businessman, Hanson had the annoying habit of hovering over his customers. Donald made his choices fast, leaving with four rolls of film, some darkroom chemicals and a box of printing paper.

"Just take this off what you owe me for the tripods."

"I'll do that now," Hanson said, opening his ledger.

The thought of selling three more of his tripods to Hanson at a profit of five dollars each left Donald feeling wealthy. His next stop was the dry goods store, where he spent nearly four dollars, the most he'd ever paid for a new pair of shoes.

From a distance, it looked like Clarence and Naomi were having an outdoor market. Several men were examining a collection of planes, chisels and files sitting on the sawhorses and door that Clarence used for a temporary workbench. A neighbor was carrying away Naomi's old sewing machine. Donald saw her slip some bills into the pocket of her dress, then speak to a woman who was looking at glassware in a crate.

Donald looked into the garage. Except for old Mr. Hammers examining the sleeve of an overcoat hanging on a nail, the space was empty. Clarence had everything in the yard. Donald started to ask, but Clarence spoke first.

"You been Saturday shoppin' I see. Your ma said to remind you about goin' to Mrs. Carhart's today."

"I didn't forget, Pa. Say, what's all ..."

"What's she got in store for you today? More books, you reckon?"

"No, just someone she wants me to meet. Say, Pa, what's all ..."

"And you bought yourself some new duds it looks like."

Clarence was prying; something he seldom did. Naomi waved at Donald from across the yard, saw Clarence, then turned quickly to a prospective customer.

"You have time to stop by the post office on your way home?"

"Sure, Pa, I was going to anyway."

Clarence grinned like a fisherman with a bite. "You expectin' mail?"

"Maybe." Donald said, certain now that Naomi had told him about Clara. Donald refused the bait.

"What are you doing, Pa, having a sale?"

Satisfied with teasing Donald, Clarence was ready for the next topic. He looked around the yard.

"Didn't plan to have one; the sale jus' happened. I went to clean the garage this morning, and afore I knew it, folks passin' by was askin' if this or that was for sale. Your ma and I raised near twenty dollars already, and we're just getting' started."

"But what made you want to clean out the garage today, Pa?"

"We're thinking of gettin' an automobile and needed a place to store it." Clarence pulled Donald closer. "We figured with Cletus comin' home and him bein' blind, a car might come in handy."

"Good thinking, Pa."

"How much for that chair?" A man pointed and Clarence turned away from Donald.

"Dollar-fifty, and I got three more jus' like it yonder round the side."

The man took a couple of steps to see where Clarence was pointing. "Sold," he said, shaking Clarence's hand.

Back in his shed, Naomi had laid out Donald's best trousers, a clean white shirt, a tie and his dark blue jacket. His new shoes would go just fine.

"First impressions make a difference, dear boy," Mrs. Carhart said in Donald's mind.

"Who's coming?" Donald asked aloud to his empty room.

"Just be sure you make a good impression," the room answered back. Donald laughed at himself as he buttoned the fresh collar and cuffs onto his best shirt.

From his window Donald noticed Clarence helping the man who'd bought the chairs tie them in the back of his buggy. A lady sitting up front holding the reins was smiling broadly. Two neighbors, along with several people Donald had never seen, were milling about. One man carried a bow saw that Clarence no longer used, and a woman standing beside him held one of Naomi's old lamps. The chickens, lacking interest in the neighbors or the sale, gathered at the far end of the yard to peck the ground near the burn barrel.

On impulse, Donald pulled a shallow wooden crate from under his bed. Inside were two Kodak Hawk-Eyes, one given to Donald and the other a two-bit purchase from the pawn shop. They'd been easy to repair and both looked good as new. He brought them to Naomi, who took her time inspecting Donald head to toe.

"You look just fine!" she said. "And you bought new shoes. Very nice."

"Thanks, Ma." Donald held up the two cameras. "Would you mind putting these out for sale?"

"Glad to." Naomi took the cameras, holding both against her stomach with one arm. She shaded her eyes from the sun with her free hand. "How much do you want for them?"

"Seventy-five cents each would be fine. Both of them work like new."

"If you fixed them, I'm sure they do. I'll ask a dollar-seventy five for each." She set the cameras on a nearby table. "You'd better run now, you don't want to be late for Nina's luncheon."

Donald didn't run, but he did hurry to the trolley stop. New shoes always took a few days to break in. He was happy to sit for the rest of the trip to the Carhart estate in the Heights.

On most visits Donald would enter through the back garden. Today he paused to admire Albino's prize pittosporum bushes and two stately date palms before he rang the bell at the front door.

"Good day, Mr. Brown. May I take your hat?"

"Hello, Kamal. Nice to see you."

Nina Carhart's butler was one of the most exotic persons Donald had ever met. His lean dark face was deeply lined, but when he smiled, his near-perfect teeth made him look young. As far as Donald knew, Kamal was the only name the Moroccan ever used.

"The others are in the library, Mr. Brown. Would you care to join them?" Kamal's concise English held a slight French accent. He handled Donald's simple leather cap as if it were a gentleman's silk topper, then gestured toward the room Donald knew so well.

Elsie was moving among the five guests with a tray of dry sherry. She handed the last one to Donald as he walked in.

"Thank you, Elsie."

She nodded and gave a faint smile. "You're welcome, Mr. Brown."

Her formality surprised him. Donald wondered if he had offended her on his last visit, but now was hardly the time to ask.

He studied the crystal glass in his hand, enjoying how the slightest movement made light sparkle. The library windows opened to a view of the south garden with its curving pergola. Four men stood in the book-lined room, two and two, engaged in conversation. Of the four, Donald recognized only Jules Davenport, president of the Heights Regional Bank and Trust, and a frequent guest at the Carhart home.

Mrs. Carhart's mother, Frederica Johnston, occupied a small sofa in an alcove, like a queen receiving her subjects. "Good afternoon, Mrs. Johnston," Donald said, bending slightly at the waist and extending his hand as Mrs. Carhart had taught him to do.

"Ah, hello, Donald, so good of you to come."

"Thank you, ma'am."

Frederica Johnston turned to the woman beside her. "Donald, have you met Miss Ida Templeton, the writer?"

"Oh, Miss Templeton, I've read some of your articles. It's a pleasure to meet you in person!"

"Please call me Ida. Won't you join us?"

Just looking at her, no one would guess that the handsome woman sitting politely on the sofa with Nina Carhart's mother was the famous—infamous, her targets would say—muckraker who attacked industrial tyrants and corrupt politicians with equal skill. Donald sat in a nearby chair. Frederica Johnston spoke first.

"Ida was telling me about her next series." She turned toward Miss Templeton. "Do go on."

Ida took a sip of sherry, then held the glass over an embroidered napkin in her lap. "I've been looking again at the oil industry," she said. "It has been several years since I've written much about it. I'm afraid that the situation for workers is quite grim. I fear that ..."

Raised voices interrupted her thought. She turned toward the noise and Donald followed her gaze. A lanky man with grey curls hanging over his collar was jabbing his index finger on a younger man's chest.

"I'm telling you, Clifford, that approach won't work in a monthly." Having made his point, the older man removed his finger, took a long pull of his drink, then held his glass straight down to his side, fingertips spaced evenly around the rim. "Our readers will get in-depth reporting, not the claptrap they see in the daily press!"

"Claptrap?" one of the group objected, "Claptrap?"

"Nothing personal, Mitch. I don't mean *your* newspaper."

All four men laughed. The accuser held up his near-empty glass. It held a sliver of amber liquid, but Kamal stood waiting with an identical glass on a small tray.

"Don't mind them," Ida said to Donald. She sipped the last of her sherry and nodded once when Elsie offered her another. "This argument has been going on for months in our New York office. We all work together except for Mr. Davenport. He is our banker, and ..."

Ida turned toward the library door.

Donald stood at once.

"Ah, Donald, welcome," Mrs. Carhart said as she crossed the room. "I see that Mother and Ida are keeping you entertained." Turning toward them she added, "May I introduce this young man to the others?"

Donald nodded to Mrs. Johnston, then turned to Ida Templeton. "I look forward to reading your new reports."

Ida raised her sherry glass. "I hope you won't be disappointed."

Nina Carhart looked on approvingly, then guided Donald by the arm toward the first two men.

"If you gentlemen can stop fighting long enough, I'd like for you to meet someone." She drew Donald near and introduced the finger-pointer's victim, a man in his early forties, with bright blue eyes, blond hair and a sportsman's deep tan.

"Donald, this is Clifford Murray, an excellent writer who has a special gift for discovering the truth behind stories."

"Pleased to meet you, Mr. Murray."

"That's my dad's name," Murray grinned, shaking Donald's hand. "Call me Cliff."

Nina turned to the man who had been poking his finger in Clifford's chest.

"And Donald, this noisy fellow is Leonard Hoffman, president and brains behind the *Granbury International Free Press*."

"Nina, my dear, you are too kind. I merely sign the checks."

"Nevertheless, Donald, Mr. Hoffman is a respected publisher who has gathered some of America's finest journalists for a magazine he is launching next spring. Leonard, may I present Mr. Donald Brown."

Hoffman extended his hand, gripping Donald's firmly as he spoke.

"I hear that you are interested in photography."

"I hope to become a professional someday."

Hoffman released his grip. It was surprisingly strong for a man who spent his days in an office.

"Nina has shown me some of your photographic prints. Do you have any experience with publications?"

"No sir, but I have a position waiting for me at the *Houston Chronicle*. That's one of our local newspapers."

"Yes, I'm familiar with it. I've known Mr. Jones more than twenty years." Hoffman paused, considering his next words.

"What would you be doing at the newspaper?"

"In the beginning, I would get the easiest assignments, photographing construction sites, meetings and public events."

Elsie stepped up with another tray of sherry. Hoffman fingered his own drink, while Murray and Mrs. Carhart nodded their thanks. Donald held up his glass to show Elsie that it was still half full. She smiled, turned slowly and walked away. Donald watched her go.

"Do those things interest you, Donald?"

"Sir?"

"Construction sites, meetings and public events. Does making photographs of them interest you?"

Hoffman had used the word "making" instead of "taking" pictures, a distinction that caught Donald's attention. He and Mrs. Carhart had discussed it many times.

"I know those subjects are mundane, sir," Donald said carefully, "but I see every photograph, no matter how simple, as an opportunity to do more."

"Oh? What do you mean by that? Photography is just a matter of capturing an image using a simple box and a few chemicals, don't you think? The job of the person holding the device is to get the exposure right."

Donald glanced to Mrs. Carhart, whose eyes said, "Go on." He sensed that she was studying his performance, as a coach might evaluate a young athlete.

"When I have a camera in my hands, I see more," Donald said. "I notice things others might not see, then capture them in the frame."

"Very poetic."

The men standing nearby had stopped their conversation, as had Ida Templeton and Mrs. Carhart's mother, still sitting together on the sofa.

"So you consider yourself an *artist?*" Hoffman said a bit too loudly.

The man's words were clear, but Donald knew he meant something else. This was no idle question. Hoffman's mood had turned serious, combative and cold.

"No, sir, I don't see my images as art."

"What then?"

"My photographs are documents."

"Documents? What do you mean by that?" Hoffman's shoulders may have relaxed a fraction of an inch. Hard to tell.

"Documents, sir. I want my pictures to tell a story, so that the person who sees them gains an understanding of what's happening, even if they can't read."

Hoffman relaxed and took another sip of whisky before speaking.

"That's a great deal to ask of a photograph."

"Yes, but it can be done. I think photographs should be read, as one would read a book or a newspaper."

Hoffman looked past Donald and nodded toward the adjoining room, where Kamal waited.

"So, you believe a good photograph tells a story? But tell me, Donald, are you ever concerned that the story might be wrong?"

"Yes, sir, I think about that often." Donald paused while Hoffman thoughtfully placed his empty glass on Kamal's tray and took the fresh one.

"Go on."

"Yes, Mr. Hoffman. I think it is possible to reveal the truth with a photograph, but it's also possible to lie, as easily as a person can lie with words. I believe it is the photographer's duty to tell the truth to the best of his or her ability."

Hoffman smiled and clamped his free hand on Donald's shoulder. He raised his glass and looked him in the eye.

"So do I," Hoffman said.

He turned to Mrs. Carhart, still gripping Donald's shoulder. "Nina, I like this boy already."

Nina hadn't noticed that she'd been holding her breath. Now, as Donald continued his visit with Leonard Hoffman, it was time to move on. She patted Donald's arm and stepped away toward the two gentlemen a few feet away.

She addressed the older one first, a man whose most striking features were his shiny bald head and muttonchop whiskers. Nina spoke to the powerful banker as if he were a childhood friend.

"Well, Jules, I understand that you are financing Leonard's latest venture."

Davenport and the man beside him both laughed.

"At least that's what Leonard thinks," the banker said, loud enough for the publisher to hear.

Chapter 28

"Need a ride, Don?" Cliff said, pointing to his two-passenger coupe parked near the curb. Compared to Jake's rough-and-tumble Model T, the tidy green Nash seemed like a sporting, no-nonsense car. Cliff had left the upper half of the windshield and the side windows open, so even though the roof was black and the day warm, the tan leather seats inside felt cool when Donald opened the door. Cliff cranked the engine himself, then got in next to Donald.

"Where to?" Cliff said as they headed north on Heights Boulevard.

"I live on Dennis Street, near the orphanage."

"You'll have to show me where that is, I'm new to Houston."

"Circle back here at 18th Street, then head south."

The Nash handled the brick street more smoothly than Jake's tin lizzie, and it didn't rattle as much, probably because of the white balloon tires. Cliff looked at ease, with one hand gripping the top of the steering wheel, the other on its side.

"Say, Don, you held your own with Leonard. He can be difficult. I saw him talking to you all through the meal. Did he offer you a job?"

"It's more of an apprenticeship, but yes. He used an odd term."

"Stringer?"

"That's it. He said I could photograph stories in this area for his new magazine. The company will pay my expenses and something extra every time they use one of my pictures. Turn left at the next intersection."

"And he will give you the assignments?" Cliff stuck his left arm out the window to signal the driver behind that he was turning. He slowed for a bicycle crossing Washington Avenue, then waited again for a buggy to pull over in front of the feed store.

"That's what I liked most about Mr. Hoffman's offer." Donald said. "He, or one of the editors, will give me assignments, but he also wants me to keep my eyes open for stories that would fit the magazine."

"He asks that of the writers as well," Cliff said. "It's one reason I agreed to join the venture several months ago. Leonard plans to give us a great deal of freedom to develop leads."

"Leads?"

"Story ideas. I like to have at least three good leads at a time. It keeps me on my toes."

"Three good leads," Donald repeated, "I like the sound of that. How many are on the staff now?"

Cliff thought for a minute, moving the fingers on his left hand to keep count.

"Ten in New York. Four in Washington D.C., two in Chicago, two in Los Angeles and two in San Francisco. He's looking for someone in Denver. Looks like you and I are the staff in Houston."

"That's all? I thought he would have more in Texas. Oh, turn at the next street."

Cliff signaled with his left arm for the right turn, his arm out the window, bent smartly at the elbow, hand pointing up. Donald chuckled to himself. Jake would rather die in a crash than signal what he planned to do.

"Say, Don, have you done any writing?"

"Only what I put in my journals, but Mrs. Carhart thinks I could be a good writer."

"Work at it, Don. If you stick with Leonard, he'll push to see what you can do. Someone who can take the pictures and write about them is a real asset."

"You're a writer. Are you a photographer, too?"

"I have a camera, but that's about it. I took a couple of pictures that my former editor used, but his standards weren't high. Leonard expects only the best."

"Then you must be a very good writer."

Cliff looked at Donald and grinned. "I try."

Before they reached Dennis Street, Donald remembered he wanted to check the Stokes' postal box for mail.

"You're sure you have time, Cliff?"

"I'm glad to, Don. Where's the post office?"

They stopped in a small asphalt parking lot adjacent to the building. Cliff left the engine running while Donald ran in. He walked quickly down a wall of ornate brass boxes, each with a combination lock, until he found the right one.

Through the small glass window, Donald could see there was mail. Two turns right to three, one turn left to nine, then back to five. The thick door swung open. Inside, an envelope addressed to Mr. and Mrs. Stokes, and a post card from Galveston. Donald snatched the card. On the front, a rotogravure illustration of the seawall and buildings along the boulevard. He flipped to the back side to read Clara's one-line note.

Galveston, 13 Sept., 1918
Dear Donald, It was a pleasure meeting you as well.
Regards, Clara Barnes

The energy drained from his arms and legs. He forgot the prospect of a challenging job with a new publication. Donald slipped the letter and Clara's card into his pocket and walked toward the post office door. Only when he reached the steps outside did he remember Cliff waiting in his car.

"Bad news, Don?"

"Not exactly. I was expecting too much, I guess."

"Too much of what?"

"I got a card from someone I met a few days ago, but she didn't say much."

"That's too bad."

Cliff sat for a moment, the engine of his car still idling. Donald looked straight ahead, resting his elbow on the open door and touching his thumbnail to his front teeth.

"Where's your house, Don?"

"Oh, Cliff, sorry. It's just a few blocks from here. I think I'll walk."

"Suit yourself. Here is my card. Until Leonard hires more people in Texas, we won't have an office, so this address is the boarding house where I stay. If I'm not there, leave a message with the landlady."

"Thanks, Cliff. I'll be in touch."

Donald stepped back from the car and felt a solid thump when he closed the door. He was halfway home before he realized he should have offered his own address and the Stokes' telephone number.

Clarence kept a burn barrel near the alley gate in the far corner of the yard, and that's where Donald found him, loading a few combustible items that hadn't sold. Clarence balanced a heavy apple crate on the rim of the barrel. He was holding an old copy of *Popular Science* magazine and muttering to himself. He didn't hear Donald walk up.

"No reason for throwin' this away, 'cept for The Queen Herself demands it."

"Hi, Pa."

Startled, Clarence nearly dropped the whole box into the burn barrel. Luckily, it wasn't lit.

"Hi, Donny, I didn't know you was there. I think I don't hear so well any more."

"What's in the box?"

"Some perfectly good magazines your ma says I got to throw away."

"Are those the ones you've had in the garage for years?"

"I read 'em when they come in, then store them in case I want to read 'em again."

"But you never do."

"Now, don't go takin' her side. There's valuable information here." Clarence found an issue that was barely a year old. Cockroaches had eaten the top edge of the cover and half the spine, but otherwise it was in good shape, except for the mildew smell.

"Now look here." Clarence held open an article called *Listen to the World*. The photograph showed a man seated at a workbench, wearing what looked to be metal earmuffs connected by wires to an electrical device. His left hand rested on one dial, but his eyes had a glazed, far-away look. The pencil in his right hand was poised over the beginnings of a message he was writing down.

Clarence tapped his finger on the page.

"This here's an article about buildin' a crystal radio set. With one of these, you could listen to signals from around the world!"

"But you don't know Morse code."

"You sound just like your ma." He put that copy back in the pile and dug for another. A fat silverfish, annoyed by the light, scurried down the outside of the crate.

"How about this? *Build Your Own Apple Press for Five Dollars.* I might want to do that some day. Your ma is always after me to do something with the extra apples from her tree."

Donald laughed. "All right, Pa. I see your point. Let me help you put them on the high shelf above your workbench. Ma won't see them there."

Clarence relaxed. "Good idea, son. Let's do it afore she comes back out here to check on me."

From her kitchen window, Naomi watched Donald carry the box of smelly, roach-infested magazines into the garage. She let the curtain fall back into place. "My boys," she said aloud, smiling and shaking her head.

A minute later, Clarence came up the back steps and into the kitchen.

"Jus' need matches for the burn barrel," he said, grabbing two from the dispenser near the stove, then walking quickly back toward the screen door.

"Did everything fit?"

"Yep, I'm fixin' to light the fire now."

"That's fine."

Clarence looked at Naomi, sensing trouble. He stopped, one foot already on the back porch.

"Anything else afore I go?"

"No, just tell Donald to wash his hands good before he comes in the house."

"How was the luncheon?" Naomi said as Donald took his seat at the kitchen table. Clarence was right behind, but he hurried down the hall to the safety of the bathroom. Naomi was surprised when Donald didn't go straight to the cookie jar, as he normally did.

"The luncheon was fine, Ma. I met some interesting people. One of them is a publisher from New York. After talking to him, I made a decision about the newspaper job Jake lined up."

"Oh?"

"Yeah. I'm not going to take it."

"What will you do?"

"Well, everything depends on the Army now, but if they don't want me, I'll photograph for Mr. Hoffman. He's starting a new kind of magazine, one that features pictures just as much as the stories."

"Like Collier's Weekly?"

"No. *Collier's* has illustrations. Hoffman's new magazine will use only photographs."

Naomi finished rolling her pie crust and began pressing it into the bottom of a well-used pan. She used a knife to trim the excess dough, which she mashed back into the larger lump still in her mixing bowl. She patted the sides of her apron, then wiped her hands on a dish towel before turning to Donald.

"When do you start?"

"That's up to the Army."

"Have you heard from the draft board yet?

"No, Ma."

Naomi leaned forward and glanced down the hall to see if Clarence was within earshot, but he remained in the bathroom.

"Did you hear from Clara?"

"Yes, she sent a card, and you got a letter." Donald fished them both from his pocket and laid the letter and card side-by-side on the table.

"You don't sound happy. What did Clara say?"

"Not much, Ma, just that she enjoyed meeting me."

"That's all?"

"Yes." Donald rested his chin in the palm of one hand, elbow braced on the table. Naomi thought for a moment before speaking.

"Donny, did you write to her?"

"Sure, Ma, I mailed it Thursday morning.

"A letter?"

"No, a post card."

"A post card? Donny, what were you thinking?"

"Well, Ma, I didn't have time to write much, so I figured a quick note would be all right."

"You go to your room this minute and write that girl a proper letter! A post card! Good Lord."

Naomi fussed at Clarence, but seldom raised her voice to Donald. Still, the thought of writing to Clara cheered him. He headed for the cookie jar, selected four, then poured himself a cool glass of milk.

"Good idea, Ma." Hands full, Donald pointed toward the table with his chin. "Don't forget your letter."

Naomi watched Donald carry his snack across the yard. He'd spoil his appetite for supper, eating so late in the day, but she didn't mind. She eased the screen door closed after Donald disappeared into his shed. White smoke from the burn barrel drifted across the yard. Its woody smell permeated the kitchen.

Down the short hallway behind her, the toilet flushed. Naomi turned to the letter on the table, picked it up and froze.

"You'd better see this," she called as soon as Clarence opened the bathroom door. "We got another letter from the Red Cross."

Clarence stood behind his wife briefly, resting his hands on her shoulders. Naomi didn't move.

"Let's see what it says."

"I'm afraid."

"Well, don't be. If it was bad news, the Army would've sent a telegram, don't you think? Sit down."

Clarence took the envelope from Naomi's hand, rolled his hips to the right in his chair and pulled a knife from his left pants pocket. He folded open the blade, slipped the point under the flap, then pushed it neatly from one side to the other.

The typewritten letter inside was on Red Cross stationery—American this time, not British. As before, someone else was writing for Cletus, but this time the letter was less than a week old, and it had come from New York.

As Clarence read, Naomi reached for his hand and his strength.

Am. Nat. Red Cross Service Center
New York, N.Y.
September 7, 1918

Dear Mr. and Mrs. Stokes,

Cletus has asked me to convey that he arrived safely in New York and that our medical personnel have cleared him for transport by hospital ship to either the Port of Galveston or Port of Houston in the next few days, depending on the available vessel.

Your son is doing as well as can be expected, considering the effects of nerve gas on the body. He says he feels stronger each day, although only a portion of his eyesight has returned thus far. He is able to walk for short distances. One of our staff will advise you as soon as we know his approximate arrival date. Cletus sends his love to you and his brother.

Cordially yours,
Willa M. Grimes,
Assist. Transport Document Coordinator

Clarence read the letter aloud a second time, then laid it on the table. He patted the top of Naomi's hand, which was still gripping his own. Her eyes, brimming with tears, never left the window as she spoke.

"When do you think our boy will be home?"

Clarence cleared his throat. "Well, let's see. If he did leave a few days after this letter was mailed, that means he could've left New York Wednesday or Thursday. Today's Saturday, so I figure he's somewhere at sea, like the letter says, on one of them hospital ships."

"How long would that take to get all the way from New York?"

"By sea? I reckon the better part of ten days, maybe two weeks dependin' on the kind of ship and the weather. It's still hurricane season, you know. If a storm come up sudden while they was in the gulf, they'd likely have to put into port somewhere to ride it out."

"So when could he be here?"

"For certain by the end of the month."

Naomi squeezed her husband's hand once more, then pushed her chair from the table.

"I've got to tell Donny." Naomi was already at the screen door. "He's writing to that girl in Galveston, the one I told you about."

Chapter 29

Donald took the news about Cletus as a positive thing, although he could see the pain on Naomi's face. He hugged her, lightly stroking her back.

"Things will work out, Ma. It's just going to take Cletus time to heal."

"I hope you're right, Donny, I certainly do."

Naomi clung to Donald a moment more. "Well, standing here won't bake the cornbread and cook the beans." She stepped back, brushing flat the front of her dress. "Will you be ready to eat in an hour?" She glanced at the three remaining oatmeal cookies and the glass of milk waiting on Donald's desk.

"Sure, Ma, I'll be hungry."

Naomi wasn't so sure, but at least she felt better about Cletus when she walked back to the house to start supper.

In his shed, Donald pulled a tablet from his desk, sharpened a pencil, took a bite of cookie and began. The words flowed so easily that he wrote for half an hour without stopping, and only then to light his kerosene lamp.

Saturday, September 14, 1918
Houston, Tex.

Dear Clara,

Thank you for your card, which arrived today. So much has happened in the last few hours, so much has changed, I hardly know where to begin.

First, let me say that I did register for the draft on Thursday a.m., as you knew I planned to do. For all the worry it has caused over the past few months, the actual thing took only minutes, and I was greatly relieved when it was done. Now I must trust fate. I expect to receive the notice to take my physical any day now. That is the next step for everyone. Whether the Army wants a soldier with eyes like mine, I do not know. I am certain that I can contribute in some way, even if it is not at the front.

Maybe it will be the same for Elton. Despite his asthma, he was accepted for military service and is due to report to Camp Logan soon. By the way, Jake let me know that he will meet Elton at the train station Sunday afternoon, and I plan to accompany him. By the time you receive this letter, he will be home.

Another big event is that Cletus will be coming home. His eyes and lungs have been damaged by nerve gas, but there is hope he will recover. I don't know the day yet, but he is coming by ship, either to Galveston or the Port of Houston.

The "change" I mentioned above came as a surprise earlier today at the home of Mrs. Carhart, where I was invited to lunch. Four of the guests were in the publishing business: two writers, one newspaper editor and one book publisher. The other guest, besides myself, was the banker who is financing a new magazine for Mr. Leonard Hoffman. You may know of him, since his New York company has printed several medical textbooks.

Mr. Hoffman is starting a new kind of magazine, one that features more photographs and fewer words. He says faster film and better lenses are making it easier to get good pictures "in the field." Those were the words he used. I like the sound of them.

When Mrs. Carhart introduced us, Mr. Hoffman's attitude was cold and his questions tough, but I knew he was testing me. When he saw that we have the same ideas about photography, he warmed considerably. We spent the rest of the time talking about how pictures should be made. "Making" pictures is another of his terms. He uses it the same way Mrs. Carhart does.

The very best thing is that Mr. Hoffman offered me a job, making pictures for his new magazine! I told him "yes" right away, but later wondered if I had made a mistake. It is not a regular paying job. That worry was completely gone after I talked to Clifford Murray. He is a writer who gave me a lift home in his car. It looks like Cliff and I will be working on magazine stories together before long.

I hate to tell Jake that I do not want the newspaper job after all.

Everything, of course, depends on the draft. Uncertainty has become the most difficult thing for me.

Well, Ma is calling me for supper, so I will end for now. I am enclosing one of the pictures I made of you on Wednesday. I hope your nursing studies go well, and that you have time to write to me soon.

All the best,
Donald Brown

"What do you mean by that?" Clarence said, dipping cornbread in the juice of the red beans on his plate. "How can you call it a job if they don't pay you regular?"

Naomi and Clarence had been grilling Donald for ten minutes, ever since he mentioned the position with Leonard Hoffman's new magazine. Donald squirmed in his seat and his neck began to ache.

"I'd be a stringer, Pa."

"Ha! A stringer is what you put fish on after you catch 'em."

"In the news business, a stringer is someone who works for a newspaper or magazine, but only when there's something to write about or photograph."

"Like part-time work?"

"You could call it that, Pa, except I'd be keeping my eyes open for news stories all the time."

Clarence shook his head and spent a few seconds with his fork, mashing cornbread into his beans.

"Don't seem right to me."

Naomi had enough of being quiet. "Papa, don't be so hard on Donny. I'm sure he knows what he's doing."

Clarence looked at his wife, but pointed toward Donald with his fork full of cornbread and beans. Juice dripped on the table as he spoke.

"The boy jus' told us he's goin' to be a part-time photographer, but to do that he's got to spend all his free time looking for things to photograph. What kind of job is that?"

"Pa, it's a great opportunity."

"Yep, an opportunity to go broke." Clarence grew quiet then, but only because his mouth was full. Naomi spoke next.

"Donny, are you sure?"

"I'm sure, Ma. And Mr. Hoffman said they'd give me assignments, too, so I don't have to find all the stories myself. He wants to publish a national magazine. If some of my pictures are in it, people all over the country will see them!"

"And how many people have subscriptions to this magazine?" Clarence was back on his horse.

"Well, nobody yet, Pa, the first issue hasn't come out."

"Hah! There you go!"

"Pa, you don't understand." The fact was, Donald didn't understand either. He only knew what he'd heard over lunch.

"Mr. Hoffman has publicity people in New York. They're advertising the new magazine, generating interest so people will look forward to the first issue. He says some folks will even buy them as keepsakes, just because it's something new."

"Then what?"

"Well, then people will see what a fine magazine it is. They'll buy them from newsstands, and if they like what they see, maybe they'll take out subscriptions."

"And then what?"

"Merchants will see that the magazine is good, and that a lot of people are reading it, so companies will buy advertising."

"And what then?" Clarence was relentless, but Donald finally saw his point.

"And then I get paid."

Back in Donald's room, uncertainty overwhelmed him once more. Was the magazine offer good? His enthusiasm had been clear. Now he had doubts. The *Chronicle* position was a sure thing: fifty dollars a month to start. In a year, he could be making sixty-five. That kind of money is hard to turn down. But forget the job; would the Army want him instead? And how much help would Naomi and Clarence need when Cletus came home?

He found a match and lit the kerosene lamp on his desk. When he slid the glass globe back over the brass clips, the harsh light cast a shadow that went from the heels of his shoes, across the floor, up the far wall and half way across the ceiling of the shed.

"Think, dear boy, think!" Mrs. Carhart said in Donald's head.

"What if my pictures are not good enough?"

"Then you will try harder!"

"But the magazine is not a sure thing. Who knows when I'll get paid? At the newspaper, I could have a paycheck in two weeks."

"Nothing in life is a sure thing, Donald. You might be in France three months from now."

"But ..."

"But what? With this war, in three months, you could be dead."

Chapter 30

Sunday, September 15, 1918

Donald played with Bosco in the yard, then finally went into the garage to talk to Clarence.

"You goin' to pick up Elton or not?" Clarence said.

"Yeah, Jake's just late."

"Seems normal for him."

"Well, he gets things done." Defending Jake was becoming automatic for Donald.

"Say, thanks for helpin' me move them magazines yesterday." Clarence pointed with a screwdriver to the crate on a shelf high above his workbench. "Your ma don't suspect a thing."

Bosco, sniffing a corner of the freshly-cleaned garage, suddenly perked his ears and ran into the yard. Donald followed, with Clarence limping behind.

Jake's hand was poised over the klaxon, but he saw Donald and Clarence first and only waved. Both of the neighbor's coon hounds stood with noses to their own picket fence, waiting, like Bosco, for the horn.

"Howdy, Clarence. Some World Series, eh?"

"Yep, sure was. I thought the Cubs had a chance this year."

Jake laughed as he flipped open the passenger side for Donald. The little half-door squeaked out as far as the hinges allowed, then bounced halfway back before Donald caught it.

"Get in, Don, we're late."

Not "Sorry, I'm late," Donald thought, but "We're late," as though Donald shared the blame. He jerked his cap down tighter on his head and settled in for the ride downtown.

Clarence waved as he turned back to the garage, but changed his mind and went into the house to find Naomi.

Donald could tell that Jake was in a good mood. "You look pleased with yourself. Did you win more money on the game?"

"Yeah, but that's not the reason. Foley told me Friday that he'll keep my job for me until I get back from the war."

"What!" Donald yelled over the engine noise and rattling car.

"Foley said he'd keep my job open ..."

"Until you get back from the war?"

"I told you I was thinking about it. I still don't like the idea of being a soldier, but with Elton going to Camp Logan in a few days and you registered for the draft, I suddenly felt like I was sitting on the bench for an important game."

"I can't believe it. What happens now?"

"Well, I explained to the draft board on Friday that my folks are better and don't need my help so much. They thanked me and were glad to cancel my deferment. They changed my status to A-Prime."

Donald laughed. "That sounds like a grade of fresh meat."

Jake turned to look at Donald, serious this time.

"It is."

The Interurban from Galveston pulled in at a quarter to six. A man and his wife were first off, followed by a nun and six acolytes with their bags. Two young women without luggage stepped down next, then stood waiting a few feet away.

"There he is," Donald said. He reached up for Elton's left arm while Jake took the right.

"Here, pal, let me help you down."

Elton looked good, Donald thought. His jaw was barely swollen, although there was still a prominent bruise. He moved gingerly down the steps, but then stood easily enough on his own.

"Jake, Don, thanks for picking me up."

The two young women inched closer, their faces framed by enormous yellow hats.

"How was your trip, El?"

"Fine, Jake, thanks to these nice ladies." Elton gestured toward the pair. Jake himself would have been pleased to know either one.

"Don, Jake, meet Idis and Laura Beckham." Both women nodded and smiled, but their attention remained on Elton.

"Are you sure you'll be all right?" Idis said, slipping her arm through Elton's. Her sister took his other arm, concern on her face as well.

Jake and Donald stepped back. Jake's mouth opened, but nothing came out. Donald asked the question for him.

"Elton, are you coming with us?"

"Uh, no. The Beckam's driver has a car outside. Laura and Idis said they'd be happy to drop me off on their way home. Sorry you made a trip for nothing."

"Elton told us about his terrible automobile accident," Laura said. "He's lucky to be alive!"

Donald smiled toward Jake, who finally found his voice.

"Yes, Elton is certainly lucky."

"Well, I'll be damned," Jake said after Donald had cranked the engine and settled into the passenger's seat. Donald shook his head and laughed, but Jake had more to say.

"Bruises and all, Elton looked more relaxed than I've ever seen him around women. Maybe all his trouble in Galveston was good for him."

"I wouldn't know, Jake. Women are your field."

Jake backed up from his angled parking spot directly into the path of a two-horse dray. The man on the wagon jerked at the reins. Jake waved "thanks" with his right hand as though the wagon had stopped to let him out. The man yelled and shook his fist, but Jake drove on.

"Me? What about you?" Jake said. "You and Clara got along fairly well."

Donald knew that protesting would only invite more teasing.

"Yeah," he said. "That was a surprise."

Jake took a detour past his rent house on Travis Street. All three tenants were paid up, so there was no need to stop. One of them, a pretty woman about Jake's age, waved from the front porch.

"Jake, who's going to watch your property if you go in the Army?"

"You suppose your folks would be interested?"

"What did you have in mind?"

"They'd keep some of the monthly rent. I'll pay for any repairs to the house and advertising if they need new tenants. Naomi could handle the business side, and Clarence could take care of maintenance."

"They'd like the extra income, especially with Cletus coming home."

"Oh?" Jake slowed the car just slightly when the brick pavement ended and they continued on a rutted dirt road. "Cletus is coming home?"

"He's badly injured. His outfit was attacked with nerve gas. He's nearly blind now and has trouble breathing."

"Sorry to hear that. Your folks must feel terrible. Clarence looked sad when I picked you up. I thought it was because the Cubs lost. How's Naomi?"

"She's taking it hard. She must have cleaned Cletus' room three times already. Now they're thinking of buying a used car, so they can take Cletus around to places he needs to go."

A mongrel dog raced into the street and ran alongside their car for a block, barking through the dust the whole time before finally giving up the chase.

"How about you, Don? What do you think?"

"I'm worried. I'll help my folks with Cletus as much as I can. I could be at Logan myself soon enough, but I suppose they'll get by all right. One of the letters said Cletus was getting stronger every day and that some of his sight had come back, so maybe he'll recover."

Jake turned onto Dennis Street about three blocks from Donald's house. He was driving slowly now, shoulders relaxed, hands together gripping the bottom of the steering wheel.

"You know, the three of us could be at Logan at the same time." Jake looked at Donald and grinned. "You think the Army can manage that?"

They rolled to a stop near the Stokes' back gate. Bosco greeted them from behind the fence and waited patiently for Donald to pull his ears. Donald remained in the car.

"Jake, there's something else."

"About Cletus?"

"No."

"Your folks?"

"No."

"Clara?"

"About the *Chronicle* job."

"Let me guess. You got a better offer and were afraid I'd be mad."

"How did you know?"

"Sixth sense. Besides, our jobs don't matter any more. With you, me and Elton maybe going to war, we've got a lot more to worry about than the newspaper business."

Chapter 31

Thursday, September 19, 1918

Naomi and Clarence dressed in their finest clothes. They took the trolley as far as the Ford dealership on Main Street and from there, visited several others. Now they both wished they knew something about motor cars.

"Yep, this here's just what you need," the man said, patting the fender of a 1915 five-passenger Ford. After looking at several used Chevrolets, Buicks and even a Packard, Naomi and Clarence were back to the Ford dealership. Every pitch was the same. Every dealer had exactly the car they needed. Their heads ached and their feet were sore, but the Stokes were determined to buy their first car.

"Tell me again," Clarence said, "how come this one's better than the '14 model we seen on the other lot?" The salesman sighed and began explaining it once more.

"Lots of reasons," he said. "Non-skid tires on the back, a magneto horn you can hear two blocks away, tapered springs front and rear, and look," he stepped in front of the radiator, "this one still has brass trim. Most car companies don't use brass any more. But the main thing is that the '15 model has electric headlights."

The salesman lifted his hand from the top of the radiator and cupped the curved back of the headlamp as though he were cradling a newborn's head. "Ain't no comparing kerosene to electric lamps. With these, you can see where you're going."

"I don't suppose we'll be driving much at night," Naomi said coolly.

Undaunted, the salesman pressed on. "Well, ma'am, then how about these seats?" He opened the passenger door and gestured with his hand at the imitation leather. "You won't find this quality in the '14 model."

Naomi got in. With the top down, there was plenty of room for her Sunday hat. She sat for a moment, adjusted her backside and declared, "The upholstery is nice, but the seat's not very comfortable." She got out again, clutching her small handbag waist-high in front of her, waiting for the salesman to respond.

Clarence was beginning to like the car, but he knew that Naomi would make the final decision, whether she said it out loud or not. Lord help us men, he thought, when women get the vote.

When the salesman appeared stumped, Naomi spoke again.

"Let me see the rear seat."

The salesman opened the rear door and helped Naomi onto the running board. She hesitated, looked around, then stepped in and sat. Her gloved hand lingered over the padding, which extended to each side for more comfort. There was plenty of leg room, and she really liked the wide metal bar on the rear of the front seat. It gave passengers something to grab onto when they climbed in back.

She gave the bar a solid tug.

"This is perfect for Cletus," she declared.

Naomi patted the seat. "Come see what you think."

Clarence climbed in beside his wife. Naomi squeezed his hand and smiled.

"We'll take it," he said.

"Excellent, sir. Will you take your car now or should I have it delivered?"

"Better deliver it," Clarence said. "Neither one of us can drive."

"This was in our box, sir." Donald handed a small card to the elderly gentleman behind the post office counter. Young Bentley, the previous clerk, had shipped out to France in the early spring. Bentley's replacement, well past retirement age, adjusted his spectacles down near the tip of his nose, tilted his head back and peered at the note in his hand.

"Mr. Brown? Yes, you received a package."

A package? He wasn't expecting anything from Sears or his photographic supplier in St. Louis. He was happy enough to find three letters in the postal box. Now a package. He fingered the envelopes. The first two were from the Army: one for Donald and one for the Stokes. The third was from Clara. He smiled, and a woman passing by smiled back.

"Here you go," the clerk said a minute later.

"Thanks."

Donald took the letters and package to a nearby table. The parcel, wrapped in brown paper and tied with twine, was also from Clara. It weighed well over a pound. He decided to wait to open it.

Whatever was in Clara's package rattled a bit, Donald thought. Why send a letter and a separate parcel? Why not stick the letter in the box and save the two-cent postage?

Bosco acted happy to see him, but ducked Donald's hand in favor of the box. Whatever was inside, the dog was interested. He followed as far as the kitchen door, then whined at being left outside. Donald tossed the rest of the mail on the table and opened Clara's letter first.

Tuesday, September 17, 1918
Galveston, Tex.

Dear Donald,

Thank you for your nice letter and lovely photograph. Since my nursing classes have resumed, I'm afraid that I have only time for a short response now, but I do have news to relay.

First, it cheered me to learn of your exciting prospect with the magazine! I know you must be happy. Even if military service interrupts your plans, it is good to know that someone as important as Leonard Hoffman is interested in your work. Yes, I do know of his company. It published two of the textbooks we are using this year.

The news from here is that, after you left last Wednesday, I searched again through Mama's collection of pictures. I was looking, of course, for any that might have been taken by the same person who photographed you as a baby. I think I have found one.

The photograph was taken at the old Galveston wharf, as it looked before the 1900 storm. The style reminds me of the picture of the man (your father?) lifting a small child. The same person is holding that child in his arms (she looks younger), and both of them are looking down at a uniformed man seated at a desk.

The print is of excellent quality, with only slight water damage to the paper along the right side. I nearly overlooked it, because it is a bit smaller than the photographs taken in the room. I chose not to enclose the new print in this letter for fear it would be lost in the mail. Please advise if you prefer that I send it to you.

Kind regards,
Clara Barnes

P.S.—I packaged some cookies for you last night and mailed them separately on my way to class this morning.

Another photograph! Donald was reading Clara's letter for the third time when he heard a car horn outside. Not Jake's this time, something new.

He wasn't prepared for the sight. Two motor cars had stopped near the back gate. The first was a shiny new Ford 2-passenger Model T. Its driver remained at the wheel.

The second Ford was an older model, shiny and black. The top was down. In the back seat, Naomi and Clarence sat like royalty. Their driver stepped from the car, walked around to Naomi's door, opened it and offered her his hand.

Clarence, dressed in his best suit and tie and wearing his bowler hat, waved at he stepped from the running board.

"Hey, Donny, look here at our new automobile."

"Don't move! Let me get a camera!" Donald ran for the shed.

Bosco stood with his paws atop of the fence, tongue out, wagging his tail. Clarence turned to his driver, thanked him, and watched as he climbed in next to the driver of the first car, which then pulled away. Even Naomi, who had no interest in machinery, looked pleased.

Donald returned with the largest of his Kodak folding cameras open and ready to use. He looked down into the viewfinder and began gesturing with his free hand.

"Step closer to me. That's good. Pa, step a little closer, and turn so that your left shoulder is closer to me. Ma, you're just fine. You look like the queen herself!"

Naomi laughed and Donald snapped the picture.

"Now, Pa, put your right hand on the door, like you were opening it for Ma."

Click.

"Yeah, go ahead and open it a bit. That's good."

Click.

"Now look at Ma like she was your lady friend."

"She is!" Clarence called back as Donald clicked again.

The three of them were laughing still when Donald held the screen door open for Naomi and Clarence. Naomi saw the letters first.

"What's that on the table?"

"We got mail. I was just reading a letter from my friend in Galveston."

"You can say her name, son," Naomi said as she opened an unmarked letter addressed to Mr. and Mrs. Stokes.

"Did Clara send them cookies too?" Clarence said, reaching for the box.

"Yeah. Try one, they're good."

"This is about Cletus," Naomi said, holding a short typewritten note on Red Cross stationery. Donald and Clarence stood silent as she read aloud.

Am. Nat. Red Cross Service Center
New York, N.Y.
September 14, 1918

Dear Mr. and Mrs. Stokes,

I am writing again to let you know that your son, Cletus, left New York September 11 on a U.S. Navy medical transport scheduled to arrive at the Port of Galveston on Sunday, September 22. All troops will be seen by doctors from John Sealy Hospital and either admitted, cleared for further transport, or released to family members. Please forgive the brevity of this note. We have so many to write and there are too few available aides. Cletus sends his love.

Cordially yours,
Willa M. Grimes,
Assist. Transport Document Coordinator

"Sunday!" Naomi said, dropping her hand and the letter to her side. "Cletus will be home in three days!" She put her hand to her mouth and walked quickly down the hall, taking the letter with her. Donald and Clarence heard the bedroom door close.

"What's wrong with Ma?" Donald said. "That sounded like good news to me."

"Things can rattle her at first," Clarence said. "She just needs time to think. By this evening she'll be herself, barkin' orders to you and me like a drill sergeant."

"You got the car just in time."

"Yep. All I got to do now is learn to drive it."

"I can help, Pa. Jake taught me last year. It's not that hard."

Clarence poured himself a glass of milk as he considered the offer.

"Mind if I have another of your lady friend's cookies?"

"She's not my lady friend, just someone I met in Galveston."

"That's not what I hear."

Before Donald could protest, Clarence saw the second envelope on the table. He pointed with his cookie hand.

"That your notice to take the physical?"

"September 30, 9:00 a.m." Donald answered. "I'm surprised it's not sooner."

"What happens next, assuming you pass?"

"If they want me, I suppose I'd get orders to go to Logan. Elton reports next week, but he's hoping for a few more days to recover from his injuries. Could be that Elton and Jake and I are there at the same time."

"I thought Jake had a deferment on account of him bein' sole support of his sick parents."

"He says they're better now. Anyway, Jake cleared it with the draft board, and he certainly won't have trouble passing the physical."

Clarence shook his head. "I told your ma that boy wasn't a slacker, no matter what folks say."

It was dark enough to turn on the electric lights in the house, and Naomi still hadn't left her room. Clarence and Donald both knew better than to disturb her about supper. They decided to forage on their own.

"Let's see, we got cheese and milk here in the icebox, Donny, what did you find?"

"Cornbread from yesterday and a box of soda crackers. Do you see any jelly in there?"

Clarence clinked the bottles of milk aside to reach the back of the icebox. "Yep, there's some strawberry jam and butter, and a jar of leftover beans."

"And we've got these cookies, Pa." Donald set the cornbread and a tin of Nabisco crackers on the table next to Clara's package.

"Then I reckon we ain't goin' to starve right away," Clarence said as he added the butter, jam, cheese and milk to the table.

"Nobody's going to starve in my kitchen," Naomi called from the hallway. You just leave those things on the table and come back in twenty minutes." She reached for her apron, which popped loudly when she flapped it in front of her. "Now, scoot! Leave me to work!"

Clarence stopped when the telephone rang, a forkful of scrambled eggs and red beans halfway to his mouth. Naomi's tea cup clinked in the saucer. Since the news about Cletus, every call made her jump.

"I'll get it," Donald said, heading down the hall.

"Hello? Yes, this is the Stokes' residence." Donald covered the mouthpiece of the wall-mounted telephone and called back to the kitchen from the hall.

"Long distance."

Clarence reached for Naomi's hand.

"Yes. No. Yes. Thank you." Donald covered the mouthpiece again.

"The operator is connecting now." Naomi squeezed her eyes shut.

"Hello? Oh! Hi! Just a second." Again, Donald's hand went to the mouthpiece, but he still held the receiver to his ear. "Clara is calling from Galveston."

Naomi breathed in relief, then her back stiffened as she said to Clarence under her breath, "That's not right, a young woman calling a man on the telephone, especially at this hour. And long distance, too!"

Clarence looked down at his pocket watch. "Eight thirty-five. At least she waited 'til the rate went down."

Donald put his hand over his right ear and pressed the receiver to his left. "Please say that again."

Clara's voice in the earpiece was tinny and strained, as if she were speaking to him through a long metal pipe.

"Donald, can you come to Galveston Saturday? It's important."

"Of course, Clara. I just need to help my folks on Sunday. Cletus is arriving on a Navy transport."

"Oh, it's good to hear that! Donald, I'll be at the wharf myself. The student nurses are helping the hospital staff. Anything I can do to assist your family ..."

The line crackled and Donald found himself looping the receiver cord over his knuckles like a length of rope. He raised his voice, although it probably didn't help.

"Clara? Clara? Thank you. Can you hear me?" The static grew momentarily louder, then the line cleared.

"Donald?"

"I'm here. You said it was important that I come to Galveston this weekend."

"Yes. The man in the photograph."

"Sorry?" The connection faded again.

"The man ... (static) ... holding a little girl ... (static) ..."

Donald strained to hear. The hallway, lit only by electric lights from the kitchen, grew darker. Donald glanced toward Naomi and Clarence, who were standing at one end, watching and worried. He turned back to the phone, almost shouting in the mouthpiece.

"Yes, Clara? The man in the photo? What about him?"

"Don..." Clara's voice cracked, but the line was clear. She drew a deep breath. "Donald, I found him."

When Naomi, Clarence and Donald returned to their meal, none of hem noticed that the scrambled eggs and red beans were cold.

"You said she found someone?"

"Yeah, Ma, that new photograph gave her the idea."

"Sounds peculiar to me," Clarence said, taking the cracker tin Naomi had left on the table. "Pass the cheese. Thanks. Sounds peculiar, someone turnin' up after eighteen years."

Clarence used his knife to cut four squares of cheese. He thoughtfully stacked four soda crackers beside them on his plate before speaking again.

"Your lady friend has a lot of gumption."

"She's not my lady friend."

Clarence smiled, but didn't press the point. "So anyhow, she shows that picture of the man holdin' a little girl to a fella at the port. Then what?" He took his first bite of cracker and cheese, then leaned back in his chair as he chewed.

"Clara recognized the old Port of Galveston, the way it looked before the 1900 storm. The photograph was taken in an area where immigrants used to register when they arrived."

"Your folks was immigrants?"

"I'm not sure. I couldn't understand everything, but a port supervisor said one man in the photo was an immigration agent, and it was October, 1899. He was certain because of a ship in the background. It was the last time that vessel was in port before it sank."

"October? Donny, that was less than three months before you were born. Did the supervisor recognize the man holding the little girl?"

"I don't know, Ma. The line got so bad after that, I couldn't understand anything Clara said."

Clarence finished the last of his red beans and sopped the juice with cornbread. He took another bite of cracker and cheese.

"Some of them immigrants had it near's bad as slaves when they come here. They borrowed money for passage, then worked years payin' it back. You figure that's how it was with your kin?"

"I don't know. That's all the information I have." Donald looked up at Clarence and Naomi. "Whoever the man is, Clara thinks she found him. She wants me to come to Galveston Saturday."

"You're going, aren't you?" Naomi said. Without looking down, she tapped her fork on the plate, even though she'd finished the last of her eggs.

"Will you be all right?"

"Pshaw, Donny, why wouldn't we?"

"I'll still be with you when Cletus comes in, and Clara has offered to help."

"Of course. Don't worry about us, we can certainly find our way to Galveston. You can meet us at the station when we get in. Go see Clara and find out what she knows about your real family."

His *real* family? Naomi wasn't worried about the trolley ride to Galveston. Donald slid his arm across the table and squeezed her hand.

"Ma, you and Pa and Cletus are my real family. Whatever Clara found in Galveston is just history."

Chapter 32

Saturday, September 21, 1918

For once, Donald woke before the rooster. Briefly, he considered finding the arrogant fowl and waking him. In a fit of foresight the night before, Donald had left his glasses where he could find them easily in the dark.

Bosco lay sideways on his blanket, legs twitching in a fitful doggy dream. When he heard bare feet on the floor, he raised his head, blinked a few times, then squeezed his eyes shut when Donald lit the kerosene lamp.

Clean pants, shirt, underwear and socks were folded neatly in the chair. Donald's new shoes, freshly polished, sat on the floor nearby. His travel bag waited by the door. The first Interurban left Union Station at 6:00 a.m., and Donald planned to be on it.

He peeked outside. The Stokes' house was still dark, but Naomi and Clarence knew he was leaving, so they'd said their goodbyes last night. He planned to meet them in Galveston Sunday morning. With any luck, Clara would know by then when the hospital ship would be in and how long it would take for Cletus to be examined and released.

Donald used a bar of soap to lather his face. He flipped open his razor and wiped the steel blade several times across his leather strop to hone the edge. With the fingers of his left hand tugging up on his cheek, Donald raised his chin, stretched his neck, lifted the razor and cut himself on the second stroke. A minute later, he did it again, this time nicking his cheek.

Donald swore quietly but clearly each time. Bosco ignored the remarks, knowing they weren't aimed at him. Seconds later, the screen door creaked.

"Where'd you learn to talk like that?" Donald turned to see Clarence peeking through the screen. Behind him, the kitchen lights were on.

"Morning, Pa." Donald turned back to the hand mirror hanging by a nail on the wall. "I thought you weren't getting up until after I left."

"Your ma had different ideas. She's in there now making coffee and something for you to eat on the train." Clarence stepped into the shed, squatted for a moment to scratch Bosco's head, then steadied himself on the end of the bed to stand up.

"Oof! That's getting' harder to do each year." Clarence rubbed his knees. "Reckon I'll need a cane afore long."

"You're tough as a boot."

"Boots wear out, you know."

Donald rinsed the last of the soap from his face, trying hard not to get blood on the towel. He studied the little mirror, first turning his neck, then his cheek and upper lip to survey the damage. He fished a scrap of tissue paper from the drawer, tore off three small tabs and stuck them over his wounds. Blood stuck the paper to his skin.

"Looks like you come up two bits short in a knife fight," Clarence said. "Got your bag packed?"

"I'm not taking much, since we'll be back Sunday night." Donald looked over to Clarence, who had settled into a chair by the door, rubbing the top of his leg. Not like him, Donald thought.

"You all right, Pa?"

"I'm fine. I was jus' wonderin' about the car."

"The car?"

"How hard you figure it'd be to drive down to Galveston instead of takin' the train?"

Donald turned from the mirror to face Clarence. "Don't try it, Pa! Driving a motor car is different from driving a buggy."

"Folks at the Ford dealer says it's easier. At least a car will go where you point it and stop when you want. They showed me how to start the engine and where to put the gas and oil. I even drove 'round their parkin' lot with the salesman while your ma waited in the office. Didn't hit a thing. Drivin' ain't so hard."

"You'll be a fine driver before long, but please don't take your car to Galveston tomorrow."

"Donny?" Naomi called from across the yard. "Donny? Don't leave yet. I've got something for you to take."

Donald walked to the screen door, raising his voice for Naomi to hear. "Just a minute!" He turned back to Clarence. "Promise me you won't."

"All right! All right," Clarence said, raising his hand in defeat as he unfolded stiffly from the chair. "Thunder, you'd think that Ford was a damn steam locomotive! I seen women drivin' the things, but all right, I reckon I can wait a few days to get some lessons."

"Donny?"

"Coming, Ma."

In the kitchen, Donald slipped Naomi's sandwich bag into his duffel. He wrapped an extra shirt around the coffee thermos and put it next to his folding camera, journal and pouch of unexposed film.

"Is that one of Nina Carhart's books?" Naomi asked, pointing to the red one.

"No, that's from Clara's library. *Cyrano* is a play about a soldier who loved a beautiful lady, but never told her because he had a funny nose and was afraid she'd turn him down."

"You done read it?" Clarence asked.

"Finished last night. I may read it again on the way to Galveston."

Naomi left the kitchen briefly and returned with a small but elegant envelope she'd closed the old fashioned way, with a dribble of red wax and her initials pressed into it while the wax was still hot. The seal had been a gift from Clarence, and Naomi saved it for special correspondence.

"What's this, Ma?"

"A note for Clara. Just give it to her when you get there."

"You don't even know her."

"That doesn't matter. Just give her the note, and don't open it first."

He hesitated, so Naomi pressed on.

"Donny, your friend offered to help with something that's very important to us. I just want to tell her how much we appreciate it, and that we look forward to meeting her."

Donald watched the sun rise over the prairie south of Houston as the Interurban made its way toward Galveston. The car was surprisingly full, but many of the passengers were trying to sleep.

Too alert to doze, Donald fished his duffel for Clara's book. He slipped off his glasses, put the open page almost to his nose and began to read. A minute later, he was in Paris in 1640, with Cyrano, sword drawn, confronting a rival.

The 21st Street depot was alive with businessmen and tourists when the car pulled in. Soon the trolley would reload, possibly adding a second car, and of the many people now waiting on the platform would be on their way to Houston.

Donald slipped Clara's letter between the pages of *Cyrano* to mark his place, then searched his shirt and jacket pockets for his glasses.

They were gone.

He stood too quickly and bumped a fellow traveler trying to retrieve his satchel from the overhead rack.

"Careful there!"

"Sorry, sorry."

Donald had only minutes. He jammed his hands in his side pockets and again came up empty. He squinted at the seat, patting his hand back and forth across the leather several times without luck. Most passengers had left the car when a kindly, high-pitched voice behind him spoke up.

"Look there, sir, just beneath your seat."

Donald squinted and saw only the shape of a slender young woman, dressed in white.

"Thank you, Miss."

Donald got to his knees and began patting the floor. Nothing. He bent farther over and looked for himself. Finally a bit of sunlight caught the edge of a lens, and he was relieved to find his glasses were none the worse for having spent most of the trip on the floor. He slipped the loops behind his ears, settled the heavy lenses on his nose, then stood to face his helper. She wasn't so young after all, but behind her own thick lenses, her green eyes sparkled.

"Thank you again," Donald said, touching his cap.

"I understand completely, young man." Donald returned her wide, sweet smile.

"I was beginning to get nervous!" he said.

"And I was delighted to help." She touched her elegant white hair.

"Besides, it has been a very long time since anyone called me *Miss*."

Donald checked his pocket watch against the station clock. Seven fifty-five. Plenty of time before meeting Clara at noon. He needed to get his bearings and wanted time to think.

A man reading a newspaper caught his attention. He had the bearing of a soldier, but dressed in civilian clothes.

"Excuse me, sir, is there a city park nearby?"

The newspaper dropped to the man's lap. Donald jerked back. What he saw resembled a face, but it was not the face of a man. The left half, including the entire nose and chin, was a mask. A very good mask, Donald thought, and like nothing he'd ever seen. It was expertly painted to resemble flesh. Spectacles without lenses looped behind the man's ears to help hold the device in place.

"Yes?" the mask said.

"A … a park, sir. Do you know if there's a public park nearby?" Donald had grown up being the butt of jokes. He knew the startled looks of strangers. Now he feared how his own reaction must appear. Still, he could not stop.

"I'm sorry to have bothered you, sir."

"No trouble. A park you say? Well, the closest is Central Park, just over there, about two blocks." He pointed with his cane. The mask spoke clearly enough, but the painted mouth didn't move. The sound it made was muffled only a bit.

The man's good eye focused on Donald, who was growing more curious than shocked. The mask was beautiful in its way, clearly crafted by an artist with love and great skill.

"I'm sorry to stare at you, sir,"

"I'm used to it now." The man lifted his newspaper, flipped it twice to straighten the pages, then resumed reading.

"Sir?"

The masked man put his newspaper down slowly. The painted eye showed no annoyance, but the working one did.

"Yes?"

"May I ask you, sir, about your …"

"My mask? Good God! Most people aren't so direct!"

"I don't mean to be rude, not in the least, sir." Donald heard his own words as if listening to someone else.

"What, then?" the stranger said with growing impatience. Donald looked side to side, then back. No one was close. Why had he spoken at all? When he saw the poor fellow's condition, why couldn't he just look away, or if he must talk, then pretend not to notice the mask?

Donald remained rooted to the spot, silent, staring, and waiting to hear what, if anything, would come from his own mouth next. Finally, something did.

"I'm a journalist, sir. Your mask fascinates me."

"Ha! Now you're mocking me?"

"No, sir! I am not making fun. I suspect that you've been injured in battle. I've heard of wounded soldiers fitted with masks, but never expected that they were so masterfully made."

The man's good eye softened and his shoulders relaxed. Donald guessed him to be about thirty, although he sounded much older. He'd been handsome, too, judging from what remained of his face.

"A journalist, you say? What newspaper?"

"Not a newspaper, a magazine. A whole new type of magazine, in fact, with shorter stories and more photographs than words."

Again, the man grew tense. He tightened the grip on his newspaper until half of it was just a wad in his hand. He barely contained his rage.

"Is your magazine a *freak show*?"

"Not at all! Nothing like that, sir!" Donald half expected a blow from the man's cane. He felt the strap of his duffel digging into his shoulder and shifted it to the other side.

"The publisher is Leonard Hoffman. He prints books of all kinds; important texts and references."

"I know his books. I was a teacher before the war. Go on."

The former soldier released the grip on his ruined newspaper and let it fall beside him on the bench. Donald continued, recalling Hoffman's enthusiasm when he described the project over lunch.

"The magazine—he hasn't named it yet—will tell stories with photographs. Some people call them 'photographic essays,' but the idea is to cover important subjects, respectfully, accurately and without bias."

"And you think my mask is something people want to know about?"

"I think it is something people *need* to know about, sir. Newspapers talk of war like they are reporting a football match, with a winning team and a losing team and people cheering from the stands."

The wounded soldier held up his hand wearily. "Believe me, it's much more than that."

"I know!" Donald didn't mean to raise his voice. Now he lowered it again. "At least, sir, that's what I am coming to know. I think most civilians don't understand the terrible sacrifice soldiers make. We buy war bonds. We sing war songs and plant victory gardens, but all we really see of war are the posters and flags and parades. Someone needs to tell the whole truth."

"Son?"

"Yes, sir?"

"Have a seat."

Chapter 33

Clara said to wait for her at the front entrance of Sealy Hospital. A light rain had begun, so Donald climbed the steps to the second floor entrance and took shelter under the tall portico. The base of the concrete arch was damp and cool to his touch. Only after he laid his duffel in a dry corner and leaned back against the side wall did Donald recognize where he was. It came like an electric shock.

> *... Saturday, upon returning to the hospital from the restaurant, I was standing at the entrance pouring water from my boots when a woman clutching a baby rushed by me through the door. I followed and found her pleading with a nurse ...*

Donald looked down at his own wet boots. Was this where the doctor stood? Are those the steps the frightened woman climbed with me in her arms? He pushed open the heavy doors and stepped into the hospital lobby, still hearing the doctor's words to his wife.

> *... The poor woman's clothes were soaked through. ... She was sobbing, trying to explain that she had been caught out when the street cars stopped running ... another child nearby ... she could no longer manage the rising water with a baby in hand. Would the nurse please keep him until she returned?*

"Until she returned," the woman had said. But she did not return. So this is the place, Donald thought. He stood motionless, fighting tears. He felt a gentle hand on his back.

"I didn't think, when I asked you to meet me here."

He turned to find Clara, her hand now touching his shoulder.

"Donald, are you all right?"

"Hello, Clara."

"Is this where you were left on the day of the storm?"

"Yes. I didn't realize it until just now." Still troubled, he looked around. "It's smaller than I imagined."

Clara laughed. "And you were much smaller the last time you were here!"

"You're in uniform," was all he could think to say.

"All the student nurses wear the same smocks and caps. Next year I'll get my proper uniform."

"Clara?"

"Yes?"

"It seems longer than ten days since I saw you."

"Did you get the cookies I sent?"

He laughed. "They were a great help. I couldn't have survived this long without them."

Donald and Clara almost touched hands, but stopped when they saw a pair of grim-faced matrons glaring from behind the reception desk.

"Where's your bag?"

"By the entrance."

Donald held the door as Clara stepped out under the portico. He retrieved his duffel from the corner, hoisted the strap over his shoulder and glanced to the clearing sky.

"The rain has stopped. Let's find somewhere to eat. I'm anxious to hear what you know about the man in the picture. The telephone connection wasn't clear."

Clara smiled and took his arm as they stepped down toward the street.

The restaurant she suggested was two blocks away. As they drew close, Donald wondered if this, too, could be the place mentioned in the doctor's letter. Was this where he ate his last meal before the storm?

"The light's better near the window," Clara suggested. Donald held her chair, then sat across from her. Curtains over the lower panes shaded the table from glare, leaving the upper windows framing the sky.

"Did you bring the photograph?"

"Of course." Clara opened the handbag in her lap, but a waiter appeared before she could hand over the print. On his suggestion, they ordered the Saturday lunch special: breaded speckled trout with fresh vegetables.

"Here," Clara said when the young man had gone. Donald took the envelope, lifted the flap and removed the print.

It was just as Clara described on the telephone. A man holding a child was talking to an immigration agent who was seated at a table. In the background, a harbor. It could have been a boring photograph, but it was not. There was a sense of action, even though the man was standing still. There was tension between the two men, and restlessness in the child. The photographer had captured it all in one shot.

Clara leaned forward when she spoke.

"See, the print is not mounted on cardboard like the other three. That's why I overlooked it the first time I went through Mama's collection."

Donald removed his glasses, set them on the table and raised the photograph near the tip of his nose.

"I also brought the picture of the man lifting the little girl," Clara said, handing over the print.

Donald held the second print next to the first and flicked his eyes back and forth between them. "Thanks, Clara. You're right, there's a similar style to the photographs, and this may be the same man in both. His face is turned a little too far to … "

"Your bread," the waiter said, placing a basket between them on the table.

"Thank you," Clara said, leaning back.

Donald looked briefly toward the waiter, then resumed studying the prints.

"Anyway, the man's face is turned a little too far to be sure it is the same one, but the …"

"And your salads," the waiter said, placing small plates of greens first in front of Clara and then Donald, who had to move his elbows to make room.

"Thank you," Clara and Donald both said at the same time.

Donald waited to see if there was anything more, but the waiter had gone to another table. Donald couldn't be sure without his glasses, but he could see that Clara held her napkin to her mouth. He suspected she was hiding a smile.

"Clara," he said, once more looking at the print, "you found this man? Did you meet him yourself?"

"No, but I talked to someone who recognized him."

"Who?"

"An Anglican priest."

Donald dropped his hand and the photo to the table, but did not replace his glasses before looking up.

"A priest?"

"An Anglican priest. Church of England. I thought about how the man in the photograph was dressed and the way he trimmed his moustache. And look here." She pointed to the print. "See the walking cane draped over one arm? Very British."

Donald raised the print back near the tip of his nose.

"But why the Church of England?"

"Just a guess. Immigrants look for familiar things when they come to a new country. If this man did come from England, he was most likely Anglican and might have joined a local church. There were two in Galveston in 1900. At the second one I visited, an older priest took one look and recognized the man as a member of his congregation. He'd been coming to the same church for the last eighteen years."

"Did he mention a family? A wife or daughter?"

"No, the priest said he keeps to himself, and always comes to church alone."

Donald placed the photos on the table. He slipped his glasses back on so he could see Clara's face. He wanted to touch her hand, but held back.

"Have you spoken to him?"

"Only by telephone."

"How did he sound?"

"Skeptical."

Clara took a bite of her salad. Donald hadn't touched his. "You told him that you had a photograph of me?"

"I told him I had a photograph of Donald Brown as a baby, and I thought that the two of you might be related." She cut a slice from the quarter baguette the waiter had left on the table. Donald did the same for himself.

"He wouldn't recognize my name. The nurses at Sealy called me Donald."

"That's what he said, that he didn't know anyone named Donald Brown."

"But his last name is Brown?"

"No, it's Payne, Geoffrey Payne."

"Was he excited at all?"

"I thought he would be, but it was odd. He was reserved. I don't think he believed me."

"Did you ask if he'd lost anyone in the storm?"

"He said yes, but nothing more. I think it made him suspicious that I wanted to know."

"Where does he live?"

"He didn't say."

"But you asked if we could meet?"

"Yes. At first he refused. Finally, I convinced him that the two of you should at least see each other once. He softened a bit and agreed to meet us in Central Park at three o'clock today."

"Today." Donald slid his fork under a leaf of lettuce.

Clara's fork clattered into her plate. He looked up, surprised to see the beginning of tears. She drew a sharp breath and covered her face with both hands.

"What is it, Clara? Did I say something wrong?" She shook her head but didn't speak. Seconds passed before she put one hand on the table and eased it forward. Donald did the same until their fingertips touched.

"Oh, Donald. I was so *sure* at first, so excited! I called you as soon as I got home from talking to the priest. When I reached Mr. Payne the next day, I thought he would be overjoyed to hear that someone he thought was lost had survived the storm. I wasn't prepared for his reaction. You warned me not to assume things. I wish I had listened."

Clara withdrew her hand and reached into her bag for a handkerchief. More than anything, Donald ached to comfort her.

"At least he agreed to meet us, Clara. That's something."

"Yes. I'm sorry." She dabbed her eyes, then continued. "I'm sorry," she said again, struggling for the right words, "sorry that it's not different. I don't know if this man is related to you, I just wanted it to be true. It had to be true. I couldn't believe my luck when the old priest recognized Mr. Payne. We may just be bothering some man who'd rather be left alone. I was expecting too much." She looked down, holding the handkerchief to her nose.

This time Donald took Clara's free hand in his own and held it tight. He waited a moment for her to recover.

"Clara? Look at me. Clara? Listen. This is extraordinary what you've done. However it turns out, I will never forget how much you're trying to help. That means more to me than discovering my whole family tree."

Chapter 34

The sunshine felt good on their faces. Only a few damp spots lingered on the sidewalk to remind them of the brief midday rain.

"The park is less than a mile, and we have to walk past my house. You can leave your bag on the way."

"That's a relief, I'm tired of lugging this around." Donald grinned as he tugged at the duffel strap and slung it over his shoulder.

Clara's street looked familiar; Donald was learning the lay of the town. Galveston was beginning to feel like home.

His home.

"No one has your room in the carriage house this weekend," Clara said as they crunched up the shell driveway between her bungalow and the guest house next door. Clara waited under the arbor while Donald put his bag away. She was surprised at the look on his face when he returned.

"Are you all right?"

"Sure."

"You look pale."

Donald wiped his jaw with one hand. He adjusted his cap.

"Are you nervous, Donald? Do you need to sit? We have time."

"No, let's go."

"I was here two hours ago," Donald said as they walked down one of the park's wide paths that led toward a monument in the center. "I sat with a man on that bench, right over there." He pointed to Clara's left.

"I didn't know you had other acquaintances in Galveston."

"I didn't until this morning. We met at the trolley station."

"Do you often strike up conversations with strangers?"

Donald laughed. "I guess I do, but this man needed to talk."

He stopped walking. He thought of the soldier's mask, and how his face looked without it. He shuddered, closed his eyes and drew a deep breath. He let it out slowly, remembering every scar.

Clara pressed his arm to her side.

"Donald?"

He opened his eyes.

"Donald, what is it?

"Too many things at once."

They walked on.

"Look, Donald," Clara said a moment later, "is that him, near the monument?"

Ahead, a lone man sat in a wheelchair, legs covered by a red plaid blanket. Donald asked Clara for the photographs she'd brought. He stepped from the center of the path into the shade of a tree. Clara looked again at the two prints in Donald's hands, then away toward the wheelchair and back.

"It could be," she said.

Donald recognized the walrus moustache, although it was now white. Eighteen years will do that, he thought. The man was heavier, too, and he wore a bowler hat.

"The poor fellow," Clara said, "sitting there alone." She heard Donald breathing deeper and turned to face him straight on.

"Ready?"

"Give me a minute. This is harder than I expected."

Clara's forehead wrinkled, then relaxed. "I think I know," she said. "You're right to be worried."

"Clara, I don't ..."

"No, let me finish." She put her fingertips on Donald's arm.

"This man we're about to see is probably no one you ever knew. Our meeting could be over in a minute. But maybe not. If he is really a relative of yours, or knows someone who is, then things will change for you." She stopped and looked up into his eyes before continuing.

"Donald, you're opening a door without knowing what's on the other side. A few minutes from now, for better or worse, your life could be very different."

Donald looked to the distance, drawing another deep breath. He exhaled slowly, looked back to Clara and forced a smile.

"Either way, I've got to know."

Clara took Donald's arm and spoke first when they reached the wheelchair.

"Mr. Payne?"

"Humph," the man snorted as he scowled briefly at Clara. He spent a few seconds longer on Donald.

"Mr. Payne? I'm Clara Barnes. We spoke yesterday by telephone."

"I remember."

"This is the young man I wanted you to meet. Donald, this is Mr. Geoffrey Payne."

Donald offered his hand. The man in the wheelchair released it as quickly as he might the handle of a hot pan.

"Pleased to meet you, sir."

"Humph."

"Mr. Payne," Clara said, "We don't wish to waste your time, but if you have a moment, perhaps we could move to that table."

"Let's get on with it," Geoffrey said, dropping his hands to the side wheels.

"Let me help you, sir," Donald said, reaching for the back of the chair.

"I am perfectly capable of moving this confounded thing myself!"

Donald backed away as Geoffrey Payne struggled to roll across the damp grass. The chair's thin rubber wheels dug shallow groves in the soil, but the man was surprisingly strong. He stopped at one end of a park table, locked the wheels in place and slumped forward, hands clenched in his lap.

"Here we are, then," he said stiffly. "I'm listening."

"Mr. Payne," Donald began, "I lost my parents in the 1900 storm. I have no idea who they were, but I think you might."

"You say your name is Brown?" Payne stared straight ahead as if he were talking from behind a closed door. "Brown's common enough. What makes you think I know anything about you?"

"We have a photograph, sir." He nodded to Clara, who reached for her handbag. A rubber ball rolled near Donald's side of the table. He retrieved it and tossed it back to a clutch of boys playing nearby.

"A photograph?"

"Yes, sir. A photograph of a man who looks like you, sitting in a chair and lifting a little girl in the air."

"Let me see!" It was the first sign of interest.

Clara handed him the print. Geoffrey Payne clutched it with both hands. He stared long enough for the sound of children to fill the air. He lightly touched the image of the girl before he spoke.

"Gracie."

He said the name softly, then his voice and eyes hardened again.

"Where did you get this?" He looked suspiciously at Donald, but Clara answered for him.

"A friend of my mother's found it a few days after the storm, Mr. Payne."

Geoffrey turned to face Clara.

"Where?"

"In the ruins of a house, upstairs, between some books that were still on a shelf."

"Good Lord," Geoffrey said, his defense breached. He struggled, like a fighter reeling from a good punch.

"I haven't seen this photograph in eighteen years, but this doesn't prove who you are. What makes you ..."

"We have another photograph, sir, taken in the same room."

Geoffrey's hand trembled as he took it from her.

"Wesley!" he cried, then covered his mouth with the back of his hand. Tears formed in the corners of his eyes.

"Wesley?" Donald asked.

"Of course! This is Wesley Brown, a dear, sweet child who died in the storm. Oh, God, the memory still hurts. Wesley and his mother, both lost the same day!"

"Was her name Maude?" Clara asked. Geoffrey flinched as if she had poked him with a stick.

"Yes, how did you know?"

"I have another photograph just like this one, sir," Donald said.

"Mine has writing on the front."

"What writing?"

"The words 'Maude Brown's baby' are in pencil across the bottom of the card."

Geoffrey Payne leaned forward, both hands flat on the table as Donald continued.

"A woman was forced to leave me with a nurse at John Sealy Hospital in the early afternoon of September 8, 1900. A physician on duty wrote a letter to his wife and described to her what happened. I have the letter."

"The day of the Great Storm?"

"Yes, sir."

Geoffrey's hand shot across the table to Donald's arm. "You are Wesley Brown?" His eyes went wide, searching for anything familiar in Donald's face. Geoffrey had looked frail, sitting alone in his wheelchair. Now the hand on Donald's arm had a young man's grip.

"The nurses at Sealy didn't know my name, sir, so they called me Donald."

"This can't be! I thought Wesley—I thought you—died long ago!"

Clara had seen the uniformed man when they arrived. He was alone, and had not moved from a bench on the far side of the path. He was watching them still, out of earshot, but intent on Donald's conversation with Mr. Payne. Clara, struggling to keep her own joy and relief in check, looked back to the table. Geoffrey's questions tumbled out.

"An orphanage in Houston? You grew up there?"

"Only until the age of twelve, sir."

"No! What then?"

"I was taken in by Naomi and Clarence Stokes."

"Good people, I hope?"

"Yes, sir, the best."

"Thank God."

Geoffrey dropped back in his chair. A leaf fell onto his lap blanket, but he didn't notice. In the stillness, Donald felt his strength slip away. Simply talking was an effort. He glanced at Clara, who was dabbing her eyes with a handkerchief. He turned back to Geoffrey.

"Sir, did you know my parents?"

Geoffrey sighed, looking off in the distance. "Yes, Donald, your mother was a dear friend."

"And my father?"

"A fine chap, although I didn't know him well."

"Then please tell me about my mother. What was she like?"

Geoffrey looked at Donald, again studying his face. He leaned closer.

"You have her hair, I'd say, and the shape of her chin. Take off your glasses, please."

Donald slipped them off, but held them in one hand.

Geoffrey moved his head back and forth several times. "Different eyes, I think."

"Sir, I mean, what was my mother like as a person?"

"Ah! Of course." Geoffrey settled back. "Your mother was a lovely girl, cheerful and bright. She was the sister I never had."

Donald exhaled slowly as Geoffrey continued.

"I can't remember a time when I didn't know Maude. Her parents and mine were close friends. Our fathers met in boarding school. Maude and I were the same age and inseparable as children. It was a sad day indeed when we both went away to different schools. That's why I was so happy when she eventually came to live with us, even under the circumstances."

"Sir?"

Geoffrey looked trapped. A male grackle landed on the far end of the picnic table, his black feathers iridescent green in the sun. Mouth open, the bird jerked his head, demanding a handout. Finding none, he flew on.

Clara and Donald exchanged glances.

"What circumstances, Mr. Payne?" she asked.

Geoffrey looked at Clara, turned to Donald, cleared his throat and continued.

"Wesley—I mean Donald—your mother was what some people call a free spirit."

"Sir?"

"Maude loved life, and she was loved by her parents and mine, but she did not share their views about … about marriage."

"Oh!" Clara said, suddenly understanding.

"My mother did not marry?"

"Not exactly. Your mother was unmarried at the time your sister was conceived. Maude simply announced it one day over dinner, casually, as if she meant to say a package was coming in the post. My brother and I were not surprised. Maude was twenty-three at the time, and quite familiar with the facts of life."

"My sister," Donald repeated slowly. "What year was that, sir?"

"Let's see, Maude graduated from college in '96, so that would have been the spring of 1897 when she let her family know."

"College? My mother graduated from college?" Donald saw Clara smile, as if Mr. Payne confirmed what she already knew.

"Yes, we all did," he continued. "Of course, it was easier for us men to get into university. My brother and I attended Harrow, and Maude went to Bedford."

"What did she study?" Clara asked suddenly.

"Literature and philosophy, but photography was her passion."

"Photography!" Donald gripped the front of the bench. Slowly he began to rock, bearing most of the weight on his arms.

Clara reached into her handbag and pulled out a third card.

Donald's hand shook as he took the card from Clara and passed it to Geoffrey.

"Is this my mother?"

Again, Geoffrey's eyes moistened as he touched the surface of the print. "Yes, Donald, this dear lady is your mother." He coughed, then cleared his throat. He handed the card back to Donald, then looked away to a group of five young boys engaged in a rough game of keep-away with someone's cap. He seemed to draw strength from their play. With his finger, he tapped the card in Donald's hand.

"I took the picture myself after she adjusted the camera so that all I had to do was squeeze the bulb. I'm afraid I'm not a photographer. She was a delightful person, but sadly, this picture doesn't show it."

Wind loosened more gold and red leaves from the trees, and several tumbled across the table. Donald covered the prints with his hand to keep them from blowing away. He searched Geoffrey's eyes. No longer hard, they belonged to a kind and gentle man who lived with a great deal of pain. Donald leaned closer. He struggled silently for words, and then heard them as if he and Mrs. Carhart were speaking as one.

"Mr. Payne, I am very grateful to your family for helping my mother."

Geoffrey sighed, adjusted himself in his wheelchair, then continued his story.

"But of course. You see, the Lancasters, your dear grandparents, were devastated when they learned that Maude was expecting. They truly loved Maude, but they could not bear the disgrace. Your grandfather had worked himself up through the ranks until he finally ran the London office of my father's shipping company. For their daughter to have a child without the benefit of a husband would have ruined the Lancasters socially."

"But Mr. Payne, you implied that Donald's mother did marry."

"Right you are, Clara. She married straight away. The father's name was William Brown, a young soldier she met while on a photographic trip to Scotland. As soon as she wrote to him that she was with child, he sent for her and they married in Aberdeen. She took his name, of course, and Maude Lancaster became Mrs. William Brown."

"My father was a soldier?"

"Yes. Captain Brown was a fine soldier, but he had to serve in places where your mother, especially while she was carrying Grace, could not join him."

"Sir ..."

Geoffrey held up his hand.

"My family had an estate near Liverpool. It was much easier for Maude to live quietly with us in the country during her pregnancy. It would have been impossible to keep the secret from neighbors if she had remained with her parents in London."

Clara watched Donald. He wouldn't look at her directly. He rocked again on his hands, eyes down to the photographs on the table. He finally spoke, too softly to hear.

"Did you like him?"

Geoffrey leaned closer. "Say again, please?"

Donald looked up.

"Did you like my father?"

"Ah. Captain Brown seemed a splendid fellow to me, and it was clear that he loved your mother, but his military career took him away. Maude continued living with us long after Grace was born, and Captain Brown visited whenever he could."

Wind lifted the back of Clara's straw hat. She caught it with one hand and asked the next question as she worked to pin it back in place.

"Was he able to visit frequently, Mr. Payne?"

"Not enough for Maude. The last time any of us saw Captain Brown was in the spring of 1899, just before he left for South Africa."

"The last time?" Donald asked, fearing Geoffrey's next words.

"Yes, Captain Brown served with the Second Battalion of the Black Watch. He was wounded in a skirmish with Boer commandos and later died from the infection. When Maude got the news, she was already expecting her second child."

"Me?"

"You."

Donald took a sharp breath and looked up through the trees. He laid his cap on the table and drug his fingers through his hair, pulling hard at the roots as if drawing thoughts directly from his brain. After years in the dark, the flood of news was hard to absorb. He exhaled slowly before looking back at Geoffrey Payne.

"What happened after my sister was born?"

"Grace was a lovely child, but sickly. We were all happily surprised when she improved and finally learned to walk."

Geoffrey answered the unspoken question in Donald's eyes.

"Donald, I lost Gracie in the yellow fever outbreak of 1903. There's a little stone marker in the cemetery on Broadway. It took me years to recover my balance."

Donald leaned forward on his elbows, momentarily resting his face in his cupped hands. To Clara, he seemed to be trying to slow his breathing. Geoffrey slumped deeper into the wheelchair. Clara broke the silence.

"Mr. Payne, why did you leave England?"

Donald looked up as Geoffrey paused, then answered.

"It was expected that I should go. My older brother was in line to inherit the estate and family business, so it was my duty, as the younger sibling, to leave."

"Expected?" Donald said. "Were you forced out?" He thought how his words sounded and quickly added, "Forgive me for such a personal question."

"Not at all. I assure you, leaving was entirely my decision. My family would have backed me either way."

"But why did my mother come with you?"

"She could have stayed in England with Grace. My family's estate was a fine place to raise her child, but with a second baby on the way and the recent agony of losing her husband, Maude wanted to get away."

"So you invited her …"

"Of course. I was already planning to come here, you see, so I asked your mother to join me." Geoffrey beamed at Donald and Clara.

"And that is why Wesley—pardon me again—that is why Donald was born on Galveston island, and not at my family home in England." Geoffrey patted Clara's hand. "And to think that Clara was able to deduce so much from Maude's photograph of us at the wharf!" He patted her hand again, then remembered something important.

"Look," Geoffrey reached for the picture of Donald, turned it over and tapped with one finger. "See, I was the one who wrote your birth date on the back."

Clara glanced back across the park to the man in the grey tunic, tall boots and military cap. He was standing now, feet spread, jodhpurs flared and arms crossed over his chest.

She turned to Geoffrey. "Mr. Payne, when I learned you might have been an immigrant, I thought of the poor people we see in pictures, huddled in steerage, longing for a fresh start in this country. But now I think the passage may have been easier for you."

Geoffrey laughed so loud and hard that Clara and Donald both jumped. It was enough to bring the man in uniform trotting toward their table. Geoffrey, still laughing, reached again for Clara's hand.

"No, dear, the passage was not difficult for us at all. My father owned the ship!"

Chapter 35

"Is everything all right, sir?"

"Yes, Clayton, please bring the car around now."

"Yes, sir!" Clayton touched the bill of his cap, wheeled on his boot and trotted away as quickly as he'd come.

"Now then, if you two have time for a short trip, there is something I would like very much for you to see."

Clara spoke for both of them. "Yes, of course, we'd like to go."

Donald seemed unable to move until Geoffrey turned and beckoned with a gentle wave. Suddenly energized, Donald rose from the table, stretched both arms and stepped into place behind Geoffrey's wheelchair. He lifted the handles and leaned into the task.

Clayton held the rear door of the car open as Geoffrey stood from his chair, walked the last few steps with the help of his cane and climbed in. The driver took the wheelchair around to the back, where he strapped it to a sturdy rack.

"Wesl ... Donald, would you mind riding up front with Clayton? With this leg, I need extra room to get in and out."

"Of course, sir." Donald waited as Clayton held the door for Clara to get in back with Geoffrey, then reached for the handle of the right front door.

"Other side, sir," Clayton said. "This car is British."

Donald walked around and climbed into the front seat. Clayton sat to his right behind the wheel. Donald touched the wood trim, which was finished as well as any piece of furniture he'd ever seen. Not even Mrs. Carhart's Cadillac was this fine. Every gauge had brass fittings. The cherry wood steering wheel was polished to a mirror shine. A small golden figure of a woman with angel's wings graced the far end of the hood.

"What is this?" Donald asked as Clayton engaged the car's electric starter. The engine caught immediately and ran quietly enough for their conversation to continue in a normal voice. Donald touched the firewall, but there was almost no vibration. Clayton smiled.

"This, sir, is a Rolls Royce, the finest motor car in the world."

"I've never seen one before."

"Are you asking about the car, Donald?"

The glass partition that normally separated the driver from the passengers was open. Clara and Mr. Payne looked as if they were resting in a comfortable parlor, with huge glass windows to either side, and a handsome oval porthole of beveled glass on the rear wall behind them.

"My father sent this three years ago as a birthday gift. A complete surprise, I should say. Clayton came with the car. He is a superb driver and a Rolls Royce mechanic to boot. Clayton, do tell Donald about yourself."

"Nine years building these cars before joining Mr. Payne's employ," Clayton said as he accelerated onto Broadway. Several pedestrians stopped to watch the massive Rolls Royce go by.

"I also designed some of the components that are now standard on this model. Mr. Royce himself hired me in 1906, and gave me this gold watch when I left." Clayton patted his pocket and the smart gold chain that looped out to a button on his uniform.

"Why did you leave?" Donald asked, then worried if he was prying.

"Ever since I was a lad in Manchester, I wanted to come to America. This was my opportunity, and besides, Mr. Payne pays better than Mr. Royce." Donald heard Geoffrey laugh from the back seat.

Clayton guided the Rolls smoothly up a long circular driveway. A ragged double row of oleanders lined the path, which was laid in a herringbone pattern with alternating shades of brick.

"Clayton," Geoffrey called from the back, "please ask the gardener to look after these oleanders; they need trimming."

"Yes, sir."

Donald noticed Clayton's lingering smile.

Clayton stopped the Rolls in front of a white marble landing that was as wide as the car was long. He held the door for Clara and Geoffrey, then moved to help his employer up the steps. Donald opened his own door and stepped around the back of the car toward Clayton.

"If you walk about, sir, mind the peacocks." Clayton glanced back at Donald. He nodded his head toward several large birds strutting near the gazebo. "They bite."

"A glass of sherry, my dear?" Geoffrey was standing now, leaning heavily on his cane. He motioned Clara and Donald into the drawing room, then crossed to its well-stocked bar.

"Yes, thank you," Clara said.

"And Donald, how about you?"

"I'll have whatever you're having, sir," Donald said, instantly fearing a mistake, but not enough to take it back. Geoffrey nodded solemnly and began pouring their drinks.

"What a beautiful room," Clara said, slowly turning to take it all in.

"What do you call that, sir, when the center of the ceiling is missing and you can see to the second floor?" Donald asked.

"That's a mezzanine. It allows light from the second story windows to illuminate the drawing room."

Donald's eyes followed the railing all the way around the upper floor. "It's like having a balcony all around."

The room was filled with interesting objects. While Geoffrey mixed their drinks, Donald was drawn to a pair of portraits hanging in a small alcove. Electric lamps over each painting illuminated the canvas.

Geoffrey made his way toward them. "These are my parents, Jonathan and Melissa Payne. I am happy to say that they are both alive and well. Perhaps you can meet them some day."

"I'd love that, sir," Donald said, knowing that if he ever did travel to Europe, it would more likely be with a gas mask and a gun.

"Here you go, then," Geoffrey said, handing a sherry to Clara and balancing drinks for himself and Donald in the palm of his other hand.

"My heart medicine," Geoffrey said, raising his crystal glass. He held it aloft in a toast. "Ah, single-malt Scotch. It does me good, Donald, to see that you appreciate fine spirits."

Donald looked skeptically at the amber liquid. He sniffed and felt a warm rush in his nose. Geoffrey winked at Clara and smiled. Donald raised the glass to his lips, then drank as if it were a cup of warm beer.

"Ackkk!" Donald jerked forward and cupped his left hand under his chin to keep Scotch from dribbling to the floor. It spurted, instead, from his nose.

"Ackkk!" He convulsed again, trying to keep the rest of it in. Heat rose up his nostrils and raced down his throat. Heat spread across his chest. He drew a frantic deep breath and covered both nose and mouth with his handkerchief. In a raspy voice he managed to say, "excuse me."

Geoffrey chuckled. He took Donald's glass and ambled slowly back to the bar. Clara's face shifted from concern to relief. "You said you had something to show us, Mr. Payne? Did you mean the paintings?"

"No, Clara, not the paintings." Geoffrey raised his hand toward a simple but well-crafted staircase leading to the mezzanine. "There's something upstairs that will interest you more."

Donald had recovered somewhat. He took a few breaths. Geoffrey smiled toward Clara and gestured for Donald's arm. Together, they took the stairs slowly, Geoffrey raising one foot and then the other to each new step. At the landing he stopped to rest his leg. A generous space opened at the top with room enough for a pair of comfortable chairs.

"This is sweet," Clara said, pointing to a child-sized reproduction of the adult chairs. In it, a porcelain baby doll sat alone, eyes open wide.

Donald gazed over the banister into the room below.

Geoffrey coughed before he spoke. "You see, Donald, I bought this house soon after your mother and I came to Galveston. The core of it was built by a retired navy captain in 1885. He fancied the mezzanine. I think it reminded him of his ship. Your mother and I made minor changes to make the house more suitable for her and the children."

Clara turned to Geoffrey. "Donald lived here?"

"For nine months, yes."

Donald felt himself sway. Geoffrey's hand tightened on his arm.

Geoffrey pointed his cane toward a closed door. "I seldom enter this room because it makes me sad. I make sure it is aired and dusted regularly, but other than that ..." He reached for the glass door knob. His eyes were fixed on Donald.

"Yes, sir?"

Geoffrey let the door swing wide.

"Donald, this was your mother's photography studio."

His feet refused to move. He felt Geoffrey release his arm and Clara's hand on his back. "Oh, Donald," she said, "it's all just the same! The chair, the wallpaper, even the books against the wall and the little clock on the chest of drawers."

Donald wanted to inhale the room. He walked around the perimeter, studied the high ceiling and marveled at the French skylights.

"Those windows were the devil to install," Geoffrey commented, pointing up with his cane. "But Maude insisted she needed them. I think you must have agreed, because you were never so happy as when you were in this room with your mother."

Donald stepped to the center of the room. His hand glided over the top of the large studio camera, feeling the smoothness of its wooden sides. He lightly pinched the leather bellows and admired the polished brass trim.

Geoffrey watched with pride.

"What's in there?" Donald pointed to a door that had black fabric over the transom glass.

"Her darkroom," Geoffrey said.

"May I?" Donald said, walking toward the door.

"Of course. Everything in this room belonged to your mother, so consider it yours."

Donald opened the door slowly. There was no chemical smell, but a shelf full of brown bottles stood empty, clean and ready for use.

"She had a fine darkroom," Donald called over his shoulder. He looked for a button on the wall, then realized that this room had never been wired for electric lights, although it did have copper water pipes along the wall. A pair of matching paraffin oil lamps with ruby lenses hung from their mounts at each end of the wide, shallow sink.

"What are those?" Geoffrey asked from the door.

Donald followed Geoffrey's gaze to a collection of cardboard boxes marked "DuVoll's" and "Darko" and "Kodak," each with the warning, "Open only in very subdued or ruby light."

"Printing paper, sir, and those boxes on the highest shelf contain dry photographic plates."

Donald examined the glass beakers and a matching set of white porcelain trays. He tipped a small set of balance scales with one finger, watching for a moment as the opposite side tipped up. He examined one of the film developing tanks, and then a funnel. Each object lingered in his hands—his mother's hands—Donald thought.

"Are you all right?"

"Oh, yes, sir." Donald struggled for something to say. "The printing plates and paper are too old to use," he called out, "but everything else is in perfect order."

Geoffrey smiled. "My boy, it would do me good to see someone use this studio again, and your dear mother would have wanted it to be you. I hope you will visit here often."

Donald, lost once more in thought, didn't hear. Geoffrey cleared his throat.

"Donald, this room is exactly as your mother left it on the day she took you and Grace with her on the trolley into town."

"Sir? The day of the storm?"

"Yes."

"Wait! My sister was with us?"

"No, my boy, At some point, Grace and the nanny became separated from you and your mother. They found refuge in a house that survived the storm. I didn't learn about it for two days, until they were able to make their way back here. I was beside myself, looking for them. Of course when the nursemaid turned up with Grace, it gave me hope that you and Maude were ... were still alive, but ... I ..."

Geoffrey sniffed and pinched the bridge of his nose. "Your mother went into town that day to visit another photographer. That's where the other pictures of you were found."

Clara moved closer and lightly touched Geoffrey's shoulder. He sniffed again and smiled at Clara. "Right you are. Stiff upper lip. Best stick with the present—and the happy news that Maude's son has returned!"

Chapter 36

"If you'll excuse me now, I'll see what the cook can rustle up."

Clara laughed. "Rustle up?"

"Oh dear. My parents would be appalled at my speech," Geoffrey said. "I've lived in the States too long."

"Thank you, sir. We'd love to have supper with you."

Clara watched as Geoffrey slowly took the mezzanine stairs down one by one. Donald stood silently, his hand on the back of the chair in the center of the room. A moment later, she joined him.

"Donald? This is your mother's studio. What are you feeling? What do you think?"

Donald laughed. Clara stepped away, anger in her eyes.

"I didn't mean to be funny."

He laughed again.

"Donald! Stop it."

"I'm sorry, Clara, it's not what you said. I'm laughing at myself."

"I don't understand."

"It's just that Mrs. Carhart asks me the same questions whenever we talk about the photograph of me on this chair. She wants to know how I feel. She tells me to think, but it's always frustrating. I never had an answer, because I didn't know what she meant. Now, for the first time, I do."

"Please tell me, Donald ..."

"Look! What's that?"

Clara, startled, followed Donald across the room. He stopped before a narrow oak cabinet. It was a sturdy piece, about five feet high and outfitted with several shallow drawers, each centered with a small brass frame just above the handle.

"Oh boy."

"What, Donald?"

"My mother's negatives."

A label on one drawer read Oct.-Dec. 1899. Donald opened it. Inside, a double row of glass panes—larger ones on the left, smaller to the right—stood on edge, each supported by grooves cut into the wood.

Clara peered in. "Why two sizes?"

"The five by seven-inch plates were used in her studio camera." He nodded back toward the tripod in the center of the room. "The smaller ones fit the camera she carried outside the studio, probably that one over there." He pointed to a field camera resting on a shelf across the room.

His fingers stepped from the edge of one negative to the next, as if they were walking from the front to the back of the drawer. He pulled a negative from the second row, then turned toward a wall sconce and held it up to the electric light.

"See, this was taken on a ship, perhaps on the passage from England." He turned so Clara could see.

"That must be your little sister and Mr. Payne standing against the rail."

"Yes. And the photo you found of him talking to the immigration clerk? That negative could be in this drawer."

Donald slid the glass plate back into its grooves, closed the top drawer and pulled out the second. Its hand-written label read Jan.-Mar. 1900. There were fewer negatives than in the first drawer, and most were the smaller size. He pulled a glass plate about the size of a playing card and held it to the light.

"See, here is one of my mother and ..." Donald removed his glasses, set them on top of the cabinet and brought the negative near the tip of his nose. He squinted and closed one eye. "Yes, my mother in bed with a baby."

"You!"

"Me."

"Who is the other lady?" Clara said, on tiptoe, peering around Donald's shoulder.

"I don't know, but I think Mr. Payne took this one."

"Why?"

"It's out of focus."

Clara laughed.

Donald hesitated, still looking down at the glass plate in his hand.

"It's strange, Clara."

"Strange?"

"I thought that if I could only discover who my parents were, I'd somehow be a different person."

"And now?"

"Now I wonder if dwelling on that was an anchor holding me back. In this room, I feel the gap between me and the past is closing, as if I'm on a train moving out of the station. Does that make sense?"

Donald stopped looking through the negatives and rested his arm on the open drawer. He felt his pocket for his glasses, then decided to leave them off. He looked in Clara's direction.

"By studying the one photograph I had, by analyzing every detail, I thought I could touch the past. I had dreams of being here. That's why this room is so familiar."

Faint voices downstairs let them know the supper table was being set. Clara moved closer. She patted Donald's chest lightly several times. He loved the feel of it.

"Yes, Donald, it all makes perfect sense."

Donald had left his glasses off, as he did sometimes when he wanted to look inside himself rather than out. With her hand still on his chest, Clara was close enough for Donald to see, at least in soft focus.

Clara preferred Donald's eyes without the distortion of his thick glasses. She spoke softly.

"Mrs. Carhart is not here, Donald, so I'll ask for her: Now that you know who your parents were, and now that you're here in your mother's studio, how does it make you feel?"

Donald's hands went to Clara's shoulders. He held her gently for a few seconds before answering. "I think Mrs. Carhart wanted me to know that whatever I am and whatever I become is up to me, but she could never have imagined finding all this."

"And now that you're here?"

"For the first time, dear Clara, I feel whole."

Clara and Donald heard boots and a cough in the hall, giving them time to step apart. They were surprised to see Clayton, the chauffeur, rather than a butler.

"Mr. Brown? Miss Barnes? Supper will be served in fifteen minutes."

"Thank you, we'll be down soon," Clara said.

Donald patted his pockets for his glasses. Clara retrieved them from the negative cabinet and put them in his hand. He made no move to put them on. Clara paused, studying his eyes before she spoke. She patted his chest again.

"Donald, I need to freshen up. Why don't you stay here and come downstairs when you're ready?" Not waiting for an answer, she closed the door softly behind her.

Donald stood alone in his mother's studio, motionless, no longer aware of his arms or legs, or even his feet on the oak floor. His mother was here. They breathed the same air. He laughed, lightly at first, then as freely as if someone had told an excellent joke.

"What do you see, dear boy?"

He laughed again.

"Everything!" he said aloud.

"What do you see?" Mrs. Carhart repeated, her voice flat in his mind. Donald, suddenly frustrated, felt his jaws growing tight.

"What do you want me to see?" he said to the empty air.

"Keep looking."

Donald crossed to his mother's secretary. He pulled the lid toward him to form the writing desk. Inside, an orderly row of nooks and a narrow shelf formed the rear of the cabinet. Several pens stood on end in a small vase. A hand-held blotter, well used, lay beside it. Donald reached for a small black book, five by seven inches on its sides and half an inch thick.

"My mother's journal," he said aloud.

"Just like your own," Mrs. Carhart replied.

Donald pressed his hands on the front and back covers, letting his warmth soak in. The books were indeed alike. Donald knew that this was not the only journal his mother kept, just the last one. He shifted the book to his right hand and lifted the cover with his left. The first page was blank, save for a handwritten name and date.

Maude Elizabeth Lancaster-Brown, September, 1899

Donald turned the page and read the first entry.

Monday, 25 September, 1899, Liverpool Harbor
How I dread the next three weeks at sea! Geoffrey is exceedingly kind, but
there is only so much a man can do. At least he is good with little Gracie,
which will give me time to rest as the doctor says I must. I pray that the
child I carry will be strong.
* I am filled at once with hope and fear for the new lives we pursue.*
Our ship sails today! Not an hour passes without wishing my dear
husband was alive and with us still, but that is not to be. Only time will
tell if I have made the right decision.

An inch-wide ribbon marked the page of her last entry. Donald was
disappointed to see only a mundane note and short list of errands for the
following day.

Friday, 7 September, 1900
A quiet day. Geoffrey off tonight with friends from his club. Weather
sultry. Newspaper says rain possible this weekend.

Saturday, 8 September,
— Pick up mounting cards and prints from Essex's.
— Need new Sunday dress for Gracie
— Visit Mrs. Hixon

Donald closed the book and slipped it into his coat pocket.
"What are you waiting for?"
"What?" he said aloud.
"Her camera, dear boy. Your mother's camera."
Donald returned to the center of the room. It was all as he had
imagined: the tripod, the camera, the chair. For years he had longed to be
in this room. Now, among all the joy and surprise, he knew he was also

afraid.

"Inhale ... hold ... exhale ..."

"All of this will be here tomorrow," he said aloud. "Besides, the others are waiting."

"They can wait. Do it now."

Donald stooped forward. He lifted the black cloth that hung from the rear of the studio camera and looked at the ground glass plate. The screen was dark, the glass reflecting Donald's own face. Without looking out from under the cloth, he reached around to the front of the bulky camera and removed the brass lens cap. His fingers found, then depressed the lever that opened the shutter. His reflection disappeared, replaced by the view through the lens. In the focusing glass, the chair and room appeared upside down, as he knew they would.

From the hallway, Clara had heard Donald's voice. She slowly opened the studio door. The big camera sat on its wooden tripod in the center of the room. Donald stooped behind it, head and shoulders hidden under the thick black cloth.

She watched his hand reach for the squeeze bulb hanging by a thin rubber hose from the lens. His fingers closed around it as slowly and gently as if they were holding a fresh egg. Clara stepped back into the hallway. The studio door clicked faintly as it closed.

Under the dark shroud, Donald felt years slip away. He studied the view. His hands belonged to someone else. One adjusted the focus for maximum depth of field. The other reached forward and cocked the shutter of the heavy lens. The image on the glass disappeared.

In the darkness of the cloth, a young boy laughed. Donald peeked around the left side of the camera and saw the boy in the chair. Donald opened his eyes and mouth wide, making a playful face at the child.

The boy, suddenly delighted, leaned forward, left hand on the arm of the chair, right hand in his lap. His little forefinger and thumb just touched.

Blood pulsed in Donald's neck and rushed in his ears. His mother's fingers and his own tightened on the rubber bulb. Sweat ran down his back. It dripped from his brow. The scene is just as Mother left it. The only thing missing is her son. Wait ... Wait ... *Squeeze.*

Click.

At last, he is here.

Donald's head jerked up, startled from his dream. He knew how foolish he must look. He stood awkwardly. The black cloth pulled from the camera and hung on his shoulders. Half of it draped over his head. He lifted the fabric from his glasses. His eyes darted left to right, then back to the closed door. He was grateful to find himself alone in the room.

"Inhale ... hold ... exhale ... hold."

He heard a quiet knock, but the door remained closed.

"Donald?"

"Yes, Clara?"

"Supper is ready. Can you come down?"

"I'll be right there."

Chapter 37

"Will you join me in another Scotch?"

"No thank you, sir." Donald returned Clara's grin. "One is my limit."

Geoffrey refilled his own glass from the decanter he'd brought to the table. He took his time pouring, careful not to spill a drop on the tablecloth. He didn't speak until he'd finished and replaced the crystal stopper.

The cozy dining room was just off the kitchen. Electric wall lamps remained off in favor of candle light, and the warm glow made Geoffrey appear younger. His eyes revealed a softness that wasn't there earlier in the day.

Geoffrey studied Donald over the rim of his full glass. "So, it looks as if you know something about cameras, my boy."

"Donald is a photographer and journalist," Clara said.

Geoffrey sipped his Scotch before responding. "Hum, a photographer and a journalist? Photo-journalism. Any future in that?"

"I aim to find out, sir."

"What sort of …"

The kitchen door thumped open, flooding the quiet candle-lit dining room with harsh electric light. A jovial woman with rosy cheeks and bright red hair backed in, bottom first, balancing a silver tray with three steaming bowls of potato soup and a plate of rolls.

"I'm hoping you're hungry now," she said in a thick Irish accent. "Eat hardy. The pork chops will be out by the time you're done with this."

The cook gave Clara an approving wink, then quickly as she'd come, disappeared into the kitchen. The door swung back and forth on its hinges several times. When it closed completely, Geoffrey felt free to explain.

"Most of the staff is off tonight; Bridget and Clayton are doing extra duty."

Geoffrey drained the last of his Scotch and reached for the full bottle of Texas wine.

"I think you will enjoy this selection from my supplier in Val Verde."

Donald and Clara each sipped at their wine and nodded approvingly. Geoffrey swallowed half of his in one gulp and refilled the glass.

Donald dabbed a small chunk of bread in the bottom of his bowl to retrieve the last drops of soup. Clara refrained. Geoffrey was about to speak when the dining room once more filled with electric light. Bridget backed in, again moving the heavy door with her rear, and carrying in her hands a silver platter with the main course.

"Pork chops from the butcher and greens from me own little garden," she said cheerfully, serving Geoffrey first. "And you, miss, and you, sir." The cook completed her task in a way that reminded Clara more of service in a simple country inn than the home of a wealthy man.

Geoffrey, bemused, thanked Bridget and waited until she'd returned to the kitchen.

"It is so difficult to find proper help," he said. "Not like in England, I can assure you." Geoffrey refilled his wine goblet, spilling a bit on the table.

Donald swirled his wine gently, lost briefly in its deep garnet hue. "Sir, could you tell me more about my mother's interest in photography?"

Geoffrey grew thoughtful. He sipped his wine more slowly.

"It was much more than an interest, my boy. Photography was her life. It meant so much to Maude that we decided straight away to find a house where she could have a proper studio and darkroom."

Clara traced the delicate scroll etched into her wine goblet. "Was she happy living here?"

"Oh yes, dear. Maude was so pleased with her studio that I could hardly get her out of it for meals."

"And this house, sir," Donald asked, "was it badly damaged by the storm?"

"It survived nearly unscathed. If Maude had gotten home from town that day, she would probably still be alive."

Geoffrey fell silent, and Donald and Clara let him eat in peace. Once he seemed himself again, Clara pressed on. "And you've lived here ever since the Great Storm?" Donald was grateful for her questions.

"After the storm," Geoffrey said, "I retained the nanny to care for Donald's sister. When little Gracie passed in '03, I dabbled in business, but found I had no talent."

Donald heard voices in the kitchen. If Geoffrey objected, he didn't say. A minute later, Bridget backed in with bread pudding and coffee.

"Are you still in business, sir?" Donald asked after Bridget had gone.

"No, the accountant looks after my investments and pays the bills. I still meet with associates for companionship, but I'll have none of the business world myself."

"There is something I don't understand, Mr. Payne."

"Yes, Clara?"

"When I called to let you know that you might have a relative who survived the storm, you sounded reserved on the telephone."

"No, my dear, I was not reserved. I was entirely rude."

"But why? I thought you would be happy."

Geoffrey tipped a dash of brandy in his coffee, then stirred with a small silver spoon. "Coffee is the thing in this country," he said. "I used to drink nothing but tea." He added more brandy, stirred that in with the rest, then answered Clara's question.

"I was thrilled the first time someone claimed to be the boy I knew as Wesley. I made a fool of myself, crying on the telephone. I even wired money for the scoundrel to come to Galveston. That was three years ago. It happened again last year, so yours was the third such call."

"Why would anyone claim to be someone they were not?"

Geoffrey sipped his coffee, then held the cup a few inches from his nose, closing his eyes to savor the aroma of warm brandy. He opened his eyes slowly and explained.

"People consider me a wealthy man, my dear, and the smell of money attracts charlatans and cheats. I'm afraid that when you called, I released my wrath on you. My first thought, seeing the pair of you today in the park, was that yours was the best fake yet."

When they'd finished with dessert, Geoffrey suggested they retire to the drawing room for a nightcap. He tried to stand, but dropped heavily back into his chair, making a loud scraping sound against the floor. The room instantly flooded with electric light as Clayton burst through from the kitchen.

"Are you all right, sir?"

"Clayton, dear fellow. In my cups, again, I'm afraid."

"Ah well, no harm done, sir. Let me help you."

Geoffrey looked up at his guests, who were now standing by their chairs.

"Donald, Clara, will you excuse me? I feel a bit light-headed."

"Of course," Donald said. "Clayton, do you need help?"

"None at all, sir. I'll be back in a few minutes."

Donald could see the way Geoffrey flung his arm over Clayton's broad shoulders that this was not the first time the chauffeur had helped his boss this way. Clara and Donald decided to wait in the drawing room for Clayton to return.

"Some of this reminds me of Mrs. Carhart's home," Donald said, examining a large cloisonné vase resting on a three-legged Art Nouveau table.

Behind him, Clara laughed.

"What?"

"Donald, you should see this."

He turned and looked to where she pointed.

"Those funny boxes?"

"Yes. They're wonderful."

"They're crooked."

Clara laughed again. "That's part of their charm," she said, lifting one. "It's called tramp art."

Donald looked closer at the little box. He opened the lid, then closed it again. He leaned closer, lifted his glasses, then dropped them back on his nose.

"The whole thing's made of matchsticks and bits of tin."

"And this box is made of tongue depressors, just like we use at the hospital."

Donald shook his head and began examining the room's odd décor with more interest. Here, a gathering of miniature iron frogs. Nearby, an company of lead soldiers, each uniform hand-painted down to the last button. Donald opened an album on the table and found a set of rotogravure travel cards. One entire wall of the room displayed posters, handbills and souvenirs from the 1900 World's Fair.

"He's quite the collector," Clayton called out as he entered the drawing room. Donald was surprised to see the chauffeur so completely at ease. Clayton still wore his smart grey uniform, but now the top buttons were undone.

"May I use your first names?"

"Certainly," Clara said, speaking for them both.

"Donald, Clara, won't you please sit with me?" Clayton gestured toward the most comfortable chairs in the room. "There is something you should know about Mr. Payne."

Chapter 38

"Say Bridge?" Clayton called toward the kitchen.

"Yes, love?" Bridget called back.

"Could we have a sip of coffee and some tarts?"

"In a minute, love."

Clara and Donald traded looks, then turned back to Clayton.

"Bridget is my wife," he explained.

"Where is Mr. Payne?" Donald demanded.

"Resting in his room. He should be up again soon."

"I don't understand. I thought this was Mr. Payne's home."

"Oh, it most certainly is. I mean no disrespect. I have the deepest admiration for Mr. Payne."

"Are you really the chauffeur?"

"Yes, Donald, I am indeed the chauffeur."

"But ..."

"And I am the gardener, and the accountant, and Mr. Payne's personal secretary, and anything else he needs. I am also his friend, and he is mine."

"Mr. Payne said that most of his staff had the night off."

"That's not exactly true, Donald. Bridget and I are the staff."

Clayton leaned forward in his chair and cleared space on the low table between them. Bridget appeared with a small pot of coffee and four cups. Donald and Clara politely declined, but Bridget sat with them and poured for Clayton and herself.

"Bridget and I are Mr. Payne's only employees," Clayton repeated. "Sir Jonathan Payne sent us here to care for his son, which we've been doing for the past three years."

Clara sat back into her chair, her hand raised to her mouth.

"I don't understand, Clayton." Donald glanced again at Clara. "Mr. Payne seems capable enough."

"Yes, Donald, he seems capable, but he is not. Without help—ours or someone else's—he would be penniless in a year. Although Mr. Payne is one of the kindest men I've ever known, he is not fully in touch with reality. It wasn't always so. I'm told that he was fine when he came to Galveston in 1899. When he lost you and your mother on the same day, and then your sister three years later, it hurt him terribly."

"Is that when he began," Clara paused, searching for the right words. "Is that when he began to change?"

"Yes, he has changed, Clara. Mr. Payne is a proud man who lives in the past. This ..." Clayton swept his hand toward the rest of the room, "this is the way he grew up. He is more comfortable thinking of us as servants, and Bridge and I don't mind. It has become something of a game we play. I think Mr. Payne knows who we really are, but we never discuss it. The three of us live here as a household. We each have our role, and we function quite well."

Donald pointed toward the portraits of Jonathan and Melissa Payne hanging in the lighted alcove.

"Mr. Payne's parents?"

"Both gone, God rest their souls."

"Oh dear," Clara breathed.

"But who pays your salary?"

"Bridget's salary and mine are paid from a trust established by Sir Jonathan Payne's will. A solicitor in London oversees the trust and we receive a monthly allowance, which I manage."

Clayton sipped his coffee, then set the fragile china cup in its saucer. He looked directly at Donald.

"Sir Jonathan and Mrs. Payne passed away more than two years ago. Soon after, Mr. Payne's brother drove the family business on the rocks. There was little left of the shipping company or the estate, other than the fund that provides for Mr. Payne."

"What about the car?"

"The Rolls Royce was truly a gift from Sir Jonathan to his son, just as he told you this afternoon, and it was part of the ruse that brought us here.

Mr. Payne knew his son would not accept being cared for by strangers, but if the car arrived a gift, with me the chauffeur and Bridget as cook, then we fit perfectly into his world."

Bridget, sitting beside her husband, nodded her head. "If it helps dear Mr. Payne for us to pretend," she said, "then we don't mind."

"Clayton will drive you home," Geoffrey called out. He walked slowly into the drawing room, sliding his slippers across the floor and steadying himself with his cane. His thinning hair was neatly brushed. A handsome silk dressing gown covered his pajamas, although Clara noticed that the hem of the gown had been repaired by someone whose talents didn't extend to sewing.

"Donald, Clara, I seemed to have fallen asleep. Please forgive me."

"Of course, sir."

Bridget hastily gathered the coffee cups and set them on her tray as Clayton buttoned his tunic and rose to steady Mr. Payne. "Are you feeling well, sir?"

"Certainly Clayton, I just need to say goodnight to our guests." He rested one hand on Donald's shoulder and the other on his cane as they walked carefully toward the front of the house.

Ahead, waiting in the foyer, Clayton begged with his eyes for Donald and Clara to continue the game. Donald nodded to assure Clayton, then turned to Geoffrey.

"Will you be all right, sir?"

"Of course, Donald, I just need to stay here and rest my sore leg."

"What happened to it?"

"A squash injury, I'm afraid."

"You squashed your leg?" When Clara laughed, Donald knew he'd said something foolish. Geoffrey smiled and put his arm over Donald's shoulder, drawing him close.

"No, my boy, squash is a game you play in a closed room, using racquets and a small rubber ball. It was very big when my brother and I were students at Harrow. In fact, the game was invented there. I still love to play, although I seldom beat Clayton here."

Clayton, hand on the door, grinned at the remark. Geoffrey looked at Clayton, clapped his hand on Donald's shoulder, leaned closer and whispered loud enough for everyone to hear. "You'd think the fellow would be smart enough to let his boss win now and then, especially since I own the court where we play."

Geoffrey shook Donald's hand and kissed Clara's. Once again he thanked her. Donald agreed to return soon. For now, emotion overwhelmed him.

"Mind the steps," Geoffrey called from the doorway.

The Rolls was still in the driveway. Clayton held the door for Clara and Donald to get in. The passenger compartment was even larger than Donald thought. He stretched his legs straight out and found a good twelve inches more between the tips of his toes and the back of the seat in front. Clara leaned forward to give Clayton her address.

When she settled back into the soft leather seat, she stopped near the center rather than sliding to one side. Her shoulder touched Donald's in the darkness, and neither of them moved away. Clayton adjusted his rear view mirror, smiled to himself and set off, determined to find a longer, slower route to Clara's house.

Chapter 39

Sunday, September 22, 1918

Donald smelled the fresh biscuits as soon as he stepped under the arbor. He took a moment to admire Clara's victory garden in the early morning light.

"I enjoyed the note from Naomi," Clara said cheerfully when Donald opened the screen door. She had the north and south windows open, and a light cross-breeze gently moved the curtains.

"Good morning, Clara."

"Did you sleep well?"

"Yes, thanks."

"Help yourself to the coffee. I'll have the eggs on in a moment. We meet your folks at the Interurban station at 10:00."

"And the hospital ship will dock around noon?" Donald crossed the kitchen, filled his cup and refilled Clara's before returning the pot to the stove. It was taking him longer than normal to wake up.

"That was yesterday's wireless report. I'll telephone the hospital to confirm right after we eat."

Donald opened the icebox and set out the butter, cheese and strawberry preserves. Clara had already set the table. Each time they were together, he felt more at ease. Without being asked, he took a knife from the drawer and sliced the tomato.

Clara brought the biscuits and a steaming bowl of scrambled eggs to the table. Instead of sitting across from him, she took the end chair to sit diagonally at Donald's right. Their knees almost touched.

"Donald?"

"Yes?"

"Try not to be shocked when you see Cletus."

"Oh?"

"Aside from his injuries, he will almost certainly be different from the man you remember. He may seem older, or more quiet. He might anger easily. Every case is different, but he will have changed. The homecoming could be awkward, especially for Naomi and Clarence."

"Thanks, Clara. Then we all have to be patient and help him as much as we can."

"I know you will. I just want you to be prepared."

"They're not on this one, either," Donald said, scanning the last of the passengers getting off of the 11:00 Interurban from Houston. He looked at his pocket watch and automatically checked it against the big clock high on the wall in the 21st Street terminal. "They should have been here an hour ago."

"Are they usually late?" A sudden gust of wind blew through the open station, causing Clara to clutch the side of her skirt and put her hand on her student nurse's cap to keep it from blowing off.

"They're never late," Donald said. "You could set your watch by either of them. Something must have happened."

Clara looked around the platform, which was already clearing of passengers.

"Donald, you can stay here and wait for the next train, but I need to be with the other nurses on the dock when the hospital ship comes in."

Donald didn't like the idea of Clara leaving on her own, but he couldn't think of anything better.

"All right, I suppose that's best. You go ahead and I'll ..."

" 'Scuse me, sir," an elderly porter said, tipping his cap.

"Yes?"

"Man outside says you got to come right now." The porter pointed toward Church Street and indicated which way to turn.

"A man? What man?"

"I don't know, sir. There was two white men and a woman. The lady was none too happy. One of the men says for me to look for a white man with thick glasses and tell him to come right away. I don't see no one but you what fit the description. The big man give me a nickel to come find you."

Donald dug a nickel from his pocket and pressed it into the porter's rough hand.

"Thank you. Clara, let's go."

Clara held the side of her skirt with one hand and her cap with the other. The terminal, open as it was at both ends, funneled the wind. A sheet of newsprint tumbled wildly across the tracks. Donald put his hand on the back of Clara's arm as they hurried toward the street and around the corner of the building. Donald saw Clarence first.

"What? Pa, you said you wouldn't drive the car!"

"Nothin' to it," Clarence said, looking proud as Andrew Carnegie himself. He posed by the driver's side, arm crooked on the door and right foot resting on the running board of his gleaming black Ford. The touring car was parked at an angle to the curb. The car's black canvas top was up, and in the shadows Donald could see Naomi sitting in the back. She was not amused.

"Where's Jake?"

"Now what makes you think Jake had somethin' to do with this?"

"Where is he, Pa?"

Donald couldn't help but laugh when he saw his friend strolling toward the car, whistling like a pedestrian just crossing the street. Jake acted surprised to see Clarence. He stopped, looking at the car as if seeing it for the first time.

"Hello, Mr. Stokes." Jake produced a long, slow whistle as his hand glided over a shiny fender. "Does this fine motor car belong to you?"

That was it. That was as long as they could manage the charade before both men laughed. Donald shook his head.

"You had us worried, Pa. You were supposed to be here an hour ago—on the trolley!" Clarence raised his hands in surrender as Jake helped Naomi from the opposite side of the car.

"I just couldn't see buyin' this fine automobile, then leave it sit in the garage. Jake come by yesterday and said he'd drive us down."

Naomi stood next to Jake on the passenger side, not quite glaring at her husband, but close.

"You wanted to drive this car even though it took an extra hour and cost more than the train."

"It didn't, Mama, if you figure six dollars for three round-trip tickets and another ticket for Cletus one-way. We saved at least three dollars."

"By the time you fix that flat tire, I suppose it will cost just as much, and it did take longer."

Clarence started to protest, but Naomi adjusted her shoulders in a way that meant she'd finished what she had to say. She relaxed and smiled.

"Donald, are you going to introduce us to your friend?"

"Oh! Clara, these are my folks, Naomi and Clarence Stokes. Ma, Pa, this is Clara Barnes." Clarence tipped his bowler hat and Naomi stepped up onto the sidewalk to shake Clara's hand.

"So nice to meet you, my dear."

"Thank you, Mrs. Stokes. That was a lovely note you sent."

"Please, dear, call me Naomi." The way Naomi smiled and patted the top of Clara's hand let Donald know they were going to be friends.

Clarence rode up front. Donald sat with Clara and Naomi in the back. Jake even cranked the engine himself, the first time Donald had seen him do that in two years.

Jake guided the car to the corner and turned north on 22nd Street, driving from there to Wharf Road. He found a parking spot two blocks from the dock.

"I see some of my classmates." Clara turned to Naomi. "You can wait over there in the shade. I need to tell them I'm here."

Donald, Jake, Naomi and Clarence found a bench in a large warehouse that was open on one side to the wharf. Behind them, a handful of workers pushed two-wheeled carts full of trunks, suitcases and crates. The larger freight was being hauled on mule carts and drays. A noisy chain-drive truck had just finished delivering a load of cut lumber, but Donald guessed an average ox wagon could have hauled more with less smoke and fuss.

For all their effort, the men moving crates and luggage and lumber were just an incidental part of activity on the wharf. Cotton was king. Thousands of bales lined the open dock and filled the warehouse, awaiting shipment to markets around the world.

"Smoke?" Jake asked Clarence as he pulled a foil pouch and small pack of rolling papers from the side pocket of his coat.

"Thanks. Never acquired the habit. Besides, it's a lot of bother to roll the darned things."

"Cheaper than Luckies in a pack," Jake countered.

Jake creased a single square of cigarette paper in half, then unfolded it to form a v-shaped trough between the fingers of his left hand. With his right hand, he dipped a pinch of tobacco from the pouch in his lap and sprinkled enough onto the paper for one smoke. He folded over the top of the pouch, rolled the paper back and forth between his fingers to form a neat cylinder, then licked the edge to seal it closed.

"You sure, Clarence?"

"Too much bother," Clarence repeated as Jake struck a match.

Naomi and Donald sat at the far end of the bench, watching the empty lumber truck rumble onto Wharf Road. As the noise faded in the distance, Naomi could again talk without shouting. She kept her voice low so Jake and Clarence wouldn't hear.

"Donny, I like Clara. I admire the way she smiles and how she looked me straight in the eye when she shook my hand."

"Thanks, Ma. Clara's had a rough time, losing her dad in the storm, then her mom passing suddenly last year. She worries about her brother in France, but she manages the house well enough on her own."

"She told you all that?"

"Clara never complains; she just talks about nursing and what she wants to do with her life, and how nice it will be when her brother comes home."

"I see." Naomi looked away from Donald to where Clara stood in a group of student nurses, listening to a doctor who seemed to be in charge. Naomi shaded her eyes from the sunlight, which had just found its way under the edge of the warehouse roof.

Medical personnel had gathered on the dock. Near them, six military ambulances, their drivers and perhaps two dozen uniformed soldiers stood by with stretchers. A short distance away, to the left of where Donald and Naomi sat, family members were just beginning to gather behind a length of rope that soldiers had erected to keep visitors back. Two of the early arrivals compared the time on their pocket watches.

"I see the ship," Naomi said. Donald looked to Naomi's lap, where she had twisted her handkerchief about as tight as it would go.

Naomi, Donald, Clarence and Jake walked over and were among the first standing behind the rope barrier, which Naomi gripped with her gloves as if it were a lifeline. Donald looked back. Within minutes, a small crowd had gathered and more were on the way. He suspected that many of the wounded soldiers' relatives and friends did not live close enough to Galveston to come. For those men, homecoming would be delayed.

A woman near Jake was first in the crowd to shout.

"Look! There, near the rail. Billy! Billy!" The woman waved furiously. A soldier on deck waved back with his good hand.

Docking took another ten minutes. A narrow steel walkway was lowered to the wharf. Finally, a sailor at the top of the gangway lifted a temporary iron rail from its pins and motioned that it was safe to go down. Nurses and assistants helped some of the soldiers, but most in the first group walked on their own. Some had visible wounds, with bandages on their heads or arms. Others were missing limbs. Some were sullen and withdrawn, but most of them frantically searched the crowd for familiar faces. Everyone looked unsteady on dry land after nearly two weeks at sea.

One by one, the wounded either found their loved ones or realized that no one had come to welcome them home. Clara and the other volunteers watched for those, and did their best to fill in. One arriving soldier broke from a nurse who was leading him to the receiving tent. He walked instead, using crutches to compensate for a missing foot, into the arms of a couple just a few feet from Naomi and Clarence. The three of them clutched each other desperately. Naomi watched, but didn't speak. Her Cletus had not yet appeared.

The halting parade down the gangway continued for another half hour. A short line of soldiers—those who could stand—formed at the registration desk. Several early arrivals were seen briefly by medical staff and released. One ran to a young woman who ducked under the rope to greet him halfway.

"I see him," Clarence said. "There, about twenty feet back from the gangway."

"Yes!" Naomi began waving, then remembered that Cletus couldn't see. He gripped the rail with his left hand; his right hand rested on the shoulder of the man in front of him. Someone else's hand held Cletus by the shoulder and so on down the line. Only the leader in front could see.

"Papa, he's so thin!" Naomi said, squeezing her husband's arm.

There were at least a dozen men in line with Cletus, all inching forward one shuffling step at a time. Some still had bandages over their eyes, but others, like Cletus, wore dark spectacles.

"Cletus!" Naomi shouted. Donald and Jake did the same.

Clarence cupped his hands around his mouth. "Over here, son!"

On the ship, Cletus cocked his head to one side, then lifted his hand from the rail and waved in the direction of the voices. If he smiled at all, it was faint.

Clara reached Cletus first at the foot of the gangplank, while her classmates helped other men in the line.

"Cletus Stokes?"

Cletus squinted at Clara through his dark lenses, surprise showing in the lines of his face. He could see shapes at least, and that was an improvement from the week before.

"Yes?"

"I'm Clara Barnes, one of the student nurses and a friend of your brother."

"Oh?" Even the short walk down the gangway had left Cletus short of breath. Clara pulled him from the line, taking a moment to set the hand of the person behind on the shoulder of the man in front.

"I'm so happy to meet you, Cletus. Welcome home."

As Clara led him slowly toward the registration tent, she looked closely for clues to the hidden damage Cletus might have suffered behind his sightless eyes.

"Donald talks about you a lot."

"Nothing terrible, I hope."

Clara was encouraged that Cletus could walk without hesitation, and relieved to see him smile.

"Nothing terrible at all."

Clara stayed with Cletus through registration, then escorted him across the dock to his family. Instead of leading Cletus by the hand as the other volunteers were doing with their blind patients, Clara looped her arm through his and pressed it close to her side. Walking toward Naomi and Clarence, they looked like any young couple taking a stroll. Jake and Donald lifted the rope to let them through. Naomi couldn't hold back tears as Clara put his hand in hers.

"My boy!" Naomi sobbed—relieved, happy and sad all at once.

Clarence wrapped his arms around them both, resting his forehead against the side of his son's head, while Donald patted his adoptive brother's shoulder and rubbed his back. Naomi's hand, clutching her son's head, knocked off his uniform cap, which Jake picked up and held at his side.

Clara turned away, but Donald reached for her hand and drew her close. "Thank you."

She squeezed his hand in return. "I need to assist the others. Can you wait for me?"

"I'm going to help my folks to the car. I'll be back."

It was nearly two o'clock by the time Jake had the Stokes loaded in their car and ready to return to Houston. Everyone spoke at once.

"It's so good to have you home!"

"Thanks, Mom."

"We got your letters."

"Sorry I can't write for myself anymore."

"Shush, now, you'll be writing again before long."

"I can see things, but the light still hurts my eyes."

"Your room is all ready."

"Can't wait to be home."

"We can pull down the shades."

"Sure, Mom. How's Bosco?"

"Fine, dear."

"Nice car, Dad. When did you get it?"

"Tell you the whole story later, son."

Cletus wheezed, and everyone held their breath. He recovered in a moment, trying to ignore the burning in his lungs.

"Hey, Don, I like your lady friend."

"She's not my lady friend," Donald protested with little conviction.

Cletus laughed. "Well, Don, if she's not your lady friend, then I want her."

"I guess we can talk about that later, too."

"Everybody set?" Jake called from the front of the car, one hand on the fender and the other on the crank.

"Ready," Clarence called from the front seat.

"Ready," Naomi and Cletus echoed cheerfully from the back.

Jake gripped the outer edge of the right fender and rotated the crank handle down toward the ground. He pulled up and hard to the right. The engine sputtered and died. He tried again. The second time it caught.

"Nothing to it," Jake said as he climbed behind the wheel and adjusted the spark advance. The engine smoothed into a noisy idle.

"Just the right touch," Clarence said over the clatter. He glanced back at his son and wife holding hands in the back seat. Donald, standing by the driver's door, leaned over and spoke quietly to Jake.

"Thanks for bringing them in the car. It means a lot to Pa."

"I know," Jake said. "All this," he pointed over his shoulder with his thumb, "means a lot to me, too. You coming back to Houston tonight?"

"I plan to."

"I'll stop by your house tomorrow."

Jake started to put the car in gear, but Donald touched Jake's forearm, which was resting on top of the door. He felt the engine vibrating through the fabric of Jake's coat as easily as if he'd put his hand directly on the car.

"Jake?"

"Yeah?"

"We met someone who knew my mother."

"Knew your mother?"

"Clara found him. He was in Galveston all this time. He brought my mother here from England."

"Clarence mentioned it. So your folks were poor immigrants?"

An image of the ride home in Geoffrey Payne's Rolls Royce made Donald smile. He stepped back from the running board and raised his hand goodbye.

"They were immigrants all right, but not exactly poor."

Chapter 40

The most severely injured were last off the ship. Stretcher bearers took them directly to waiting Red Cross ambulances. Each vehicle carried four men. As soon as one ambulance pulled away for the short drive to Sealy Hospital, another took its place. Donald spotted Clara walking alongside one stretcher, talking to a soldier with bandages on both arms. Nearby, a doctor suddenly fell to his knees.

Clara rushed to his side, gently easing the young physician onto his back. His eyes were half closed and his face pale. She drew a small cloth from the pocket of her smock and placed it under his head, then borrowed a soldier's duffel to raise the doctor's feet. She briefly held her cheek near his mouth and nose to check his breathing. She pressed her fingers against the side of his neck. Donald lifted the barrier rope and started toward them, but one of the medical staff reached Clara first. Donald stopped short, just close enough to hear their conversation.

"What happened?" said a balding man in a white coat.

"Doctor Lewis fainted," Clara said. She turned and asked an approaching nurse's aide to bring a cup of water. People flowed around them, with steady rows of wounded and medical staff moving to and from the hospital ship.

The man on the ground began to stir. Clara stroked his forehead. The doctor—no older than Clara herself—looked up and tried to gain his bearings. He finally recognized Clara as one of the student nurses. He sat up, but Clara put her hand on his shoulder and asked him not to stand.

"Did you see that man's face?"

"Whose?" Clara said.

"A wounded soldier." The doctor pointed feebly in the general direction of a stretcher team sliding its charge into one of the ambulance bunks.

"I lifted the cloth from his head. He had no face." The doctor began shaking quietly, hands covering his eyes. Clara wrapped one arm around his shoulder. The older doctor moved on to other patients, just as the nurse's aide rushed over with the water that Clara had requested.

"Here, drink this."

"I'm sorry. I should be more professional."

"You're only being human," Clara said. "Nothing to be sorry about." She helped him to his feet and led him to an empty chair behind the medical tent.

"Wait here until you feel better, Doctor Lewis. We're almost through with the patients."

Donald watched, taking care to stay back from the moving line of stretchers. There were fewer of them now, and finally, the parade of wounded stopped. Most family members and friends had either retrieved the men they'd come to meet, or followed them to the hospital.

Clara joined Donald after the last ambulance had gone.

"Did your parents leave?"

"They couldn't wait to get Cletus home."

Clara waved goodbye to several colleagues and classmates. She led Donald toward the registration tent, which two soldiers were now helping to dismantle. She pointed to one battered duffel left behind.

"I saved his bag. Soldiers brought all of the luggage off the ship after you left."

Donald hoisted it with one hand. Not much, he thought, for someone who had been gone more than a year.

Clara slipped her arm through Donald's as they walked past the long open warehouse and out onto the city streets. Donald loved the easy way Clara touched him, without hesitation or reserve.

"Are you leaving soon?"

"I thought I'd go back tonight in case Naomi and Clarence need help with Cletus."

"Your brother seems like a nice man."

"Pa worries he won't be able to work."

Near the end of the wharf, a flock of raucous gulls swarmed after a bucketful of fish heads, guts and tails that fishermen had thrown into the water. The sounds and the warm salt air felt thick and comforting and real.

"I hope Cletus will recover," Donald said. Clara looked at him as they walked.

"I've seen men come back from much worse injuries. Some regain their eyesight completely after a mustard gas attack, but his breathing problems can last longer."

"You must be exhausted, Clara."

"I am—and hungry. Let's stop by my house, then find a restaurant. I don't feel like doing another thing today."

They walked as far as Avenue C, lost in their own thoughts. Clara still worried about the wounded she'd seen, and Donald wondered how his family would change, now that Cletus was home.

"I hear the telephone," Clara said as she put her key in the lock. She left it there after opening the door and hurried to answer the call.

"Hello? Yes, this is Clara Barnes. Yes, operator, I'll take the call. Oh, hello, Mr. Payne. Yes, fine, thank you. Yes, Donald is here. Just a moment."

She handed the receiver to Donald and went to retrieve her house key from the lock. Donald stood, resting his hand on the sloping front of the telephone.

"Hello, sir. Yes, we just got in. Yes, the Stokes are driving Cletus back to Houston now. Me? I was going to return on the Interurban this evening." Clara watched for a moment, then stepped out of sight into the parlor.

"Tonight? Yes, I think that would be fine. Just a moment."

Donald put his hand over the mouthpiece and called out.

"Clara, would you like to go back to Mr. Payne's home? He said he had something to discuss with me."

"Of course, that would be lovely."

Donald spoke into the receiver, holding the heavy earpiece tightly to his ear only out of habit. The connection was quite good.

"Yes, sir, we'd like to come. In an hour? Yes, we'll be ready."

Donald hung the earpiece on its hook and turned to Clara.

"Clayton is coming in an hour to pick us up."

Clara tugged at the sides of her skirt and curtsied.

"A chauffeur is coming for us in Mr. Payne's Rolls Royce? Yes, Mr. Brown, that would be lovely, indeed."

Geoffrey Payne himself opened the door. "Donald, Clara, welcome. I hope you weren't rushed."

"Not at all, sir," Donald said. He, at least, was telling the truth. Donald had only to put on a clean shirt and wipe the dust from his shoes. Clara needed another fifteen minutes to get ready. Seeing her was worth the wait, but not until they reached Mr. Payne's home and she removed her shawl did Donald see the full transformation.

Clara's floor-length gown, although years out of style, retained every bit of its original elegance. A single strand of pearls made her look like a princess, and each time she moved, Donald caught a fresh breath of lavender. He wanted to touch the delicate color she'd brushed on her cheeks and lips.

"You are ravishing, my dear," Geoffrey said, kissing her hand. Englishmen are funny about hands, Donald thought.

Geoffrey motioned them into the house, but rather than the drawing room, he showed them to his private study. The room was surprisingly small, with barely enough room for the three leather chairs, a round table, and an oval writing desk in the corner. Even the fireplace was small, although there was no need for a fire just then.

"My little retreat," he explained. Donald thought of Mr. Booth and his "office" at the back of the hardware store. Mr. Payne's had a small stained glass window, mounted within a carved frame that seemed equally old. The whole thing was lit from behind by four discrete electric lights. Clara asked about it first.

"Saved from the ashes," Geoffrey said. "When the Earl of Essex began dissolving the monasteries in 1525, many of their beautiful stained glass windows were destroyed. This little gem reminds me of the tribulations mankind has managed to survive." He raised his hand to the window, looked at his glass of Scotch and set it down without taking a sip.

Clara looked to Donald and back. Although they'd met him only the day before, they both saw a change in Geoffrey. He rang a bell and

Bridget appeared in the doorway.

"Yes, sir?"

"Please bring some hot tea and sweets." He thought better, then asked, "Or would you two prefer coffee?"

"Tea is fine, sir," Donald said. Clara smiled and nodded her head. She hoped that no one else heard her stomach rumble.

"Fine. Tea it is," Geoffrey said, "and please, Bridget, take away this drink."

Geoffrey motioned for Clara to sit, then he and Donald took their own chairs at the round table. Clara and Donald looked puzzled.

"Are you all right, sir?" Donald asked.

"Yes, perfectly well, and far better than last night."

"Last night, sir?"

"I'm afraid I was in my cups. Too much to drink, my boy. You may have noticed that I'm quite fond of spirits. In the excitement of finding you, I forget to count."

"That's all right, sir. It was a wonderful dinner."

Geoffrey laughed. "If you say so. I don't recall the last few bites."

Clara felt a rumble again. She'd been on her feet all day and was looking forward to more of Bridget's cooking. Hidden below the edge of the table, she pressed her hands to her stomach.

"So you see, Donald, I've had more time to think, this time without the benefit of Scotch. What I would like to discuss is your future. What are your plans?"

"I want to be a photographer, sir, and possibly a writer. I have a position waiting that may include both."

"What sort of position?"

"I would be on call to photograph stories for a new magazine."

"On call. I see. And what about the draft, Donald? Are you registered?"

"Yes, sir. I signed up in Houston last week and will take my physical at the end of this month."

"So soon? Dear me."

"The military needs a lot of men."

Bridget entered, jolly as the night before. She winked again at Clara as she set the tray of tea and scones on the table. Clara noticed that Bridget was careful to position the silver tray in a way that kept the dented corner away from Geoffrey's view.

"I'll serve," Clara said after Bridget had gone. She slid forward in her chair, held her hand over the top of the pot to keep the lid from slipping off, then poured tea into three cups. She gave Mr. Payne the one that wasn't chipped.

"Pass the scones, please. Thank you, Clara."

Clara held the tray for Geoffrey, passed it to Donald, then selected a scone for herself and immediately took a bite.

Geoffrey spent longer than necessary loading his biscuit with the proper amount of marmalade and cream cheese. He spent the time gathering his thoughts.

"Donald, you may have guessed that I am a man of some influence." Clara and Donald glanced at each other, unsure what to expect.

"I'll be frank. Perhaps I could speak to someone on your behalf, to keep you out of this terrible war." Geoffrey took a large bite of his scone, chewed forcefully and wiped a dab of orange marmalade from his chin. Still chewing, he settled back in his chair to wait for Donald's response.

At first, Donald didn't know what to say. When he finally spoke, Clara and Geoffrey were both shocked by the certainty of his reply.

"No!"

"But, Donald ..."

"Sir, I appreciate your offer, but I cannot have you or anyone else intervene on my behalf."

"What if you are drafted?"

"Then I will serve."

"And if you are rejected because of, well, because of your eyes?"

"Then I will have been rejected, on my own merit, not for some other reason."

"Have you thought this through?"

"Yes, for quite some time."

"Donald, then what about a job—a real job—either now or after you serve? What do you like? Shipping? Banking? Manufacturing? You have a bright future. I know many people who could help you. A word from me is all it would take to get you started. Think of what the money and position could mean, should you ever want to, say, get married and have a family."

Geoffrey leaned forward, placing both hands on the table. He looked eagerly at Donald.

"Thank you, sir." Donald's eyes glowed behind the thick lenses. He'd never been more certain in his life.

"Photography makes my blood flow." He smiled gently at Geoffrey. "If I don't follow my dream, I fear I will regret it for the rest of my life."

Geoffrey laughed at that and dropped back into his chair. He raised his hands to shoulder height, then slapped them hard on the table. The silverware jumped.

"Oh, my, Donald, it does me good to hear those words again."

"Again, sir? How so?"

Geoffrey, still chuckling, raised his teacup in a toast.

"You sound exactly like your mother."

Chapter 41

"I was simply hungry before we went to Mr. Payne's house," Clara said, tugging her shawl tightly around her shoulders. "Now I am famished."

Donald looked through the open glass panel to the electric clock on the dashboard of the Rolls Royce. Still early in the evening. He leaned forward to talk to Clayton, who was driving them home.

"Clayton, do you know the Mexican restaurant at 14th and Market Street?"

"Of course."

"Could you take us there instead?"

"Certainly." Clayton turned left from Broadway, made a right on Market and stopped smoothly near the front door.

Inside, several patrons with tables by the windows began pointing. Seeing the commotion, the owner of the restaurant crossed the room, put her forehead to the glass and peered out. The largest automobile Blanca had ever seen was by the curb, and a chauffeur in a smart grey uniform had just stepped out. He paused with his hand on the rear passenger door.

"What kind of car is that?" one of her customers asked.

"Steering wheel on the right. Must be British," offered another.

"A Rolls Royce, I think," said someone from the next table over.

"Blanca, are you expecting royalty?"

"Not tonight," she said, curious as the rest.

Clayton opened the door and spoke quickly to his passengers in the darkened rear seat.

"Make a good show, you have an audience."

Not ten feet away, a dozen faces now pressed against the restaurant windows.

Donald, nearest the curb, stepped out first. He turned and offered Clara his hand. To Clayton's credit and Donald's amusement, Clayton had become the symbol of a proper English chauffeur: shoulders back, hand resting on the door and eyes fixed in the distance, all in his crisp, military style.

Clara stepped out next, placing her foot delicately on the running board. Her burgundy gown looked all the more elegant under the gas street lamp.

"Thank you, Clayton. We can walk home from here," she said.

Clayton touched his hand to his cap.

"If it's all the same, miss, I'll stay with the car until you're ready to leave. We don't want to spoil the effect."

Blanca greeted them at the door. Clara had never seen her face so red. "I'll explain later," Clara whispered before her friend could ask. A waiter appeared, but Blanca turned him way. She'd take their order herself.

The glances and stares from other tables grew less frequent, and by the time their main course arrived—more quickly than normal—Donald and Clara felt at ease.

"Enchiladas," Blanca said, placing two steaming plates on the table. Clara took her first hungry bite, then another, even before Blanca walked away.

"Delicious!" Clara said, wiping her mouth with her napkin. She sipped her *Triple-X* cream soda, fingers on the top of the paper straw and eyes on Donald. He smiled back.

"Clara, you look radiant."

"I spent the afternoon in the sun without a bonnet."

"No, your glow comes from inside."

Clara laughed. "What a lovely thing to say, but don't embarrass me here. We've already caused enough gossip for one night."

"I didn't know the invitation was just for tea."

"No harm done. Besides, I'm more comfortable here."

Clara finished her meal before Donald. She dabbed her mouth again, carefully considering her next words.

"Donald?"

"Yes?"

"You dismissed Mr. Payne's offer pretty quickly."

"Did I?"

"You seemed so confident. Do you think he was only fooling himself, that he couldn't really help?"

"No, Clayton told me that Mr. Payne does have prominent friends in business and politics. I'm sure about that."

"What, then? Why were you certain that you didn't want his help?"

"I've been thinking about my future for a long time, but until now, I've had few options."

"So when Mr. Payne wanted to help you find a job, it was easier to imagine a different path?"

"Yes, but his offer to keep me out of the military tipped the scale. That really ..."

Clara saw Blanca approaching and raised her hand for Donald to wait.

"Would you like anything else?" Blanca asked. She had many more questions in mind.

"Sopapillas would be nice, and some coffee."

Donald reached across the table as Blanca walked away. Clara's fingertips curled over his.

"I admire, that, Donald, what you said to Mr. Payne. He offered you a chance to avoid military service, but you turned him down."

"There was no question about it."

"But what about the job? What Mr. Payne suggested sounds like a much brighter future, and certainly more pay than being a photographer or a journalist. Aren't there things in life you want for yourself?"

Donald knew he was being tested, but didn't mind. He looked around the restaurant. Couples and families sat talking or simply eating their meals in silence. He thought of those in the streets and in their homes, all more or less the same. He turned back to Clara.

"How many people really enjoy what they do for a living?"

"I don't know, Donald. I suppose many simply tolerate their jobs."

"Then why keep them?"

"To feed themselves and their families? To buy the things they want?"

"Yes, but ..."

"Tell me, what do you want?"

Donald thought hard before answering. "There are things I'd like to buy, but just making money is not reason enough to take a job I don't want."

"What, then?"

Donald thought again, then touched his free hand to his chest.

"Clara, everything I really want is inside. Photography fascinates me now, so I want to be the best photographer I can be. If my interest shifts to writing, then I want to be good at that, too. If new paths open in the future, I want to follow them if I can."

Clara squeezed Donald's hand, but couldn't speak.

Clayton waited with the car as promised. When Donald and Clara left the restaurant, it caused nearly as much stir as when they arrived.

"Very good show," Clayton laughed as he pulled from the curb. "Well done!" He drove straight to Clara's house and let them out, then stood for a time on her shell driveway, acting far less the chauffeur than a friend. Clayton shook Donald's hand and bid Clara a good night.

"It was a pleasure to meet you both. I hope you'll visit the house again soon. I've never seen Mr. Payne so happy."

"The two of you seem close," Donald said. "Do you ever call Mr. Payne by his first name?"

Clayton laughed as he climbed behind the wheel. "Only on the squash court, and then, only when I let him win."

Clara and Donald watched Clayton drive away. Three blocks down, the electric taillights on the Rolls finally turned and disappeared. Overhead, a full moon peeked from behind slow-moving clouds.

Clara turned toward the house, but Donald put a hand on her arm. They faced each other in the driveway, inches apart, fingertips just touching. Donald spoke first.

"Let's stay outside for a while."

Clara didn't speak, but her eyes answered for her.

They sat side-by-side in her porch swing, slowly easing it back and forth with their heels. The moonlight glowed off the white walls behind them and the white planks beneath their feet.

"I have something to show you," Clara said. She opened her handbag and removed an envelope that Donald knew well. Inside was the photograph of himself as child. He lightly touched the print, but for the first time, he felt no urge to remove his glasses and study it closely.

"You've had this in your purse?"

"I wanted to be with you the next time you saw it."

"So much has changed."

Clara slipped her arm under Donald's and rested her head on his shoulder, savoring the cool breeze and gentle motion of the swing. Together in the moonlight, they gazed silently at the print. From the little card in Donald's hand, Maude Brown's baby smiled back.

The End

Richard Cunningham is a freelance science writer and commercial photographer. He holds a bachelor's degree in Journalism from Oklahoma State University and a master's in Science and Technology Journalism from Texas A&M University. He has been writing nonfiction articles and books for more than thirty years. *Maude Brown's Baby* is his first novel. He lives with his wife, Lily Ann, in Houston.

Acknowledgements

It takes a team to write a book. My head coach, captain and cheerleader for this project was Lily Ann, an adjunct professor of Art History at the University of Houston-Downtown. She has master's degrees in Fine Art and English Literature, and a voracious appetite for books. She is also my wife. For the 18 months it took to write *Maude Brown's Baby*, Lily Ann kept me on track, mainly through persuasion, but sometimes with a stick.

There were two genuine novelists on the team: Sarah Andre, author of the romance mystery, *Locked, Loaded and Lying*, and Kay Kendall, author of the historical mystery, *Desolation Row*. Their technical help and encouragement were invaluable.

And then, there were the readers. These are the family members and friends who, after endless badgering, finally agreed to read early drafts. Thank you, thank you dear Linda, Diana, John (aka Jack), Gina, Scott, Mom, Dad, Brittain, Cynthia, Jane, Don, Jerry, Bob, Brian, Julie, and of course, Clarence. I could not have done this without you.

Given all the help I've had, be assured that any remaining errors and typos are purely my own. —R.C.

CPSIA information can be obtained at www.ICGtesting.com
Printed in the USA
LVOW081558130613

338475LV00004B/580/P

9 781478 201519

[9]